Rage of the Phoenix

Book One of Rage MC

Elizabeth N. Harris

*To Emma
Congrats
Elizabeth
x*

ISBN: 9781708739034

This is a work of fiction. Names, characters, businesses, places, events, and incidents are either the product of the author's imagination or used in a fictitious manner. Any resemblance to actual persons, living or dead, or actual events is purely coincidental.

This book was written, produced and edited in England, the United Kingdom, where some spelling, grammar and word usage will vary from US English.

Elizabeth N Harris
Rage of the Phoenix.
Book One of Rage MC.

Copyright © 2019 Elizabeth N Harris
All rights reserved.

elizabethNharris74@outlook.com

ALL RIGHTS RESERVED. This book contains material protected under International and Federal Copyright Laws and Treaties. Any unauthorised reprint or use of this material is prohibited. No part of this book may be reproduced or transmitted in any form or by any means, electronic or mechanical, including photocopying, recording, or by any informational storage and retrieval system without express written permission
from the author/publisher.

Rage of the Phoenix.

A woman running from her past finally finds safety and a place to call home. A man who has seen and done things no man should.

Two MC's about to go to war over one woman.

Just when life is finally settled, love hits Phoenix without warning. Her past is dark and she's in a good place for her and her children. Drake a man haunted by the things he had to do to get his beloved club clean, finally thinks he may have found beauty.

Someone's past is going to bite them hard when they aren't looking for it. Before life can be lived, the dark must be faced. Who will remain standing when the devil comes looking for them?

Books by Elizabeth N. Harris

Rage MC series.

Rage of the Phoenix.
The Hunters Rage.
The Rage of Reading.
The Crafting of Rage

Love Beyond Death series.

Oakwood Manor.
Courtenay House.

Contents.

FROM THE AUTHOR. 6
PROLOGUE. 8
CHAPTER ONE. 21
CHAPTER TWO. 50
CHAPTER THREE. 69
CHAPTER FOUR. 96
CHAPTER FIVE. 120
CHAPTER SIX. 147
CHAPTER SEVEN. 172
CHAPTER EIGHT. 201
CHAPTER NINE. 229
CHAPTER TEN. 249
EPILOGUE. 277
CHARACTER INDEX. 282
AUTHORS BYWORD. 290

From the Author.

Hello and thanks for reading my first book in an exciting new series. I have been working on this idea for a while now. I'm greatly excited to see this finally come to print!

I'd like to thank several people starting, with my son Michael, the original Muggle. Thank you for your support while I whined, cried and sweated my way through editing this book and then secondly learning my way around Indie publishing. Yeah, that was hard!

My other three sons who suffered mum being homework crazy with them one minute and then writing crazy the next! You are all saints, my angels for surviving this alongside me!

Thanks to mum, Vanessa Harris, who diligently worked through editing and proofreading. You also listened to me whine for hours about plot holes, re-writes, the craziness of editing and so on and so forth.

Ben Wright, where do I begin with you? You supported me years ago when I first sent you a different story. You read it and edited it, and now through this process, you've been a rock again. Thank you for everything, your staunch support, your comments, your friendship. You'll never know what it means to me.

Maureen Turner, who was nominated by Kerry, thank you for wading through the painful process of giving honest feedback and telling me the truth!

While my stories don't resemble a living person, I did base them in Rapid City. In doing so, I may have redesigned Rapid City a little to fit with Rage MC. I do hope no one is insulted or upset by this action, it is, after all, fiction and my imagination.

Thank you to my reviewers for your constructive comments, to everyone else who proof-read the book and basically let me drive you all insane. Finally, to you, my readers, I hope you enjoy Rage MC's journey with me. Below are a couple of ways to contact me, I try to reply to every message to feel free to drop me a line.

And just for information! Reading Hall is pronounced Reding Hall, not Reading as if to read a book!

Thank You
Beth x.

ElizabethNharris74@outlook.com
Elizabethnharris.net

Prologue.

January 2010.

The woman bit back a whimper and held her bruised cheek. She pulled herself painfully up off the floor and clutched the lip of the dresser before collapsing onto the bed. The door creaked open, and she flinched thinking the scumbag had returned. Instead, her eldest child stepped into the room. In a glance, her son took in her face and the manner in which she held her body, and he knelt at her feet. He was beautiful, her boy, so handsome, one of the few bright lights in her life.

"Mum," he whispered. She smiled, holding it together. Her baby had grown into an adult before he should have. Something else she'd never forgive her abuser for doing to them. Movement sounded behind him, and she watched her daughter hurrying the younger three children away. With a glance over his shoulder, her son pulled out several one-pound coins. He held the money out to her.

"Son?" she asked frowning which hurt. His face turned in her direction, his eyes held hers, a faint hope, a slight belief in something, in them. She'd lost faith and innocence years ago. How could she wipe out the ideals he held dear? She couldn't, to do that would be the worse cruelty she could inflict on her son.

"It's okay, Mum, he doesn't know I've got money. I'd treat the little three to sweets but Mum, let's spin the wheel. I'll go to the shop and buy a Lottery ticket, it's a massive jackpot tonight, the biggest ever. Mr Wilkes will put the numbers on if we ask him." She shook her head and folded his fingers over the coins. God, he was so good to her. She understood his hope that by taking a risk, escape may be possible. Her boy, the man looking out for his family, that was on the monster too.

"No, get yourself, your brothers and sister something special," she whispered, they never had nice things to eat. Every child needed a treat. Lord knows he didn't give her money so she could spoil her babies.

"Mum, you pick the numbers or I will. Have you seen the figure on euro millions tonight? Two hundred and fifteen million pounds. Let's try our luck, it's that terrible, it has to change one day," he whispered stubbornly. "Mum, we've tried running away, it doesn't work. God has to give us a break sometime."

"Your birthdays."

"And the final two numbers? Yours and Dad's?" She nodded, and her son slunk out of the room and left swiftly. Her daughter came in with a wet cloth and laid it over her face. She clutched her daughter's hand, squeezing to convey what she struggled to put into words.

She waited until the monster returned home. He did what he wanted then drifted off to sleep. A pillow cradled her injured cheek as she rolled over and prayed to God for deliverance.

Two weeks later, his fist rammed into her face again, and she cowered as her cheekbone audibly cracked. The children huddled scared in the single bedroom the five of them shared. She trusted her eldest son to protect them. Barricaded in their room in case their stepfather's rage boiled over towards them.

She didn't understand why he raged at her tonight. The court trial had been won, the firm had given him generous praise, his expensive steak meal cooked to perfection. Meanwhile, her children shared five tins of beans and ten pieces of bread between them.

Her son had yet again gone without for his siblings. Sneaking her own dinner of two slices of bread into her pocket, she slipped them to him so he'd eat something. Her husband meanwhile fed on a steak that cost over twenty pounds. Bitterness swept through her.

The monster was scum, pure scum. He dined well every night, and her children made do with what she found to buy for twenty pounds. Twenty freaking pounds! How on earth did anyone feed five kids and themselves on twenty pounds? She starved herself near enough every day, often just having a slice of bread. The scumbag forced her to eat it in front of him, while he lorded it over her.

Things were so desperate her son had taken an early morning paper round and an after-school job at the local newsagents while her husband was at work. Mr Wilkes, the elderly man her boy worked for, knew their circumstances, she knew, he knew, but she knew he couldn't help her.

Mr Wilkes often kindly smuggled the children a treat when she was in the shop and the widower generously paid her son well. The old man kept her son's wages, so her husband couldn't find the cash. He was saving, saving to get them free. There were no limits for her shame. She'd no money, so it was impossible to save. Forced to produce receipts for everything, if a single penny was missing, he'd smile, and punishment inevitably followed.

A fist slammed into her again, and she fell to her knees. The realisation swept over her that this time would be far worse than usual. The snarl on his face, the glow of hateful pleasure that he held power over her. The scumbag loved this, the knowledge she was powerless. She was right, it was horrific. As expected, after her beating, he left the house. Strolled to the club to drink and brag about his day. Meanwhile, he left his wife in a pool of blood.

The door opened, and her boy entered. One glimpse at her, his body stiffened, anger and hate flashed across his features. He knelt and gently helped her rise. In the background, the radio played quietly. Her husband thought it hid the sounds of his fists hitting her. Even with his supposed cleverness, he was a fool. Her son walked her into the bathroom and cleaned her face and hands.

"Mum, you're bleeding from your lady parts." She looked and saw blood dripping down her legs. Waving him away, he left the room while she washed the bloody wounds. When she went back, she sat on the bed, a failure at being a mother. She couldn't rescue her kids, she'd no chance to save herself, he'd track her wherever she fled. The evil bastard had done so every time they attempted an escape. A single tear dripped down her cheek.

"Take your siblings and run, go to Mr Wilkes," she told her son. He shook his head at once in denial. "Tell Mr Wilkes everything, social services will become involved."

"Not without you, Mum." She took his face in her hands.

"Son, he's unstoppable. As long as he has me, he'll settle for just me, get safe," she argued through her cracked jawbone. It was causing her a great deal of misery, the way he'd kicked her chin, it was lucky it only felt fractured and not dislocated.

"If we leave, he will kill you," he disagreed. She couldn't deny it. Together they sat in silence. "The only thing stopping him from killing you is the fact we're witnesses." A sigh that caused pain in her ribs escaped her, she corrected her breathing, so it was shallower.

"Start packing Mum. We'll go to the hospital. Demand police from another borough get brought in, this time they must listen. Come on, you're too badly hurt, Mum, you need medical help." He rose to his feet and then they both paused and looked to the radio as the presenter's urgent voice caught their attention.

"Again on breaking news, the National Lottery urges everyone in the Devon borough of Totnes to check their tickets. The National Lottery know the winning ticket for the two hundred and seventeen million pounds bought in Totnes, Devon and remains unclaimed. One lucky winner purchased the ticket at a local newsagent. The winning numbers are…" Oh my god, she looked up, and her mouth dropped open.

"Holy shit, Mum! Where is it?" a loud cry burst from her boy.

"In my handbag, in the lining," she whispered, not daring to dream. Her son rushed to the drawers and pulled out the bag. With her luck, her scumbag husband had more than likely stolen it. Her son rummaged through and found the torn lining and shoved his hand in. An incredulous look on his face he held up a crumpled Lottery ticket.

"Mum. This is it, we're free at last!" Quicker than lightning, he ran to the door. With a bellow for his sister and brothers, he rounded them up and into tatty coats and shoes. As they were home-schooled, her husband got away with dressing them in rubbish. There were a few sets of decent clothes, which they were allowed to wear when they had to appear as a family, which was rare.

Together, supporting their mum, he and his sister got everyone out of the house and down the driveway. She weaved a little, an awful tenderness between her legs and her stomach clenched in terrible pain. The eldest two slung her arms over their shoulders and between them they carried her. She remained upright by sheer willpower.

"Where too?" her daughter asked, looking at her son, scared. He gazed at the fragile girl, and only one person came to mind.

"Mr Wilkes," the boy said, convinced the older man would be their hero. He wrapped an arm around his mum's waist, and his sister took the other side. With a tight hold on his littlest brother's hand, he made his middle brother go to his sister. The eldest of the smaller three held on to their youngest brother.

Gradually, hiding from approaching cars, they crept to the local corner shop. In the boy's mind, it took forever, but the pressure to get them to safety eased when the newsagents came into view. He banged on the glass window, praying Mr Wilkes hadn't settled for the night. The boy kept banging and eventually saw lights go on in the shop. Mr Wilkes stood in the doorway and looked through the glass. Then for a much older fellow, he rushed and got the door open and ushered them inside to safety.

The little ones were crying quietly. Mr Wilkes made soothing noises as he took them through to the back. On entering the small living room, the three younger children clung together. The old man fetched chocolate and snacks for the youngsters and settled them in front of the television.

The widower ran his hands over their heads, offering comfort and protection. Mr Wilkes ushered the eldest two children and the woman into the small kitchen and hauled out a chair into which she gratefully sat.

"Jesus lass," Mr Wilkes muttered. She put her hand up, although she hadn't checked in the mirror, her face was doubtless black and blue. By everyone's faces, she knew it was awful. Blood stained her trousers around her pelvis, and she could only imagine how she looked.

"I'll call for an ambulance," Mr Wilkes muttered looking for his mobile phone.

"Mr Wilkes, Mum, has the winning ticket, the Lottery ticket!" her son burst out, nearly bouncing on his toes. He reached out to stop the man dialling. Mr Wilkes lifted his head from where he was searching, and his eyes grew wide.

"What lad?" Mr Wilkes asked a faint hope on his old face. This was such a lovely family, he liked these folks, with their soft-spoken mum and charming children. The mother was so similar to his own dear wife, and the kids reminded him of the ones they'd never had. Stood on the side-lines watching their suffering, caused a good man untold nightmares these last few years. The children had become withdrawn and fearful, and he'd seen bruises on her, explained as clumsiness. Hate was such a strong word, and yet he hated the stepfather with a passion.

"The euro millions ticket that they're looking for, it's ours!" The boy waved the ticket he'd kept a tight grip on while holding his mum. Mr Wilkes's eyes widened even further. Oh, thank God, his prayers for the family were answered at last! Tears welled, realising what this meant for the family.

"Rigthy'o lad. I'll get things going," he choked out. Mr Wilkes acted at once, getting on the phone to the Lottery people. The phone connected, and he hastily explained the circumstances to the woman who took his call. Sally, as she introduced herself, flew into action on hearing the list of injuries. First, Sally confirmed the ticket was the single sole winner and then second, sent a limousine to collect them.

The car drove them straight to a private medical centre, where doctors treated her for cuts, bruises, lacerations and a broken wrist. Doctors stitched between her legs, where he'd kicked her so hard, the skin had ripped open. There was severe bruising to her stomach, but nothing had ruptured, something she was thankful for.

Scans revealed her liver and kidneys showed bruising and swelling from repeated blows. The monster had broken four of her fingers and her nose, her jaw was fractured as she'd suspected. The medical staff took photographs and x-rays of cracked ribs and earlier broken bones. The evidence told a sad tale of abuse.

On Sally's insistence, police from Exeter met them there. Detectives took brief statements and further photographs. Security organised by Sally waited outside the door, observing the police officers. The on-call doctor described one of the worst cases of domestic violence he'd ever seen and offered a statement to that effect.

Sally had shown up with two managers of the Lottery. On finding out the woman's condition, a solicitor arrived, whom Sally had urgently contacted to meet with them. Sally wasn't foolish, her training told her that the husband could claim half of the winnings. Instead, Mr Wilkes would collect the fortune. A signed agreement was being drawn up for

Mr Wilkes to give her the money when her divorce was completed.

It was a grey area but not illegal, the Lottery people stated if the woman said the ticket belonged to Mr Wilkes, then it did. If Mr Wilkes then signed everything over to the family when her divorce was final, who were they to comment on his generosity?

The solicitor agreed to get a binding arrangement that Mr Wilkes couldn't and (they knew) wouldn't break, to them within the next few days. For such an important document, the phrasing needed to be perfect.

Sally whisked everyone off as soon as possible to secure them in a hotel penthouse with security at the door. The detectives came back the next day and took further statements, this time bringing child specialist police officers to talk to the youngsters. The dedicated officers helped the children through the traumatic event.

Sally ensured local law enforcement remained ignorant. Because as the family had explained, every single time they called the local police, they hushed the abuse up. The monster being prominent in the legal community ensured any report was squashed. Exeter officers got an arrest warrant issued, with an emergency hearing in front of a judge for the next day.

The binding arrangement proved unnecessary they found out three days later. Unbelievably, her husband hadn't divorced his first wife. Whom he'd driven into running away by continuous beatings, just as he'd his current.

When Sally began looking for the divorce papers from his first marriage, it turned out there were none! The judge dealing with the case ordered the marriage void. Her now ex-husband was behind bars for multiple serious offences, including bigamy. The local police were under scrutiny by Exeter police, for their part in covering up domestic violence.

After a hectic couple of weeks, the family found themselves in a far better position than they'd been in for years. Sally encouraged them to keep the penthouse for at least a month. During which Sally became a steady companion to the family. Sally even took holidays from work to support them.

The woman ended a call to her barrister and chewed her lip. Sally scrutinised her carefully, she'd faith the woman would continue to survive and thrive. Look at her, after just two weeks, instead of being curled into a ball, she was making plans and putting them together. Everything she'd survived and the world had just landed in her lap. Miracles could happen!

The barrister informed the woman, another further hearing was due. Additional charges were expected. The legal team had an idea he might make bail, but everyone was hoping he didn't. Together with her son, daughter, Sally and Mr Wilkes sat and discussed the future.

"What do you want to do?" Sally asked her, getting straight to the point.

"It's a hell of a lot of money," the woman replied, thinking hard. She was still in a state of stunned disbelief that she'd won such a large amount. Besides the shock that not only was her husband a long-term vicious abuser, but he also wasn't her husband by law. Her mind was whirling.

"Honey, that's a fuck load of dough," Sally told her. The woman giggled for the first time since her beloved first husband, Justin had died.

"I want to move to America," she blurted as an image of Jessica Fletcher crossed the screen, and the little boys quieted. The three small boys had discovered Murder She Wrote, the day after Sally installed them in the penthouse. The children became instantly hooked. She pointed at the TV.

"Somewhere like to Cabot Cove but without the murders!" she mused, smiling. The kids nodded an agreement.

"I can do that easy enough, I'll set the ball rolling."

"Mr Wilkes needs to come too," the daughter said, looking up at them.

"That's not in doubt, of course, he'll come." They didn't even need a discussion over that issue. Mr Wilkes had become part of the family. He was wonderful, with a huge heart and a great stand-in grandparent for the children who'd none.

"What else is in your mind?"

"I once had a dream, I want to make it real. We've the money to carry that out," The woman continued. Sally sat forward, interested at the look in her eyes. The woman hesitantly began talking and then found it hard to stop. When she ran out of things to say about her dream, she looked at everyone. Sally gazed at her in admiration and pride.

"I can help you achieve that if you'd let me come too. I enjoy my job, but what you'd like to accomplish, it's something I'd get my teeth into, and it'll be so fulfilling," Sally said. She received a nod. Good people, Mr Wilkes, Sally, the woman needed them around her. For assorted reasons, as time ended up proving.

Chapter One.

May 2014

I wandered around the new offices and sighed in contentment. This was the final step in getting everyone settled, this magnificent building. After three years of searching, we'd found our place. I'd chosen South Dakota as the state to make a home in, making life more settled now. Sitting behind a desk, I spun my chair and let mind my drift back over the last few years. A shiver of pleasure ran through me at what we'd achieved and what I'd accomplished.

On first moving to America, we'd bought a cabin in Ouray, Colorado. Swiftly followed by a house in Camden, Maine, and we'd moved between the two. We'd loved being in Camden in the beginning, but something was missing. Instead, we turned it into a vacation house and kept looking for a home. I hadn't settled, needing that elusive more.

The kids and I had gone on a four-week trip in Sturgis five months after our move to the States. That's when we fell in love. Micah, my eldest lad, was motorbike mad and visiting Sturgis, one of the biggest bike rallies in the world made sense. I loved the bikes, the atmosphere, I just loved everything about Sturgis.

We came back to watch the rally the following year, then last year, I'd started searching for somewhere to live near Sturgis and Rapid City. We'd rented a house, and the Black Hills had fascinated me. I remembered Calamity Jane singing about them, who doesn't remember the Doris Day version?

The minute we drove through the Black Hills, I felt it, home, this was my more. To many, it might sound crazy, but the Hills called to something inside me. As we drove past an old mansion up in the mountains, half an hour from Rapid City centre, named Reading Hall, (pronounced Redding Hall) we stopped.

The place before my eyes was a sprawling mess and falling apart. The previous owners had left it to rot, and my kids somewhat horrified, found the condition of the mansion appalling. As I ignored them, I focussed on the hidden charm, the potential, and I needed a big house. Really needed a big freaking house!

My kids had gone from five to sixteen, and with my youngest twins' recent adoption being completed, Reading Hall was perfect. Mr Wilkes called the local realtor who drove out and met us there and then. The house came with sixty acres of mostly wooded land and appeared to have a fair price. There was a dangerous road leading from Nemo Road, which led to the Hall, which needed immediate repairing. Which, of course, I'd have to pay for the resurfacing.

Mr Wilkes, now a grandfather to sixteen kids, didn't think the price fair and relentlessly bid it lower. I stood by and let him bulldoze his way to a price he considered the house was worth. Mr Wilkes didn't believe in squandering money, even though we'd plenty to spare. Firmly, he told the relator that although I was rich, that didn't equate to me being a cash cow! Hiding my grin from the flustered man, I winked at the kids. Micah, my eldest lad, hid his grin too, as the others watched shocked, that I was buying the Hall.

Within three weeks at the start of January two thousand and fourteen, I owned the tatty old mansion and work had begun on it. The original designer had fixated on the gothic era, with the embellishments one expected gothic architecture to have. Reading Hall boasted twenty bedrooms, a library, and two studies, to name a few rooms.

Let's not forget a man cave my eldest sons had hijacked! The kitchen was the size of a house itself, and I adored the space, and there was a linen room. In fact, there were many different rooms I looked forward to filling. The kids had their own ideas too.

Large, carved light grey stone blocks made up the design of the Hall, it was a rectangular shape with a tower on each corner. The stone gleamed faintly in the sun once gardeners cut most of the suffocating ivy away. I assumed the person who built the Hall built it to re-create European castles which had towers, but I wasn't arguing.

Although called Reading Hall, in my mind, it indeed, looked more a castle than a mansion but hey ho! In between the towers were sturdy battlements and a vast quantity of gargoyles and grotesques decorated the walls and battlements.

Those four towers, with their leaded and stained-glass windows and wooden carved balconies, gave me a sense of safety. The towers stood guard with my gargoyles, their roofs reached into a pinnacle that had a widow's walk around each turret.

My two eldest daughters claimed the north tower for themselves, the south tower my eldest sons claimed. The east tower was Mr Wilkes and the west tower we turned into a fun tower for the smaller children and me.

My nine-year-old son loved Star Wars and so the woods to the left of us now held a full-scale replica of an Ewok Village. Rope bridges and wooden huts hid amongst the trees. The builders cleared one section of the treeline behind the Hall for a small cottage, for my housekeeper, Mrs Ames. Mr Ames was the Hall's head gardener. Eddie, my four-year-old daughter, was hooked on Lord of the Rings. So we had a mini-sized Rivendell built in a different direction from Ewok Village.

The builders demolished the old garages and built new ones to house the family cars and bikes. The architect kept the same design as the old garage which had been a converted stable block. It was quaint. We wheeled our bikes onto an elevator that took them up to a second level. There was a second garage with ATV's and snowmobiles. A full-sized ice rink was built (with only a small seating section) as my son Tye was extraordinarily talented and loved to practise.

A baseball diamond was created for Carmine who was as proficient at baseball as Tye was on the ice. Hidden amongst the trees were more cottages for the security team Sally had hired. In fact, Liz, the personal guard came with us from England, and now managed the team. Everyone loved Liz to bits.

The girls played tennis, the Hall already had tennis courts, so they were just restored. Trees hid the ice rink and the baseball diamond, as I didn't want to look at them from my bedroom window. Mr Ames restored the formal gardens with a team, and another team repaired the outside swimming pool.

It was fifteen weeks of hard work and a huge crew, but the team had done it. A little over a month ago we'd moved into the Hall. The kids soon changed their tune when they saw the renovations. While it was being restored, I'd been looking for a Headquarters for my dream.

Within two weeks of us moving to the States, (the day after our visas came through), Sally started work on my idea, and it surpassed my wildest dreams. At first, we'd used rented offices to make it come true. With my permanent move, I decided it was time to find an HQ the Trusts owned.

The Phoenix Trust was the start of it, a charity set up to help the armed forces people who were homeless. I'd expanded that to include police, EMT's firemen, rescue workers. Anyone who I thought did a public service and a hero's job. In England, the poor treatment a percentage of them received on returning from war and so on, disgusted me.

In America, so many more wounded heroes were homeless. Phoenix Trust started in Norfolk, home to many in the Navy. I'd bought a three hundred room hotel and had it renovated into two/three-bed apartments. The architect made sure the downstairs of the hotel had enough room to install a gym, a swimming pool, a sauna and a hydrotherapy pool. He included in the design a doctor's surgery, a dental surgery, three counselling rooms and a manager's office.

On top of those, I insisted on a large kitchen, communal dining room, a small cinema, a small bowling alley, a games room, a physical therapy room. Then we added extras such as a benefits office, a personal shopper, a career advisor and a lawyer's office. At first, Sally thought I was mad until she realised how well Norfolk worked.

Entrance to the Phoenix Trust or PT as it became abbreviated to, began with the client arriving. A simple hot meal was the first port of call, after that, they met the doctor for a health check. Next, we assigned them an emergency furnished apartment until their own apartment was ready. After a night's sleep, the manager sat with them for a meeting. This happened with the doctor beside them.

During the meeting, we explained what we intended to do to help them. As a client, they received a seven thousand dollar furnishing allowance to furnish their apartment. Next, they got a three-thousand-dollar personal allowance, to get clothes, toiletries, personal items such as a watch or cd player.

We often battled disbelief, to get our clients to understand that the apartment was theirs for life. And they didn't have to pay back the money given to them. They didn't have to pay for any of the services provided for them. They weren't used to being given something for nothing.

After the meeting, they went with the doctor for a full check-up, the physiotherapist and counsellor attended too. The doctor made up health charts for them, deciding what medication they needed or physiotherapy.

Everyone had assessments with a counsellor who talked to them about what help they needed. Many experienced post-traumatic stress, nightmares, anger issues, and I knew they desperately needed the counsellors.

The benefits officer met with them too. Their task was to figure out if they were getting their full entitlement of benefits. The lawyer booked a consultation with them to discover if they'd children, with whom they wanted to contact. Possibly, there were other legal issues needed addressing. The dentist worked with them on dental hygiene and any corrective issues they needed fixing.

The personal shopper helped them choose furniture for their apartment, clothes and belongings. If the client thought they couldn't manage on the street shopping, the personal shopper helped them order online.

Once they understood everything, life for them became more relaxed. I often ended up reduced to tears, at witnessing the disbelieving hope in their eyes when they got it. They had somewhere safe to be, they could come and go, and no-one desired to control them or isolate them. They'd a roof over their head, and someone cared. Someone was fighting for them and their rights and recognised the sacrifice they had made for their country.

There were now twenty PT properties across twenty states. Our plan was to get one per state. Sally set up an admin team for each state, and they chased doctors, dentists, lawyers and so on to volunteer. Anyone who'd donate a morning or afternoon, a day even.

Everyone volunteering for a PT signed a contract that they were donating a set time each week. No matter how much time they donated, they signed a six-month agreement on each renewal. If they wanted to renew, of course. Most unquestionably got job satisfaction out of it. By signing six-month contracts, it meant our people gained stability in seeing the same person for their appointments. Retired volunteers felt useful, and their skills needed again.

We maintained a level of paid staff in the renovated hotels. Maids to clean the downstairs areas and we staffed the kitchen twenty-four hours a day. Each residence came with a fitted kitchen and bathroom. We understood sometimes they needed to be around people and not alone, hence the communal dining room.

One last thing we did for them was to organise a career meeting. The meeting helped set a plan up so when healthy, they could get help retraining in a job or go back to college. If they wanted to start their own business, we'd help. A part of what we offered was a start-up loan, payable back without interest once their business started earning money.

The PT covered their college expenses if needed. We did this on a case to case basis. If the medical support found them unable to work, that was fine. We made sure they had their apartment and their entitlements, they could breathe free. We, the public, owed them that much at least!

The Rebirth Trust was the second part of my dream (RT). The RT helped abused men, women and their children escape their terrible home lives, this was an essential agenda for me. With my understanding of abuse, I knew how many times I'd sought help and failed. Most shelters were for women, rarely for men, so my RT's were a new approach.

The safe houses used the same approach as PT, buying hotels and converting the rooms into three or four-bedroom apartments. There was a heavy presence of security (provided by our own PT people who'd set up security businesses) on these, and it was visible. It was a deterrent to any abuser intending to create havoc. The men and women in these safe houses never remained over six months.

The reason for the six-month stay was simple. If the victim hadn't gone back to their abuser within the time allocated, we found they'd adapted to their new life. The safe starter houses used the same bottom layout as the PT properties. But each apartment came furnished as the families or victim didn't stay long.

Once they'd completed the time required, we then moved them to a state of their choosing. A different one from where they'd lived with their abuser, and we bought them a home large enough for their family. In a legal contract, the RT kept ownership of the property, but they had a lifetime contract to live in the house free of rent. We helped them get a new job in the locality they wished. If they had no experience, we helped them get the skills they wanted at college again. The choice was theirs.

Once they were in their new home, we gave them the same as the PT people, a seven thousand furnishing grant. On admission to the safe house, they got a three thousand personal grant and an extra one thousand per child. When they moved to their new home, their belongings moved with them, so there was no need to re-issue that grant. A liaison officer checked in with them each month and made sure everything was okay. Any issues that arose, the officer helped find solutions for them.

The RT now owned twenty safe houses in twenty states and over five hundred properties for people we'd rehoused. RT accepted referrals from women's shelters in those states, as the shelters knew that we'd go further than they could.

The clients had the opportunity of when on their feet, if they wanted to move into their own purchased home, they could. The home we were providing them returned to the RT, for someone else to use. This had happened over one hundred times so far. It worked, it meant we were achieving my goal of helping people.

For me, it meant those families had beaten the odds and become prosperous, we'd succeeded in our goal. It meant that instead of continuing living rent-free, they surrendered their homes to help further families. No one was pressured to move out of an RT property. The satisfaction we felt that these families could free up their property, couldn't be imagined.

The third part of my dream was the Eternal Trust. ET! (As you can see the Trust's linked to the word Phoenix! I believed the Phoenix as a symbol of my own rebirth.). ET was for children who'd been sold or forced into the child sex slave trade. ET's aim was to help children living on the streets, forced into prostitution by pimps. We helped children used as slaves and abused children.

Across the States, we'd opened five ET's in five different states, arrayed in large, green, wide spaces. Each ET could house one hundred children at a time. It broke my heart we didn't have many ET homes, not because money wasn't available, it was.

It was so hard to find these children because their captors held them close and well hidden. For each child rescued, ten more took their place. To give the children dignity and privacy back, we gave them each their own room. The children were given a small personal allowance that their own personal liaison managed for them.

These children had undergone frightful ordeals. ET staff worked with them until they could manage mainstream life again. A lot of victims had families and parents who were as lost, hurt and confused as was their children. The staff worked with them on a one-to-one basis. The children received educations while with us, and they began the long journey of healing.

ET offered horse riding, tennis, swimming and many other activities. ET provided intense counselling for them as well. Many of the children stayed long term, a few stayed short term, depending on their needs and their internal nightmares. No child left still suffering if we could help, staff did their best to help them heal.

Even though I'd won the jackpot, I couldn't fund this by myself. Which meant each state had a fundraising team. The fundraising state teams liaised with my Headquarters people. Several events we made standard, a winter, summer and Halloween ball, a massive cookout in the summer for a weekend. Four raffles a year and a hot guy, sexy chick auction once a year at Christmas, were other ideas we utilised.

The fundraising teams had leeway with local events, but any significant events had to go through Stefan. The state teams put forward lots of good ideas, charity sports matches, holiday auctions, sponsored runs, etcetera. The fundraising teams oversaw the contacting of companies, sports teams, the rich and famous and so on and raising money that way. They often held their own meetings with business leaders in their locality, wining and dining them into a large donation. The teams worked hard, and I was damn proud of them.

Once word got around about what we were doing, I was over the moon to note that tickets for events became hot items. The events became significantly in demand, creating lists of people waiting for a cancellation. Stefan, my fundraising director, set a minimum price for each ticket and then released them for people to bid on them.

Adverts ran on billboards, television and radio. The publicity team set websites up, and banks and shops threw themselves behind us doing one or two fundraising days a year. Even five bucks donated bought a child a tee or a man shaving foam. Every single buck donated helped. Many of our volunteers did collection days at malls and large shops with collection tins.

We publicised their generosity and allowed them to display a small plaque at their place of businesses to promote how they'd helped us. Each year, the fundraising team assembled a book giving thanks to those who donated and to the businesses. A few businesses kept those books in plain view with the page showing what they had donated.

Obviously, we had costs to pay, the heating and electric bills, for example. During the overhaul of the hotels, we'd incorporated as many money-saving schemes as we could, solar panels and wind turbines for example. The apartment renovations were something we had to pay for, there was staff wages, grants, and other things to pay.

To combat taking donations to pay wages, I'd a shrewd investment team. I gave them five million dollars of my personal money per state. The team managed it and made sure it could pay the wages needed. When I say a good investment team, these were red hot experts at turning a few dollars into thousands. They were brilliant, sheer money-making Midas's. This meant the donations helped people they were meant to help.

Each PT apartment block worked on a six million operating fee per year. Most never used this, they averaged around five million give or take a few thousand. It was wise to give ourselves a buffer because there was always a just in case scenario. The ET centres worked on a four million operating budget each. The RT safe houses worked on a ten million budget because we had to consider the cost of purchasing houses.

Once they hit their target for the year the fundraising people didn't stop, they kept going. Everything over the target we split between two accounts. The first being a 'public bank.' This we used with an eye towards opening new buildings in new states, and they were rocking it. The second account kept the money on hold, so if a state fell short one-year raising money, we had the 'bank'.

The cost of three Trust properties in one state needed twenty million a year to run, it was highly possible that we could fall short one year. Although since we started, we'd hit every target. The Trust staff were freaking amazing!

The woman I'd been four years ago was gone, and I was living my dream. I'd three charities that meant the world to me. Sixteen kids, although I only birthed five of them and a large home my kids loved. We lived in an area I adored and had two great holiday homes. There was money in the bank, my children's futures were secure (yeah, my investment broker quadrupled my own investments), and my ex was a memory.

Life had changed for the woman who'd spent her time on the floor broken and bloody. All I'd ever desired was to raise a family and be happy, that dream was lost when my first husband died. A second chance of happiness got destroyed by my ex-husband, who turned into a complete asshole. Now my life was everything I'd wished for and dreamed it could be. I was more than happy, I was content, and my life was full of love, happiness and laughter.

Bike pipes sounded outside my office doors, waking me from my musings. I peeked outside, and my lips twitched into a smile at a familiar scene. A particular band of men had changed my life, a brotherhood who crashed through my barriers. These men were rough and ready and sometimes downright crude. They loved me, and I loved them!

Hellfire MC. Imagine that, me, having an MC to call family! Our first encounter had been fraught and terrifying. I thought back to that night nearly three years ago, as I watched bikes pull onto the Rage MC forecourt opposite my building.

Nine months after moving to the States, I was driving back to my hotel in Sturgis after a fundraising event. Andrew Wainwright, a friend, had held it for the Trusts, when the car tyre blew, stranding me alone on Sturgis Road, near the I-90, leading to Sturgis. It was pitch black, and even the moon didn't want to play ball at that exact moment. The sheer darkness of the night had frightened me.

Scared, I'd attempted to get the nuts off and change the tyre myself and I couldn't. In the act of kicking the tyre in frustration and checking my phone for a signal, I heard bikes. I stepped back into the shadows of my car and saw headlights come out of the darkness. Four bikes approached.

They rode past me and then the lead biker twisted his head, caught sight of me and did a U-turn and came back my way. He parked up and swung off his bike, the biker looked me up and down, and his mouth twitched.

"Flat?" he grunted. The other riders pulled up behind his bike and swinging off their bikes, came to stand behind him. I nodded at him, unsure of what to say or do. Run screaming for the trees or ask for help?

"Bear, get the tyre iron and get those lug nuts off," lead biker ordered. A huge man trudged forward, and my jaw hit the floor at the size of him. Wow, the guy looked like he ate children for breakfast. The man was huge, with a bushy beard and dressed in riding gear.

"Honey, your phone, not a good weapon, tyre iron makes a better one," the lead biker said and let loose the grin he'd been fighting. I glanced at my hands and realised I was holding my phone up. Wrinkling my nose, I stared at the tyre iron and then back at the lead biker and felt sheepish.

"I'm a twit," I told him. He gave me that grin again, and a shiver rolled through me, he was hot, as in Tim McGraw hot and very tall. The man must have been six foot four at least, and he was lean sleek muscle.

His shoulders were broad, and his chest simply perfect. Bright green eyes that I could make out in the dim light gazed at me. Thick, dark hair, hanging just to above his collar in a sexy windblown mess and he was clean-shaven, which I liked in a guy.

"You're hot, deadly hot, but I think you need a bit of stubble, give you that extra badass edge, although you don't need it," I blurted. One of his guys at his back chuckled, and Bear raised his head and shot me a look.

"She's cute," Bear said in an amused voice.

"Yeah," Tim McGraw look-alike agreed. I jumped and stepped closer to him as sirens sounded abruptly from the dark and two cruisers pulled alongside.

A fat, overweight man got out, and he did that creepy man thing where he pulled his pants up, and his beer belly flopped over them. The lead biker looked towards him and then to my confusion, he stepped in front of me, protecting me. I peered around him and noticed the other three bikers had done the same.

"Late night," the fat officer said.

"What do you want, Sheriff?" the lead biker asked without an ounce of respect in his voice. A third car pulled up with lights flashing, and six of law enforcements finest surrounded us, but I doubted these gentlemen were the finest.

"Late night, dark road, meeting a whore in the back roads, two and two Chance," the sheriff replied

"My tyre blew, and who are you calling a whore?" I snapped at the sheriff indignant. Chance, as I guessed his name was, moved to protect me. Bear put his hand up to me.

"Drugs, guns or pussy run?" the sheriff sneered. I felt my body lock, dangerous vibes hit me from every direction, and I knew this was trouble.

"Back off, asshole. Hellfire's clean," Chance warned.

"Take 'em in. Include the pussy, in fact, that sweet piece, I'll take in myself."

"Don't resist," Chance murmured to his guys and me.

"What's the charges?" I snapped as the fat sheriff moved towards me.

"Shut up and assume the position. I'm sure you've done that plenty of times," the sheriff sniggered. The sheriff's little followers also laughed. He hitched his pants again.

"I'm not a whore. I'm a businesswoman who runs…" the sheriff interrupted me.

"Yeah, I'm sure we're familiar with your business. Assume the position," Sheriff Fatso (as I dubbed him) snarled, waddling towards me.

Dumbfounded, I watched as officers slammed the bikers up against my car and started cuffing them. The sheriff gripped my arm and flung me next to the hood of my car, and my eyes met Chance's. Shock receded, and instead, my stomach began churning in fear. I swallowed hard as Chance held my gaze, that was until I felt fat hands on my butt and legs, and then my dress being lifted.

Terror shot through me, shrieking, I kicked backwards at the sheriff. He grunted and banged my head on the car. From being forced over my hood, I was in a far more exposed position. Those fat, grasping hands came back to my butt and legs, and I screamed, nightmares flashed in front of me, memories threatened to choke me. Green eyes flared, and then Chance and another biker were moving.

Their heads snapped backwards, and the arresting officers stumbled away. Chance was around my car before the other guy, and he jammed his shoulder into the sheriff, sending him flying. Frozen in fear, I couldn't move, as two officers came at Chance who was roaring. Even with hands cuffed behind him was positioning his body in front of me, his legs splayed wide.

"Attempted fuckin' rape will put you behind bars, fuck your badges!" Chance roared, and the officers stopped moving. The sheriff came at Chance and hit him with the butt of his gun. Chance didn't move a step just glared at them as blood flowed from a cut on his head.

"You put the woman in a fuckin' car and don't touch her, clothes she's wearing, shit around her throat, the car she's driving, says money. The sort of money that'll get you fucked. She's no whore assholes and if you can't see that you're fuckin' off your heads," Chance spat out. Silence descended, the only sound was my harsh breathing.

"Look at her!" Chance roared a few seconds later. Two officers paused as his words hit, and they turned to take a proper look at me. Doubt crept over their faces.

"Put him in the car," the sheriff rasped. Fatso grabbed me and cuffed my hands behind my back. I screamed and started fighting the sheriff. In return, he none too gently banged my head for a third time into my car. Fear had taken over, and I couldn't stop. I kicked and screamed as they took me to the ground and carried me to a car.

"For fuck's sake, she's terrified!" biker three yelled out as they forced me inside. "Anyone can see that you dumb bastards!" The last I saw of him was him getting a backhand from a cop, and I lost it.

Still losing it when we pulled into the station, I was creating as much trouble as I could. I didn't make it easy for them to get me to the cell. The sheriff having had enough of my fighting, banged my head for the fourth time but this time into metal bars. Subdued now, he uncuffed me and slung me into the cell. I couldn't get my stiff arms out in time and hit the wall hard, sliding into a heap.

The four bikers walked in and were uncuffed. Then the cell door banged shut. Chance strode over to me, his movements angry. Chance bent down and helped me to my feet. With a look at my head, he ripped a bandana from his throat and threw it at Bear.

"Wet it," Chance ordered. "Woman you okay if I touch you?" he asked me.

"Yeah," I whispered dazed.

"Gonna clean you up, he split your head. Not gonna touch you anywhere else," Chance quietly said. I knew by his tone that he'd put two and two together and come up with four.

"Okay," I whispered. Swallowing hard and audibly, I reached up and put my hands lightly on his wrists.

Seconds later, I tightened my grip and leaned towards him. Something told me this man will keep me safe, no matter the cost. An emotion flashed in his eyes, but it was so fleeting I couldn't grasp it.

"Balls of steel woman," he muttered. And then took the wet bandana off Bear and began wiping my face. Once cleaned, with the bleeding stopped from the pressure he put on it, he stepped back and gave me room. His three biker brothers got as far from me as they could, signalling they respected my personal space.

"Why are we here?" I finally asked, sitting my butt at the end of a hard bench.

"Sheriff is an asshole who hates bikers, hates MC's and mine is one of the biggest and more established. Fuckin' funny considerin' that this whole part of

South Dakota is known for bikers and MC's," Chance replied.

"He's messing with the wrong person," I said. Chance stared and nodded.

"I'm getting the point darlin', you're high class and that whoever's he's just fucked with, meaning you woman, he's gonna pay the price." I nodded in agreement, Fatso would pay a heavy price, I'd have his damn job!

"As soon as I get my phone call we're out of here, all of us. I don't know why you were on Sturgis Road, I don't care. I know you stopped to help me, and because of me, Fatso arrested you."

"Not on you, if it hadn't been you it would'a been something else. Thinkin' they were watching us," Chance rumbled back. His eyes fell to my hands, following his gaze, I saw they were still shaking.

"On me," I whispered daring to disagree with the big burly biker.

"Woman, I'm gonna sit my ass with my brothers. Those assholes ain't gonna rush shit here. You wanna sit and commune, join us, you wanna stay here in a bubble, you do that. But first, put this on, you're fuckin' freezing." I hadn't noticed the temperature had dropped, and I wore my little black dress, cut low to hint at cleavage and black high heels. My shawl and heavier coat (that I kept for emergencies, which this was indeed an emergency) were back at my car.

A leather jacket was slung at me, and I pulled it on, not arguing. I got the feeling many didn't argue with Chance. I reached up to pull out my hair, and my hand caught on something sewn onto the front of the coat. Chance moved away from me and sat, legs stretched out and hands behind his head with his brothers.

The front had several patches sewn onto it. One above his right breast said President, the second said Third Gen. The next situated over his left breast was a kick-ass patch. I pulled the jacket out and studied it better.

It was a circular patch with the flames starting at the bottom and going halfway up the circle. In the middle of them was a skeleton with devil's horns on its head and holding a pitchfork. In the other hand, the skeleton held a motorbike and above the skeleton's head was a crown of flames. It was seriously badass.

Underneath the flames were the words Hellfire MC written in a bold freestyle script in white. The leather was heavy and smelt of motor oil, which wasn't disagreeable, and of man. It was a smell I was rapidly linking to Chance. A pleasant scent and I dipped my nose to inhale it in deeper.

I caught Chance's eyes on me, and he gave me a half-grin. I smiled back and shifted closer, he held his arm out, and I froze in place. Chance began lowering it when my feet took over and took me straight to him. I curled up under his arm, and he slung it around my shoulders.

I didn't say much, just listened as his brothers, communed, I suppose. None of them looked bothered by the arrest or the fact the nasty cops had ignored my three demands for a phone call. There was a toilet set in the corner. I think they expected us to share, which was icky. I was sharing a cell with four men for crying out loud. Luckily for me, none of them used it while I was awake, if they did when I was asleep, I didn't know and didn't care.

I came awake with my head nestled on Chance's muscled thigh and opened my eyes in surprise. One of his arms was around my waist and the other behind his head. Another jacket covered my legs. I was warm, cosy, and it amazed me I had fallen to sleep. Green eyes watched me as I gathered my wits.

"Time?" I asked.

"Just gone eight," Chance grumbled. He pulled out a pack of gum and offered it to me, I took it, giving him a smile of gratitude. To moisten my mouth, I sat up, chewing it and dragged my hands through my hair. It was a mess, I gave up, rising to my feet I looked at an officer.

I pinned him with an evil look, demanded my phone call and then threatened his job and livelihood if I didn't get it in the next ten minutes. The idiot sneered at me, but his partner appeared worried enough he let me out to make a call.

I could see the front desk from the cell, and I marched over to the phone. I punched in a number I knew well and waited. If Andrew didn't pick up, I was screwed, finally, a sleepy voice answered.

"You took your time."

"Phoenix?" Andrew mumbled.

"Get your butt out of bed, Andrew. I've been arrested, held in jail all night, denied my phone call until now. Add to that list I've been groped and molested by a fat, ugly, mean, old sheriff and I'm now pissed."

"What?" Andrew roared at me, oh now he was awake!

"And they left my car open with my purse, identification and phone and everything else in it. Get your ass here now, Andrew, I need the lady facilities!" I ended indignantly.

"On it," Andrew replied curtly, and I could hear him moving. I told him where I was and slammed the phone on the desk and looked at the dickhead who'd denied my phone call. He was giving me a dark look, moving towards me.

"You're fucked," I told him smugly. His partner stopped him and let me use a separate bathroom which my begging bladder needed. Dickhead grabbed my arm, bruising me again as I came out and threw me back in my cell. Chance moved fast and caught me before I hit the wall again.

"You okay?"

"We're going to be fine," I said, "the cavalry is on its way." Chance gave me an amused look, ignoring that, I waited for him to sit and leant into him again.

An hour later, the door to the police station flew open and an irate, pissed off to high heaven, male strode in. I sat up looking at the commotion. It wasn't the man I had thought would appear, but instead Antony Parker-Jones. Antony was furious, which meant someone was going to be getting a serious come to Jesus talk! Hands banged on the front desk, and I watched the fat sheriff heading at speed towards him.

"Hey, honey," I called out. Angry eyes snapped towards me, and then his glare focused on Fatso.

"Oh dear, wrong man, Antony has issues, that's why I didn't call him," I muttered, "Andrew's calmer. Andrew should have got here first as he's closer."

Chance tipped his head towards me, recognition on his face as he saw Antony. A question lurked in his eyes and then Antony drew my attention.

"Are you insane?" Antony bellowed as an introduction and waved his hand in my direction. I nodded.

"Yeah, he has issues," I repeated, nodding my head.

"Who the hell are you?" Sheriff Fatso asked.

"Oh, you're so fucked!" I whispered.

"Senator Antony Parker-Jones and the man that's gonna get your ass canned! You locked up Phoenix? Sexually assaulted Phoenix? And by the looks of her, you roughed her up." Antony's gaze hit me and his level of pissed off intensified.

"She resisted arrest! There was no sexual assault," Sheriff Fatso replied, hooking his thumbs in his belt.

"Liar!" I shouted, and Bear chuckled.

"Why was she under arrest?" Antony narrowed his eyes.

"Drunk driving," Sheriff Fatso sneered, showing no respect for the Senator of South Dakota.

"Drunk driving? You're going with that?"

"Yup and resisting arrest."

"How does Phoe get arrested for drunk driving when she left a fundraising event at my home sober? It takes thirty minutes to reach where you arrested Phoe. Which, I know because I drove past her open car. How does Phoe go from sober to drunk and disorderly in half an hour? *Do you have any idea who Phoenix is?*" Antony seethed.

"Especially since I have multiple witnesses who will testify, she was very sober," a second voice said. I got on my tippy toes and peered over Chance's arm. Andrew stood next to Antony.

"Yay, the cavalry has finally arrived. Andrew's got issues too, but he handles them better." Chance's head dipped as he looked at me with amusement in his eyes.

"Phoe's cut, and there're bruises on her face! Get Phoenix out of there," Antony continued.

"She's gonna be charged," Fatso kept up, thinking he was in charge. Even when faced with a Congressman and Senator.

"The hell she is, you say! Let me tell you precisely what will happen here. The Vice President of the United States will walk through that door, with him will be several high-ranking law enforcement officers. These trumped-up charges will be dropped, you'll be suspended and your entire department under investigation. The V.P was my guest last night and is a witness that Phoenix was sober when she left my home," Andrew calmly stated.

"Add to that, you molested her, I'm hoping there are witnesses. Do you have any idea the shit you and your dumbass officers are in?" Antony grinned.

"That woman has the President on speed dial, Phoenix lunches with his wife and kids. Phoe has more influence than you can possibly imagine. Jesus Christ, you've no apparent clue who you arrested on phoney charges!"

"That woman saves and rescues homeless heroes, abused men, women and children, and you locked her up? Ever heard of the Phoenix Trust? Rebirth and Eternal Trusts? Yeah," Andrew sneered, as Fatso paled as the realisation of who he'd locked up kicked in.

"Antony, these guys are witnesses to the fact that dickhead was molesting me, that's why I panicked and kicked the sheriff. Fatso locked them up because they tried to stop it. He stuck his fat hands up my dress and rubbed his minuscule dick against my butt," I chirped. Heated amusement hit me from behind.

"Jesus, woman, you're signing his death certificate," Chance whispered in my ear. Two pairs of irate eyes swung in my direction.

"Works for me," I whispered back.

"Get Phoe the fuck out now!" Andrew shouted, "you've caused a cluster fuck I doubt you have the dubious intelligence to understand." The officer who'd denied my call shifted his ass, I leaned into Chance, who wrapped his arm around my shoulders.

"I warned you, you'd no idea who you were messing with, they're gonna *fuck you up*." Chance looked at me as I smirked at the officer whose eyes narrowed on my face. The swagger had gone, and now he looked worried, as he should. I stepped out of the cell, and he went to lock the door leaving the four bikers inside.

"You let them go, they're witnesses to Phoe being assaulted, molested and violated. You let them out now!" Antony demanded, and the bikers stepped out of the cell.

"Sit there, honey," Andrew whispered as he watched his best friend going to town on the dirty cops. Andrew stood tall, taking his best friend's back. I walked to the bench in front of the desk and sat.

Chance sat next to me and slung his arm back around my shoulder. Bear took my other side, the other two bikers called Diesel, and Tiny took their sides. Watching, we stayed silent until the Vice President entered the building. I waved at him, and he gave me a grin. The Vice President turned an intensely frightening look on the sheriff, Fatso began backtracking as quickly as he could. Chance looked at me, stunned.

"Who the fuck are you, lady?" Chance asked, dipping his head to mine. "Why do I think you're gonna complicate my life?"

"I'm Phoenix," I smirked and held out my hand for him to shake.

That wasn't the last time I met Hellfire MC. Oh no, those boys showed up at my hotel room the next day. They interfered in my life every which way they could. Strong bonds gradually formed with the entire MC, those beautiful men. They got into the Trusts, they got into the kid's lives, they got into everything. I did the same to them, I'd no fear when I was with them. I could do, say, what I wanted, fully aware I'd get away with murder.

With my history, one might have thought I'd be afraid of big, hairy, loud, crass men. I wasn't. Hellfire MC would never hurt me, they'd kill to protect me. If anyone glanced the wrong way at one of my kids, they'd rain hellfire and brimstone on the culprit. They were present for a few of my adoptions. Chance often wondered if I'd be rescuing every orphan in the world.

My kids loved them. Mr and Mrs Ames and Albert adored them. I loved them and Hellfire for all their rough ways, they gave their big hearts back to us. I believe fate has a way of breaking even. Once, I'd been an orphan with no one, then I birthed five children and lost a cherished husband. Fate made life go horrible, and then fate handed me beauty, so much beauty, I was overflowing with it.

Which brings me to now. I stood in the Headquarters I'd dreamed of, my dreams made real, sixteen kids, three large charities and family in the form of Hellfire MC. A biker at my back whom I desperately loved but was not in love with. Yeah, life was good at last.

Chapter Two.

I wandered around Headquarters, today was Sunday; therefore, we were empty as we hadn't opened yet. The grand opening was tomorrow, I was doing the final checks before opening, and I'd wasted an hour reminiscing. Alone in the big building, I enjoyed the peace, the calm before the storm.

As soon as my house began its renovations, Sally started to look for a Headquarters for the Trusts. She'd found this empty gothic designed building and taken one look and known it was for me. I came to Rapid City for a few days to view the building, flying in from Camden and just like Sally, I'd fallen deeply in love.

The building was large, the length and the depth of ten double shop fronts. With its four floors, there was plenty of room for what I needed. HQ was situated on 6th Street near the main shopping centre. It boasted underground parking and a smaller covered parking lot behind the building, a staff stairwell connected the car park to HQ.

The architect and I'd worked hard to create the ideal office space while keeping the original features in place. HQ's front door opened onto a plush reception where visitors checked in, before being allowed through the locked bulletproof glass doors behind it. The entire ground floor held offices for our admin, legal and accounting, filing staff, etcetera. This floor was our central hub.

Tucked behind reception was the security office with our cameras and security guards. The main floor was laid out in rows of desks each surrounded by glass walls with blinds for privacy and a few closed in offices.

The first floor held offices similar but more significant than those below and closed in, which held the desks for the State Managers (SM) of the twenty states. These cleverly designed spaces made the most of the square footage. Adjoined to the SM's office was a smaller one for their personal assistant.

The SMs oversaw the Phoenix Trust and Rebirth Trust and if they had one, the Eternal Trust in their designated state. Plaques on their doors gave their name and the state they represented. SMs was responsible for how the properties were running. The SMs made sure everything ran smoothly, so I didn't have to worry. Empty offices were awaiting their own SM's. The first floor held a large conference room that we'd often use for team meetings.

I walked up to the second floor, where I glanced in, happy with the layout and design. The level wasn't entirely in use yet. One-third of the floor stood empty, waiting for when we opened in new states and needed offices for the SM's. Based on the second floor was the Investigations Team and Property Teams. The Investigation Team were tasked with specific roles, such as looking up whether someone we were bringing in was genuine, not a fraud. The team did searches for missing people who'd been brought to our attention. Cramped spaces hindered productivity, so I made sure everyone, no matter their status, had space, lots of light and room to move around.

The Property Team sought out suitable hotels to buy, or apartment blocks we could convert in a good locality. We bought hotels that were run down as they were easier to convert. They searched for the homes for RT. The Property Team built a serious network in a short space of time, so I'd lots of respect for them. Property, knew my vision, understood it and implemented it.

The third floor housed the Directors and me, even bigger offices had been built here. A large section set up in one corner with maps of each state set up against the walls. The map had blue dots for PT's, Red dots for RT's, green for ET's and yellow for RT houses. A smaller conference room was tucked away in a corner on our floor for private meetings. My office opened onto a balcony, and I loved it. Stefan's office and Stuart's office boasted balconies too.

The fourth floor held the comforts of home. A kitchen/canteen that took a quarter of the level with nice tables and chairs to sit and eat. A massive pool table took up an ample space alongside an air hockey table. There were a television space and chill-out corner.

The day-care centre took over a quarter of the space, funded privately by me. There was nothing worse than being away from your children eight, nine hours a day. I hated it and made it so the babies could be around me. Many of my staff had young children too, so I paid for free child-care for them. The architect turned the roof into a garden with several big grills, so we could have barbeques and celebrations. I thought it would be pleasant for staff to lunch there in the summer too.

Each office got a small decorating grant, as I liked my people to be comfortable with what worked for them. Their style may not work for me, but as long as it worked for them, that was what mattered. I wandered upstairs to my floor. Here we ran the Trust, I and my Directors. Decorators had been here, the offices decorated to the Directors' specs and wishes.

I stuck my head into Diana's office, the Director of Human Resources. Diana dealt with personnel issues and did the recruiting and sometimes firing of people. She'd a team of five people working for her and didn't mind travelling when needed, nor did her team.

Abigail's office, my Director of Security, was calming with pale colours. Next up was Kyle, Director of Finance, he watched over everything financial. My office took up one corner with Stefan's in the opposite corner to mine, my Director of Fundraising. Between ours was Stuart's, Director of Legal.

Other Directors were on this floor too, Property, Accounting, Investigation, Events, Public Relations, Advertising, Operations and Wages. Sally got a corner office, but it was safe to say she'd never be in it much. Sally had itchy feet and enjoyed getting out and visiting the properties and being hands-on. We often joked we'd have to nail her feet to the ground.

The offices backed up against the walls of the building. Again, like the State Managers, our personal assistants had their own areas. A massive conference table that seated forty people dominated the centre of the floor. We'd often used this at our old rented HQ so we'd brought it with us and it now held centre stage on our floor.

My office had been decorated and looked great. I'd a comfortable brown leather corner sofa with lots of throw pillows and a glass coffee table. A big old-fashioned oak desk, something Stuart and I shared in common with trays and my office laptop. On my back wall facing me was lots and lots of framed photographs. The frames' held pictures of my kids, my staff, people we'd helped, my wall was full of them. There was a small round glass dining table and four chairs if I wanted to eat alone. Thick black carpet covered the floor, and my walls were exposed brick. A rocking chair with wicker furniture and fluffy cushions were on my balcony.

Behind my desk, the wall was full of shelves. Private files sat in boxes waiting to be unpacked and for me to put them on the shelves. I hated people touching my office or my stuff, and the guys knew that so left me to it. I ran my fingers over my desk and looked outside to the office attached to mine.

Emily's, my personal assistant, office was half the size of mine and positioned in front of my door, was a riot of colour. Emily couldn't work without it, and her walls reflected her personality, a bright sunny yellow colour. When you considered how many time's she changed colours, it was amusing. We found it cheaper to use coloured film that pressed onto transparent glass and then stripped off and changed when she wanted.

The riot of colours reflected in her furniture. Colourful cushions and multi-coloured filing trays, you get the idea. To get to me, you'd have to get past her and Emily was a bulldog. Far better than any guard dog I could've bought.

Stefan's office I looked over to see and then sighed, was white and black. Stefan's walls had to be painted white because the man had an unfortunate habit of writing on them. When an idea popped into his head, instead of scrabbling for paper, he wrote on his walls. Every few months we noted what he'd written on them and then re-painted. In the old building, we'd done this six-times, so I knew it would happen here too.

With Stefan being the Director of Fundraising, we'd had to hire a Director of Events. Stefan had great ideas and was meticulous in planning them. It was too much, though, to expect Stefan's follow through on the executing stage of the planning. Stefan loved to work out the nitty-gritty, not the doing. So Stefan planned and Rayna executed.

The core of us had been together for nearly the full four years. Emily came on board straight away, Stuart the minute Sally put things into motion. Stefan soon after that, Kyle and Diana three months into the Trusts being started. We worked well together, and yeah, we fought, but we forgave and carried on. We were tight, which was good considering how close we worked together.

Sally hired Diana at the same time as Kyle, and those two immediately clashed. By now we'd learned to put Diana at one end of the office floor and Kyle the opposite end. Matters weren't helped because their assistants took their bosses backs in things, several times we'd broken up office wars.

But, when Diana got ill, Kyle took her soup and bullied her into showers and stuff. When Kyle got hurt in a car accident, Diana pushed his wheelchair. Even though she threatened several times to push him down a very steep hill, she was there for him. Such was family.

I suppose at this point I should make things a bit clearer. The Trusts belonged to me, I didn't have a board of Trustee's, and while I'd Directors, they worked for me. The final decision in all things related to the Trusts was mine. No one could over-rule me. I didn't throw my weight around, and I trusted people to do their jobs. My Directors held my full trust, and I needed them to run their departments and hold people accountable.

The old rented HQ had been based in Norfolk. When I'd found Reading Hall, I'd given HQ people the choice of a generous severance packet or help to find another job or the option most had taken.

I'd moved each of them at a personal cost to me and helped them find a house they liked. I paid their expenses in moving across the country and paid for them to have a week off so they could move in and sort what they needed too. The real estate around Rapid City had taken a considerable boost.

Any relocation expense they had come across I'd covered. Staff were moving because I wanted to live in South Dakota in Rapid City and so I owed them. Oblivious, I'd no idea how much this had meant to them. They were paid well, but it meant they weren't taking a monetary hit.

It wasn't just my Directors who'd moved. Every single SM moved, their assistants, legal and admin staff, property and investigations. Three hundred people worked at HQ, and we'd only had vacancies for just forty-two people. Of the forty-two people who hadn't relocated, they received jobs elsewhere in the Trusts, no one had become jobless.

Diana had interviewed and filled the positions that had become vacant. She'd hired people that lived locally, so I didn't have to move anyone else. It'd cost me a whack, a tremendous whack to move HQ people across the country to here. I was touched by their dedication to the Trusts, we didn't hire people who didn't get my vision and work their ass off to achieve it. I couldn't ever repay the loyalty they showed, although I could show them how much it meant to me. In making their moves easier, I hoped I'd shown that.

The staff that had relocated had no mortgage, no moving costs and no debt concerning the move. (I'd paid the monetary difference between their old home and the new home. Any mortgage left I paid for them.) Trust staff got a bonus every year that came out of my personal money. The interest on my fortune was immense.

My two hundred and seventeen million pounds was now just under one billion dollars thanks to my investment broker. He'd been rewarded exceptionally well. In fact, he could retire, but the man loved to make money! This freed me to do things I wanted to, such as paying for the staff's relocations and bonuses.

So yeah, moving everyone, covering any mortgage and clearing it, funding moving and decorating costs cost a whack, but as I said it wasn't even a blip.

Motorbike pipes roared again, and I walked to the French doors that opened onto my balcony. Ever since Sturgis, I'd loved bikes, ever since Hellfire I'd loved MC's. Pure coincidence my building was opposite a garage that specialised in bikes and one I knew linked with Hellfire.

Hellfire specialised in car designs, with Rage MC designing bikes. The two MC's split the mechanic business between themselves. That meant it wasn't a vague link between the two clubs but a strong one. Chance never explained the connection to me, though, I admit I was curious. I never pressed him, he'd tell me when he wanted too. Chance had never taken me to visit Rage MC either, although they met up often.

Directly opposite Headquarters, the Rage forecourt was plentiful and easily could hold thirty plus cars. The garage had five bays in which you could see vehicles being serviced. Two bays at the end were where they obviously completed their builds.

The garage was a long squat L shaped building with what looked to my eye an office at the end. To the left of the garage was a two-storey building I believed was their clubhouse. Rage's clubhouse was as large as the first three bays and a dull concrete colour. Three tall white flagpoles were outside and flew three flags. One was an American flag with an eagle embossed on it, the second the MC patch and the third their motto.

MC members parked their bikes in spaces to the left of the clubhouse, and if they were driving vehicles, they parked on the forecourt. From turning my body a little, I could see behind the clubhouse was a huge grassed area. Huge grills and kegs stood on stands placed randomly around. Picnic tables and chairs were scattered around the grills. Under a wooden shed with doors that closed, I could see a music centre and large speakers.

Next to the forecourt was a row of shops. The first shop was boarded and appeared empty. A second, the width of two shopfronts was called Rage Shop. The shop sold biker paraphernalia, the shop to the left was boarded up too.

Further up, if I leaned forward and looked at the corner of my side of the street, I could see the bar that Rage and Hellfire both jointly owned. I hadn't been in it yet. Without Chance or Hellfire at my back, I was unlikely too. Hells Rage was an apt name for the bar, and it appeared busy even at this time of day.

The front corner of the forecourt held the parts store, which always had people coming and going. Hellfire was flush I knew that, it appeared Rage was too. Snuggled up on my rocking chair, I watched a tall man get off one of the three bikes that had pulled in. He swung his jean-clad leg over the bike and clapped another man on the back.

Nearly breaking my neck straining to see his face, I was disappointed I couldn't, as his back was to me. A mighty fine ass was on show, though, that ass could make any woman smile. Proof of that was my own smile, I jolted as a gorgeous Native American, and his son strode out. Both wore the warrior biker uniform of faded well-fitting jeans, tees and their cuts. There was far too much raw male sexiness in Rage, and I drooled. They had an intense discussion, then the five men disappeared into the clubhouse.

I looked as my phone pinged and saw a text from Chance. 'Be in Rapid City tomorrow, Rage clubhouse after five, baby.' That was Chance short and sweet! No, how are you, what're you doing, just meet me at five! I sighed and sent him an okay back, and then my phone pinged again as Bear texted me. Curled up, watching the bikes come and go from Rage for half an hour, I had a text conversation with Bear. Surely it would have been easier to talk over the phone. Bikers!

In the middle of shelving my files around one o'clock, I heard several loud toots on a horn and music being blasted from the street. I groaned as I knew who it was. I walked to the balcony and looked at the road and there heading towards me was Bernard driving his (as I call it) beach jeep. Hanging on the bars on the back and waving madly at me was Stefan.

I adored Stefan, but sometimes he could make me want to run for cover, and this was one of them. Wiry, slender, with toned muscles Stefan wore a pair of black jeans that made him look even slimmer. Proudly, he wore a Queen tee showing the album cover of their greatest hits. Stefan's hair was short and bleached almost white by the sun.

Bernard swung into a space outside HQ and rose to his feet and waved at me, I waved back as the man blew kisses. Stefan was wriggling his hips around the back of the jeep in a kind of terrifying dance. Bernard grinned at me, turned the volume up and he blasted me with Tubthumping. I rolled my eyes at Bernard, and he shrugged and turned to look at his crazy assed husband.

A new black Dodge Dakota belted up the road, and I closed my eyes in horror as Diana pulled in beside them. Diana could be one of the calmest, most rational people you'd ever meet. Stefan though, brought out the wild in her, when he did, everyone braced!

Diana leapt out of the car and threw her arms above her head. Loudly she screamed at Stefan who grinned back at her. Swinging his hips, he jumped off the jeep and swept her up into his arms. Stefan threw Diana on the back of her pickup before jumping up with her. Together, to my alarmed eyes, they began jumping about. I bit my lip and swallowed a giggle.

Too intent on my crazy team, I didn't see people coming out of the Rage clubhouse watching us. Instead, I saw another new black Ford Ranger pickup pull in. Stuart got out and waved at me and then glared over his shoulder at the maniacs dancing on the jeep.

"I've been following those two fucknuts for hours. I desperately need a beer followed by whiskey," Stuart bellowed up at me. "Road trip from hell, Phoe you don't want to know what they did in the diner we stopped at!" Oh I did, I really wanted to know! I tried to keep a smile from my lips and saw his gaze shoot to my face. I bit my lip again instead. After all, the team had stayed behind to shut the former HQ for the last time, I shouldn't laugh at his pain!

Stuart's passenger door opened, letting Susan, his assistant out. The woman dressed in Armani head to toe and looked the ultimate professional. Which was at odds with the mischievous smile she sent me. Bernard winked at her, Susan shrieked and ran over to the jeep. Susan hitched up her skirt and clambered on the back of the jeep and began twerking.

"Susan get your ass off there now!" Stuart hollered. She responded by twerking in his direction, I guessed the trip had been wearing on him. Stuart rolled beleaguered eyes to me and hitched his butt on the front of Bernard's jeep. I looked at the street as the last two vehicles I'd been expecting arrived.

Kyle climbed out of a black (sensing a theme yet?) Jaguar and looked unimpressed. At his look, I felt my lips twitch, I couldn't help it. Like Stuart, Kyle dressed in slacks and a buttoned shirt. Unlike Stuart, he wore a tie he'd yanked around his neck while he'd been driving. Kyle swept his arm toward the three nutcases who had moved on from Tubthumping. I rolled my eyes as they appeared to be singing to be an out of tune rendition of the Bohemian Rhapsody.

Bernard was now up on the back of the jeep and holding on to Susan's waist as she shimmied and twerked for everything she was worth. Excited squeals and yelps came from the last car. A stunning 1967 black, with silver stripes going up and over it, Flashback Shelby Mustang, Emily's baby Eleanor.

Emily shot out of the car, heading straight towards Stefan, today her hair was pink with blond streaks, and I sighed. Emily was brilliant, which is why I didn't enforce a dress code on her. She wore short shorts, and a tank top that kept slipping off one shoulder, on her feet were clunky motorcycle boots.

Stefan reached for Emily and hauled her up on to Diana's vehicle. With a small smile, I watched as half of my insane staff began belting out the famous chorus of Boeheim Rhapsody. Kyle looked on in horror, his expression mirrored by Stuart. I began to chuckle, and they looked up at me. The singers started waving their arms above their heads and weaving side to side.

The looks on the two men's faces undid me and my laughter peeled out over the music, reaching those across the forecourt watching from the clubhouse. A man straightened, and his gaze came to me. I didn't see, as I was so busy holding on to my railings and laughing so hard, I began crying.

Stuart deftly reached over and turned the jeeps music off and got a chorus of boos and hisses. The singers finished without music, remaining badly out of tune, to my giggles. With a grin at me Stefan reached his arms above his head and yelled at me, in a voice I was sure could be heard across the country.

"Hi, babe! Totally awesome idea, a street party, going to get my cute butt onto it and my delicious man can sort out the catering. What do you think, Tudthumping as our song of the year? It's so us! Need to get Public Relations on it. Phoe you going to let us in or stand there laughing all day?"

"You're freaking insane!" I called to him.

"Yeah, but you're madly in love with me, so let us in Phoe," Stefan yelled back at the top of his lungs. I gazed into his eyes, recognising his feverish delight and the wheels turning the idea of a street party in his head. I walked to my desk, hit the buzzer, heard the door open and voices over-talking each other.

"We're on the third floor," I called. They stampeded the stairs, and Emily, Stefan and Diana burst in swiftly followed by Bernard. The others were staidly making their way up. This was their first-time seeing HQ, which added to the excitement. Only Sally and I had seen the finished product. Stefan saw the white walls of his office and burst in. He gave a wordless yell and threw open his doors to his balcony and walked out.

"Hey, Phoe?" Stefan yelled from his balcony, I looked out on mine. "Cool babe. I don't have to get off my ass to talk to you, I can shout." I grinned at him, Stuart's doors opened, and he shoved his own head out. A stern finger pointed at Stefan.

"Don't you dare screech across my office!" he yelled at Stefan. Who in return cheerfully flipped him the bird and strolled back into his office.

"Oh, dear," I whispered.

"You sort Stefan out, he's your responsibility. I'm not having him yelling across my office," Stuart ordered.

"Cups and wires Phoe!" Stefan bellowed from his office the sound carrying in the relative silence.

"We soundproofed your office," I whispered. Stuart narrowed his eyes at me and then grinned and slammed his doors. Music blasted from Stefan's office, and I closed my eyes. Lost in my happiness at my guys arriving, I didn't see I was being watched with intent interest from Rage MC.

The day unfolded as we unpacked and sorted through everything. I dealt with my office while

Emily went crackers in hers. Stefan was scribbling on his walls, and I raised my eyes to heaven. Emily had given him a blank pad, but he was too caught up, drawing diagrams and scribbling stuff as his mind went into overdrive. Bernard sat nodding and helping him.

Stuart was checking his law books and legal stuff had been delivered precisely as he ordered, basically the same layout as his old office. Emily got her office right and strolled upstairs where she began a vigorous game of air hockey with Susan. Kyle was sorting through his stuff that like me, he liked to place.

Around five, we had pizzas delivered, and then I sent them home. I sat in my office for a while and thanked my blessings. I gazed across the darkened office's that for now was peaceful. Tomorrow, at eight in the morning, all hell would break loose, in a good way.

I was first in at half past-six that morning, checking things for a second time when I heard the buzzer go half an hour after I arrived. Staff weren't due to arrive for another hour, but I could hear voices in the street and lots of calls and welcome and yo's and hi's! This group was early, bless them.

The staff parked under the building and walked up to the front security door. Not having security cards meant they'd not be able to use the car park barriers. Today the barriers had been left open until everyone got their security passes. I opened the main door and got pounced on by several people carrying boxes with personal belongings and stuff, and happy to see their new places at last.

For the last week, we'd covered with temps and Property Managers while the HQ staff had a week off and moved into their new homes. It was gratifying to receive the cheerful greetings I got. The receptionist hadn't relocated, the new girl obviously hadn't learnt who was who yet. To help, Emily and Susan had both agreed to operate the desk with her. But for today I was on that task.

I handed out security passes as the first bunch came in, far earlier than their eight o'clock start. I'd finished handing them out, and Emily (who'd arrived with them) took them around the building. Emily was showing them their desks when the next bunch arrived twenty minutes later. I looked up at open balcony doors, with people leaning over the balconies and heads peering over the roof shouting greetings at those on the street.

Shouts, cheers and hollers sounded as I opened the door and I missed seeing Rage MC come out of the clubhouse, put asses to bikes and watch. There was an air of excitement surrounding the staff and building, it was catching! I ended up in the street, handing out passes and stuff as my guys came on a roll.

Excitement thundered through the air with good-natured insults being hollered, slaps on backs given, delighted squeals from Directors who hadn't yet seen their offices. Stefan and Stuart going at it on their balcony's delighting arriving staff.

Stuart stormed back into his office, seconds later Pink's So What blasted out of Stefan's windows to the laughter of those on the street. Stefan appeared in his doorway, dancing wildly. Stuart slammed his balcony doors back open and shouted a few inventive insults. To everyone's glee, he slammed his doors shut while sixty-odd staff and I laughed hard on the pavement.

The staff were even happier at getting their decorating grants, again paid for personally by me. Admin staff were cruising around and checking their desks that each had a bronzed name plaque. I ended up getting everyone in and getting them to their floors. Then doing a walk around of each member of staff, handing them security passes for the doors and one for the underground parking.

Emily made sure they each knew what facilities were available, and they'd everything they needed. By two o'clock I'd spoken to everyone. I sank into the comfortable chair that swallowed me and swung to my French doors as I heard bike pipes in the road.

I knew those pipes, I rose and walked to the opening watching Hellfire pull in, I counted bikes and knew most of the MC had arrived. Chance in front on his Dyna Glide with Bear at his right on his Fat Boy, Diesel at his left riding a second Fat Boy.

A wolf whistle caught my attention, and I saw Chatter wave up at me. I waved back at him and then my attention was caught by a large flat-bed truck and crane arriving.

"It's here!" I squealed loudly, people hearing me in the street and offices. I flew out of the office with Emily at my heels. It had finally arrived! A day late, but it was here. The staff caught on, and the street ended up jammed with over two hundred staff. People spilt onto Rage's side of the street, while I directed where the symbol of the Trusts was to go.

The colossal work of art had been built by two of the women who'd used the Rebirth Trust. One was a welder, and she'd crafted a stunning Phoenix. The Phoenix's claws latched onto the wall, the wings spanned half the width of the building, its neck arched gracefully to the sky. Elegantly the head titled downwards looking at us in the street.

A woman who worked miracles and sheer beauty with stained glass had done the second part. She'd filled in the spaces left by the welder and rounded out the design. Different oranges, reds and yellows glinted in the sun, and its wings alone were serious works of art. I hopped around terrified they'd drop it, but within two hours they secured it in place, and we gasped as the sun hit and lit it up.

Hanging from one wing was a small sign saying Phoenix Trust, under the other, was another sign saying Rebirth Trust. Above the Phoenix's head was a sign saying Headquarters and under its feet gripped by claws was Eternal Trust.

I felt tears in my eyes, I wasn't the only one because I looked around and saw it. As my people went back to work, I gazed across at Rage MC, Chance was standing there, ass to bike watching me. He gave a slow nod and then walked to the clubhouse. I knew he'd waited and watched the whole time I had.

Chapter Three.

At five o'clock people started clocking off, not much had been accomplished today as everyone was still settling in. Tomorrow my people would kick ass at what they did. Half an hour later, I put the emergency phone in my bag, as I'd agreed to take the phone for the first week.

I did a walk around and checked everything was locked that needed to be and nodded at our night security guards. The guards were new but looked capable. The night receptionist was on duty, whistling away to herself. Carole had moved to Rapid City too, she was working hard on things the day girl had left.

HQ always kept two skeleton night teams. Each shift consisted of two general SMs, two legal advisors, five investigation, five property and twenty admin staff. One team started at five when day staff were leaving and left at two am. A second-team came in at eleven pm and worked till eight am when the day staff took over.

I spoke to the five o'clock team for a while. I checked if anyone needed anything, introduced security and showed everyone around. HQ kept a night team because of different time zones across the country. The Directors and I carried the emergency phone on rotation. If someone couldn't get the office or the office couldn't handle it, the phone was used.

I walked across to Rage MC and saw the garage bay doors were closed and the office lights were dark. Surprised, I checked my watch and was shocked to realise it was half-past seven. Wondering where time had gone, I saw Bears bike and strolled over, smiling I ran my fingers across it and then spied Chance's.

I walked over and wrapped around the handlebars was the silver pendant I'd given him of the patron saint of bikers, St. Columbanus. With a smile, I reached a finger out and touched the necklace that kept Chance safe.

"Hey bitch, what the fuck do you think you're doing?" a voice screeched, making me jump.

I looked up as the skank of the year with two skank sisters, stormed across the forecourt. Short skirts, barely covering their lady bits, teased out hair that looked messed up, low cut tops just keeping their boobs inside and high heels. The three witches marched towards me, I rolled my eyes and walked over to them.

"I'm looking for Hellfire. I'm guessing they're inside the clubhouse."

"Hellfire don't want no uppity bitch, get lost," Skank one said, she could have been attractive except for the war paint. I looked at myself, in comparison, I was wearing a pearl silk blouse and a nude pencil skirt. A Gucci handbag over my shoulder, I wore Jimmy Choos on my feet. My hair was still in its

French plait from this morning. Guess I did look uppity.

"Think you'll find messing with me is a mistake, I'm Hellfire." To get my point across, I gave her a grim smile. Eyes narrowed in my direction, and she got in my face.

"Hellfire don't want the likes of you, they need real women." I got straight back in her face. That was the one thing I'd learned well at Hellfire, don't back away from skanks. I was a member of an MC, not a biker bunny. Be proud and loud, Chance often told me.

"Told you once, I'll be nice and tell you again. I'm Hellfire, get out of my way, or I won't be responsible for what happens next." The tone in my voice warned her not to mess with me. With a lip curl, she returned my glare.

"Think you can take me, bitch?" Skank of the year sneered.

"I don't think, I know, but I warned you twice, what happens next is on you," I replied and turned on my heel. The skanks sneered and gloated as I walked away and pulled my phone out. I sent Chance and Bear a text and perched on Chance's bike. Tonight wasn't the night for a fight, no matter how tempting.

Skank of the year screeched and back she came. The idiotic woman reached for me and pushed hard, rocking Chance's bike underneath me. Oh, she didn't! Annoyed, I took a step forward and shoved with both hands. As she stumbled back three steps, I glared at her.

"Don't ever touch me again, or I'll break every single bone in your hand. If I'd fallen, Chance's bike would've gone over too. Think I'm trouble? Chance will rip your tiny little skank head off your shoulders," I told her, furious. A brother's bike was sacred, the skank had crossed the line. She glared at me, and I angrily regarded her.

Foul-mouthed, cursing up a storm, she aimed a slap at my face, and I caught her wrist in mid-air and twisted hard. As she shrieked, I turned with her, taking her arm up her back. I kicked the back of her knees, and she fell to the ground. Out of the corner of my eye, I saw the other two heading towards us. Skank of the year was making threats when legs strode past her and arms swept me up.

I giggled, letting go of the stupid bitch and threw my arms around Tiny who grabbed me tight. Tiny landed a smacking kiss on my cheek and put me back on my feet for Chatter to grab me next. Chatter, terribly named because the man wasn't a chatterbox by anyone's imagination, dropped a kiss on my forehead and then Bear was there.

"What the fuck? That uppity bitch was touching ya bikes. The bitch fucking hit me!" Skanky skank, an excellent moniker to rename her, snapped. Skank of the year was a mouthful.

"Bitch put hands on Phoe!" Tiny rumbled aiming a death stare at her. Darth Vader eat your heart out!

"Whore touched Hellfire," Chatter rumbled.

"Baby girl," Bear rumbled. I looked into the big man's eyes and raised my arms. Bear threw his head back and laughed.

Bear bent low and swept me up, one hand at my knees and one around my back. I snuggled into his neck, wrapped my arms around him and sighed, home. The skanks cautiously stepped back.

Chance arrived and put his hand on skanky skank and shoved her hard. She stumbled back on her stripper heels and nearly hit her knees a second time. A position I bet she was familiar with. Inner bitch time!

"Fuckin' shove Hellfire?" Chance snapped. I glanced over at him and saw his handsome face set in the 'I'm pissed' expression.

"Didn't know that bitch belonged to Hellfire," Skanky skank snapped back, and his eyes narrowed.

"Lying skank," I said loudly, signing her death warrant. "Said I was Hellfire. Couldn't have been any clearer." The woman's eyes narrowed on me, and she turned puce.

"Think I made it plain in there, I'd a woman arrivin', and you fuckin' put a hand to Hellfire," Chance growled. He got in her face, and I lifted my head from where I'd tucked into Bear's throat. Bear tilted his gaze at me, and I shook my head. Bear grinned.

"Why the fuck would we think you'd a high-class bitch arriving. We were expecting..." Skanky skank broke off and swept her hand at her body thrusting out a hip. I choked back a laugh at the disgust on Chance's face.

"Not every man likes sticking his dick in a bucket. Your pussy is so well used it screams for fuckin' mercy," Chance snapped back, I winced as Bear chuckled. Wowzer! Ouch! Chance went for the jugular.

"I protected your bike from an uppity bitch. Look at her, that's hardly the woman for Hellfire." Hey now! Skanky skank proved she'd no brain and kept pushing. Judgemental cow!

"Should I tell her I love bondage?" I whispered to Bear who choked and then chuckled. Bear squeezed me, and I winced, the man didn't realise his own strength.

"Phoe's not enough for Hellfire? Who the fuck are you to say what Hellfire wants?" Diesel rumbled, arriving on the scene and the vibes moved from bad to deadly. Skanky skank suddenly realised Hellfire surrounded me. Hellfire was holding me, and they didn't take her back, neither did Rage, who watched the drama.

"Phoenix is Hellfire," Chance snapped. "Get the fuck out of my sight before I do something, whore. Don't come to the clubhouse while Hellfire's here or I'll put you out with the trash," Chance threatened, his anger tangible.

"Let go Bearbear," I whispered. He put me on my feet, and I walked over to Chance.

Chance glowered at me from his great height, I stared up at him and lifted my arms to him. Chance didn't scare me. He glared a bit more, so I pouted until finally, he picked me up, and I rubbed my head against his chest. Through our body contact, I realised that Chance wasn't angry, he'd bypassed that to furious. I understood why. Chance had told me I'd be safe, and a skank touched me on his watch. That just didn't happen.

"Chill, honey," I whispered.

"No one touches Hellfire, what the fuck Drake? Is Hellfire no longer welcome on Rage? Hands being raised to Hellfire doesn't sit well, brother," Chance rumbled. He shot a glare over my shoulder at someone out of my line of sight.

"Misty is Misty, the bitch is dealt with, now can we move this fuckin' drama inside the clubhouse? Don't bullshit me, Chance, you know you're family," a voice snarled back. I didn't appreciate the tone in that voice.

"Not sure I wanna go inside Chance," I said, feeling uncomfortable and unwelcome. Chance stopped glowering and looked at me in stunned surprise.

"Think I'd let anythin' touch you?"

"Well, no," I admitted, that I didn't doubt. Even though skanky skank, otherwise known as Misty, had laid hands on me.

"Then we goin' inside," Chance said grumpily and carried me away. Once inside the clubhouse, I didn't have time to look around, because Pyro swept me up for a hug and kiss. Levi, Shotgun, Rooster, Banshee and finally Celt swiftly followed Pyro. I was hugged, kissed, squeezed, and passed around. Levi ended up pulling me on his lap as he ordered a Rage prospect to get me a diet coke.

I looked for Chance and found him at the clubhouse bar. Chance had a foot on a bronze rail that ran around the bar where another prospect was serving. The guy he was with leaned over and said something and Chance's eyes flicked to me. I smiled and then looked at the guy with him.

"Holy shit, when did Chance get a twin? Why didn't he tell me?" I burst out staring at the hotness of the two guys. It was off the charts! Levi gave a chuckle as my eyes flicked between the two men.

"No seriously, you're in trouble, mister. Three years!" I said, pointing my finger at Chance, who dropped his head, something I'd learnt he did when he was amused. Chance's twin stared at me with a blank face, and I noticed his eyes were different from Chance's, a soft chocolate brown. I flipped my head between the two of them.

"They're cousins, their fathers were brothers," Levi said grinning.

"It's illegal," I exclaimed, "two men shouldn't be allowed to look that hot!" I heard Chance's chuckle from where I was sitting, but his cousin didn't appear amused. I turned away, not liking him much and asked Levi about the girl he'd been seeing. Turned out, Levi wasn't seeing her anymore, as she thought she could lead him around by his dick. Ten minutes later, my ass was shifted into Chatter's lap.

This was old hat, Chatter liked to hold me, to see I was safe. He did the same with Tatiana, Big Al's old lady. Years ago, Chatter had nasty shit go down, I've never asked what, no one pried with Chatter. I realised Chatter sometimes needed to hold a woman, someone he cared for. Chatter felt deep for Tatiana and me. He was never threatening, more comforting, we sat in silence, and that was it. It was soothing and caring and yet again, home.

Ten minutes later, I was unceremoniously picked up and dumped in Banshee's lap. Shee was bitching about a girl he'd been seeing and thinking of taking to the next level. Except she'd started playing mind games. On hearing those games, I told Shee firmly to get shot of her ass. Shee nodded, already knowing what I was going to say, my boys didn't need women like that in their life.

A few minutes later, I shifted again and snuggled into Bearbear. I wrapped my arms around his neck, and he tucked me up into his big body, hooking my legs over his.

Contented, I sighed and listened to the guys talk over my head. Six weeks had passed since we'd last seen each other, a long time as usually, we saw each other at least once a fortnight.

Not a day passed when one of them didn't text or give me a quick call. We were in constant contact. Communication was encouraged on both sides, Hellfire doted on my kids and were Uncles' to them. Hellfire only having one old lady Tatiana, Big Al and Tatiana weren't here tonight for whatever reason.

Drake, as I learnt what his name was, leaned over to Chance and said something nodding his head in my direction. Chance looked over and gave me a chin lift and turned his attention back to Drake, who gave off angry vibes. Chance's cousin was confused and pissed off. After a few more minutes, my stomach rumbled, and Bear on hearing that shouted across to Chance, I needed feeding.

This commenced a round of food orders for Chinese, and I reached for my purse, and Bear slapped my hand. I glared, snagged his beard and then grinned when he did. No one could resist Bears grin.

"Out of line Bearbear," I told the man who squeezed me tight. God, I loved this man so much, my gentle giant.

"Don't push it Phoe, you don't pay," Bear rumbled, I snuggled into his chest, loving that rumble.

"I will one day."

"Nope. You pay when we come to your place, you don't pay when out with us," Bear told me. I sighed this was a longstanding argument. Hellfire knew I'd money, I spoilt them every Christmas and birthday. But the brothers had their pride, I didn't pay when I went out with them, and that was final.

I rose to my feet, needing to use the facilities, and I was walking back to the common room when I found the way blocked. I stared into frigid blue eyes and a cruel smile and bit my lip.

"Mighty friendly ain't ya?" one of the Rage brothers grinned. With a peek at his cut, I saw a Prospect patch.

"They're my club, get out of the way prospect," I said, trying to get past. Instead, the prospect began walking into my space, and I backed away and hit a wall.

"Nice ass, nice tits, bet that pussy is tight and wet, wanna share what you're giving out?"

"Back away," I whispered, fear in my eyes and clogging my throat. The prospect raised a finger and traced my throat, and I swallowed hard. He began trailing it downwards to my boobs. I pushed ineffectively letting out a wordless sound of fear as his hand clasped around my breast.

Seconds later, he was ripped from me, and the sound of fists hitting flesh reached through my fear. I looked up into Tiny's face as his arms wrapped around me. Tiny tried pulling my head against his chest, and I fought him. Chance had the guy up against the wall and was ramming his fist into the guy's face.

"Chance!" I screamed, clinging to Tiny's cut.

"She's Hellfire!" Chance roared. Idly, panic-stricken, I wondered whether I should get that tattooed on my head. Chance's fist slammed into the guy again, and he let him go. Angry green eyes turned in my direction, and I screamed as the guy ran at Chance and slammed a shoulder into him and took Chance to the ground. Chance rolled him over, and fists and blood flew.

"Bearbear!" I cried out. Bear instantly appeared and lifted me into his arms. I burrowed into him, trying to block the sounds of the fight. It was eerie. Neither club said a word, the only sounds were fists hitting flesh and pained grunts. I began humming to myself, and suddenly I was on my feet staring into furious green eyes.

Chance checked me over, and I raised a hand to touch his split lip. There was a red mark on his cheek, and tears welled in my eyes. He squeezed me and turned us to face his cousin. Still furious, Chance gathered me up and wrapped his arms around my shoulder and waist.

"Get rid of that piece of shit," he snapped at Drake who stiffened. Shit, this could be trouble. No MC President should give orders to another.

"Plug's a Rage prospect," although Drake's tone said, he didn't think much of his prospect.

"Keep him, lose us," Chance growled, Drake struggled with the order. Clearly, Drake didn't appreciate being given demands by Chance. Finally, Drake gave a head tilt to one of his brothers. The older Native American picked up the barely conscious prospect and dragged him out.

"Strip his cut, he hasn't earned it. Planned to strip Plug tomorrow, a few hours makes no difference," Drake gave the order.

"Fucked up one time too many, Plug. Lazyass, boozing, piece of shit. Never learned no matter what chances we gave ya," someone said, but I wasn't listening. I was concentrating on controlling my fear and terror. Deep breathing, I realised Chance knew I was struggling, as he held me tight and could sense the tremors running through my body.

"Pussy," Drake said, curtly. I didn't get what he meant, but Chance did.

"Phoe ain't pussy," Chance snarled.

"No pussy is worth a brother. Not even if that pussy is golden and comes with money." Drake forced the issue, pure anger in his eyes as he looked at me.

"Phoe ain't pussy," Chance repeated.

"Wanna tell me what she is 'cause woman's been in and out of laps and not one man claimin' her. Woman's spreading for your club, can't blame mine for wanting a piece. Fuck brother, you just threatened Rage, your brothers, over a fuckin' piece of pussy. Rage and Hellfire are kin! Throw that away for fuckin' pussy!" Drake roared beyond angry.

"Open your eyes, cousin," Chance snarled at him.

"Wide open," Drake shot back. Now that could have two meanings. I genuinely didn't like him.

"No man claims her 'cause she belongs to Hellfire. Phoe's fuckin' Hellfire," Chance stressed, leaning both of us forward. Drake frowned.

"My piece of shit prospect got laid out for a pussy that shares with everyone." Okay I really, really didn't like Drake.

"Phoe's fuckin' Hellfire," Chance snapped back. In temper Chance expected Drake to catch on and got angrier and angrier that Drake didn't get what he was saying.

"So fuckin' what? We've shared pussy before between the clubs. If no brother claims her, no one can blame Rage for thinkin' it's free."

"She's fuckin' Hellfire!" Chance yelled, I pressed back against him.

"I can see she's fuckin' Hellfire. You keep sayin' she's fuckin' Hellfire. Every brother can see she's fuckin' Hellfire," Drake roared misunderstanding Chance. Chance leaned forward anger coming off him in waves.

"Phoe's a sister," Chance roared. Drake stepped back in surprise, his jaw going slack. Nuh huh, now the asshole understood. Drake looked between us and then at Hellfire at our backs. The fire flared back into Drake's eyes.

"A sister? We don't have sisters," he shouted. Rage began muttering to each other. Hellfire closed ranks against them, and my eyes darted around, checking for safety.

"Hellfire does, one, Phoenix. She's in and out of laps 'cause Hellfire has her back and will go balls to the wall. Hellfire will bleed for her, Phoe's our heart and soul. No one touches her, we ain't fuckin' screwing her, Phoe is fuckin' *Hellfire*." Okay, maybe Chance needed to stop using the word fucking as it was apparent it held two connotations!

"Thinkin' you need to explain shit. I'm missing stuff, cousin. Woman said she's known you three years and you don't tell Rage, tell me, Hellfire took a sister?" Drake drawled, his eyes on me. I burrowed back into Chance's chest, and his arms tightened.

"Thinkin' to introduce Phoe tonight to Hellfire's *kin,* 'cept our kin wanna be assholes. Wanted Phoe to have somewhere safe if our woman needed it. Rethinking that idea now," Chance rumbled still angry

"Start explaining," Drake demanded.

"Later," Chance grunted.

"Better make later fuckin' soon brother, Hellfire has a sister? A sister Hellfire will go to war over, and Rage don't fuckin' know. When did the clubs take sisters? She's your soul? Hellfire got something you withhold from Rage, we wanna find out why," Drake snarled. Chance ignored him.

"Phoe?" I didn't reply. The sound of fists hitting flesh again. I looked around but saw no fight. I was having flashbacks and fought desperately against them, refusing to let the memories come back. Chance squeezed me tightly, refusing to let the fight bring *him* back.

"Phoe, woman, talk to me. Everything's good. I'm here, Bear's here, your brothers are here." Chance gently turned my head to face him, and his face took on a frightful expression. I shook in his arms.

"Phoenix," Bear called, making me look at him. He opened his arms, but I clung to Chance. Chance shook his head, and then Chatter appeared and folded me in his arms. He scooped me up, and Chance let go.

I wrapped tightly around Chatter, and he carried me to a beaten sofa and sat. Together we sat quietly until the food arrived, I remained in his arms for the rest of the night. Watching everyone with wary eyes until I left to go meet with the second night team at HQ at ten o'clock. Rage's eyes stayed on me the whole night, with far too many unasked questions.

Two days later, on Wednesday, I sat in my office and rubbed weary eyes. Kyle had been in earlier and dropped a file on my desk. He'd said something was off with California PT and RT. I'd started looking at the figures, Kyle was right. Over the last six months, there'd been a steady decline in donations, gradual at first but now noticeable. I rubbed my neck to relieve the tension and realised something was very wrong with California.

I hit my inter-office phone and buzzed Kyle and asked him to come to my office in twenty minutes. He gave an affirmative and cut the connection. I began looking back through the figures trying to analyse where the accounting was wrong. I glanced up as the door opened, and to my surprise, Drake entered. Emily came storming in behind him, with to my shock, a baseball bat in hand. She slapped it against her palm, glaring at him.

"Emily!" I gasped my eyes widening. She stopped and sent Drake a dirty look. Drake glanced at her, and his lips twitched. "We don't beat people, sheesh girl, not even unwelcome intruders," I exclaimed. However, I'd a silent wish she'd hit him before Drake entered my office. Burying that little thought, I focused on Emily, who was spitting in fury.

"Not in the office anyway, outside the office is fair game," Emily mumbled sending Drake a death stare.

"Oh boy," I muttered, I didn't need this right now.

"Asshole pushed his way in after I told him you were busy," Emily snapped, giving him the stink eye. Wonderful. Drake was two for two, he was doing well at insulting women he encountered. It's a wonder the man ever got laid.

"It's okay, he's Chance's cousin," I replied. Emily didn't stop giving him the stink eye. Clearly being Chance's cousin, didn't rank Drake very high. Emily folded her arms across her chest. Drake watched with amusement in his eyes.

"Not even Chance would push his way in," Emily glared, and I raised an eyebrow. She looked at me and sighed. "Okay, Chance would, he ain't Chance," Emily nearly spat at Drake in her dislike.

"No, he's not. Go on, honey, it's okay." Emily pointed the bat at him and stalked out, shutting the door quietly though.

She made a point of dragging her chair around so she could see inside my office. With a snarl on her face, she pointed two fingers at her eyes and then at Drake. I closed my eyes for a few seconds and faced Drake.

"What can I do for you?" I asked wearily. His gaze snapped to my face, and his eyes searched it, and then he sat on my couch. Great, he expected a conversation.

"Came to apologise for Plug, Chance explained shit," I rubbed the back of my neck as I watched him.

Drake didn't sound too contrite to me, instead, the Rage President came across arrogant and very cocksure. There was curiosity as well, he gave me a half-smile, and I kept my face impassive.

"I'm sure he did," I replied dryly.

"Yeah, so here to apologise."

"That's kind Drake but unnecessary." I propped my chin up in my hand and looked at the irritating man.

"Plug was on Rage when insult was dealt. Plug was a Rage prospect, wore a Rage cut, it's on me and Rage MC. I'm the Prez, my place to apologise." Okay, that I could understand, Chance operated the same way, so I decided to be gracious. It was unlikely we'd meet much in the future, Chance would make sure of that.

"Okay apology accepted. Anything else?" I asked, wanting him to leave.

"Dinner on Saturday," Drake stated out of the blue. I blinked. Did Drake just ask me out to dinner?

"That's kind but again unnecessary. The apology is enough." Oh lord, I wasn't going to go to dinner with him.

Drake had insinuated I was a whore spreading my legs for Hellfire, then he and Chance had argued. Finally, he'd barged his way into my office. I didn't like the man, I let that show and smirked.

"Yeah, wanna take you to dinner," Drake insisted.

"I'm sorry I don't get it." I rubbed my brow, trying to relieve the pain beginning to hammer at me.

"Want to take you to dinner, see how I'm seein' it is this. Chance is my older cousin. But he's more my big brother, Rage and Hellfire tied 'cause of us two. Both clubs never have taken a sister, now Hellfire has one. Rage didn't know shit that Chance took a sister into the MC. I wanna know, sensing you're special, need to find out how special," Drake informed me with a confident grin.

Wow, Drake was handsome and knew it. But I'd had Chance around for over three years, and I'd dealt with Drake's good looks when dealing with Chance. Drake's looks weren't going to get him far! The two men could've been twins, with their devastating charm. I'd learned to resist Chance, and I could most certainly resist Drake.

"Well, thanks but I've got plans Saturday," I said hoping he'd go away.

"Cancel, see you got to understand being Hellfire, means you're mine too." The sheer arrogance at telling me to cancel made my mouth drop open. Not to mention the last comment rankled, I didn't belong to Rage, I belonged to Hellfire. Plus cancel? The cheek of the man!

"Sorry cancelling is impossible, Chance and Hellfire are at mine this weekend for a barbecue. Family weekend," I said smugly, thinking I'd found a way out.

Drake grinned at me, calculation behind his eyes and I got the sense I'd said something stupid. The Rage President was as devious as Chance, and I needed to remember that.

"What time Saturday?" Drake asked, rising to his feet. I narrowed my eyes at the man. Despite my headache, he was annoying.

"I said it's family weekend," I told him sternly.

"Yeah and I told ya, Hellfire and Rage family, which means if you're havin' family time, then Rage is invited too. Any time?" The man who was fast becoming a pain in my ass grinned at me, and I glared at him. "Catch ya then," Drake said and strode his fine ass out. Infuriating man, I thought as I glared after him. I looked up as Kyle entered with Charlie the SM for California, and we got down to business.

An hour later, with one of Abigail's investigators included in a conference call, the feedback was there were problems. California was a big worry, it was time to nip it in the bud. Jon, the assigned investigator, would arrive in a day and we'd wait for his report.

Kyle, Charlie and Abigail left, and Stefan entered. Bless him, he took one glance at my face and pulled the blinds in the office and gave orders I wasn't to be disturbed. Emily diverted calls to the Directors, and I stayed in my office for the last hour of the day. Stefan came and offered a ride home, but he and Bernard were looking at premises for Bernard to open a restaurant. Bernard had sold his previous restaurant to come to South Dakota, the man was a fantastic chef. Once everyone had gone, I stumbled my way to the door.

I turned out the lights and managed to lock my door. Gradually, I made my way down the backstairs, calling a low greeting to the night team. Then hugging the wall, I made my way to the car. The pain was awful, my head was pounding, and my neck and eyes hurt. I'd taken my tablets but clearly had taken them too late. Bile rushed up my throat, forcing me to bend over and I choked it back.

It was taking everything I had to concentrate on putting one foot in front of the other. Dizziness hit, making me lean against the wall. I kept one thought running through my head. Get the back-up tablets I kept in my car. Nausea subsided, and I began blindly groping my way again, concentrating so hard I didn't hear footsteps behind me.

"Yo Phoenix? Drake sent me to ask what you needed us to bring… shit, you okay lady?" I looked up, seeing a blur. To my despair, I began slipping and scrabbled with my hands and found a hold on the wall.

Pings of a phone's buttons being pushed echoed, "Drake get over here now. The alley. Somethin's wrong." the voice said, and then I hit the ground. Hands caught me under my armpits, and I was hauled up, which made me retch for a second time. I choked it back again.

"What the fuck?" Drake asked as I heard his footsteps striding towards us.

"Found her like this, brother."

"Phoenix, you okay?" Stupid question, I thought to myself as I struggled to control not being sick. Did I look okay? "Go get Hellfire, Apache," Drake ordered. Someone passed me into Drake's arms, and he cradled me. Ineffectively, I batted at the spots in front of my eyes, and Drake began to lift me in his arms.

"No," I moaned as the movement made my stomach recoil. Drake stopped.

"How can I help?" Drake asked, concern in his voice. Well, that's a surprise, Drake was capable of another emotion other than anger and smug arrogance.

"Ah no, Phoe!" a voice I recognised but couldn't place, said. I thought it was one of my guys. Arms lifted me, ignoring my moans and carried me through the alleyway to my car.

"Get the keys, Drake, that car's Phoe's," the voice said.

"Got 'em Banshee." Ah, so that is who it was, Shee indeed was one of mine. There was a beep as my car unlocked.

"Open the back doors so I can get her in. In the trunk is a pillow and blanket get them."

"Got 'em."

"Right hold her while I get in, then pass Phoe gently across to me. Don't jar her head no matter what." Shee ordered Drake, and someone moved me, and I kept my focus on not being sick. Shee and Drake got me into the car. A pained whimper sneaked out as Drake gently guided my head to the pillow on Shee's thigh.

"Get Bear, need to get her home," Shee ordered. Shee gently stroked my brow and hair, knowing that sometimes that helped.

"Fuck that, I'll drive," Drake said as the car door opened and then gently shut.

"Go easy on corners, do not floor it, no matter how tempting, avoid potholes if possible. Nice and easy," Banshee told Drake.

"What's wrong with her? Migraine?"

"Kinda, Phoe suffers hemiplegic migraines. Looks like she didn't catch this one in time. We've sat through them with her a few times, ain't ever pretty Drake."

"What's hemiplegic migraines?" There was curiosity in Drake's voice, but it was fleeting, and I concentrated on my head not falling off my shoulders.

"They mimic strokes, the pain in her head paralyses her. Phoe suffers partial paralysation on her left-hand side for anything up to two weeks. There's a stutter which can last months, she'll get confused and disorientated if they aren't caught in time."

"Christ, how'd she get that?"

"Ex-husband slammed her head into a wall, causing a brain bleed and changing her migraines to these. A more dangerous type," Banshee bit angrily and kept stroking my hair.

"What the fuck?" Drake gritted out.

"Turn here, you know where Reading Hall is? That's her place, need directions?" Banshee asked, ignoring Drake's question, good for Shee. I didn't want Drake knowing anything.

"Nah, been past it, seen work being done to it. Didn't know it belonged to Phoenix." Pipes sounded from a faraway place, and I curled into Shee and concentrated on not throwing up. Oh and not disappearing down the rabbit's hole that was opening in my consciousness.

"Oh no, Miss Phoe, how long has she been down?" a woman gasped. I'd no idea how much time had passed.

"No one knows Mrs Ames, Phoe was found trying to get to her car. Can you run on and get Phoe's bed ready," Shee asked. Footsteps hurried away and then blessed silence. A movement made me heave, and I couldn't stop it, I leaned away from whoever was carrying me.

"Fuck," another voice, all these pesky voices. Even though my stomach was empty, I kept heaving, I whimpered in the bright light and heaved again. Pain, my life was pain.

"Get her stripped Bear," Shee said. I was being held up, and clothes ripped off my body.

"Shee, get a wet cloth. Mrs Ames, the strong medication, we gotta get it in her," Bear spoke up.

"What can I do?"

"Stand back until you're needed, Drake."

"Fuck," Drake muttered as I leant over and heaved again. I coughed and spat something vile up and gave up and let my body do as it wished. I could only see blackness now, with tiny little bright flashes of light.

"Woman can't focus."

"We're aware Drake, not our first go around. Phoe we going to lay you back, honey." I tried shaking my head and heaved up again. Warm hands on my face and then a wet cloth was placed on my head. I tried batting it away, but only one arm raised.

"Medication, now Drake, run," Bear said making Drake run after Mrs Ames. Footsteps faded and then returned fast. Someone sat me up, and a pill was shoved in my mouth. A glass held to my lips, and a voice urged me to drink.

Bear ordered me to swallow. Some part of me knew I had to and managed to choke them. Gently I was laid onto the bed and found my left side dead, blackness swirling and then nothing. No sound, no lights, no pain, just peace.

"How long has Phoenix suffered that?" Drake bit out watching the sleeping woman on the bed. Bear had his ass laid out on the bed and held her tight. They'd dragged an oversized tee on her, and she lay curled into a ball.

"Whole time we've known her, nearly four years. Not often and twice worse than this, we've seen Phoe laid out for weeks. Usually, Phoe takes the meds in time and just suffers a migraine. Today she obviously didn't, we'll see how bad the damage is in twelve hours. That's how long the meds put her out," Shee answered Drake.

"Anythin' I can do?"

"No. I'll come with, and we'll go back to the clubhouse. Bear's got this." Drake shot a glance at Bear.

"Phoe's Hellfire," Bear said from the bed. Drake lifted his gaze and got what he was being told and turned on his heel. He was getting tired of being told Phoe was Hellfire. He knew Chance and Hellfire had closed ranks around the woman, but he didn't need to be kept reminding of the fact.

"Mrs Ames, you need help cleaning up?" Shee asked the older woman hovering. Mrs Ames placed a hand on his arm and smiled sweetly at him. Drake wondered how long they'd known each other. The older woman hadn't batted an eyelid at Bear climbing into bed with Phoenix.

"Go, Shee, I have this, Bear's here, and Chance is on speed dial. Our girl will be okay."

"Where are the kids?" Banshee asked. Drake looked up sharply, Phoe had kids? That was something Chance hadn't mentioned. Drake saw no sign of kids being present.

"With Mr Albert and their team and the older ones. They're due back Friday. A blessing," the older woman mused her eyes drifting to Drake. There was a curiosity in them but also a warning. Drake gave nothing away that he'd recognised the warning.

He fast realised that everyone was damn protective of Phoenix. He'd felt it in his gut after Chance had explained Phoe was special, now he saw it in everyone's actions.

"That's good, give her a few days of recovery. Will you let HQ know?" Shee replied.

"Of course. HQ will run without her, she's got good people there. Go Shee, we have this covered, not our first rodeo." Shee looked at Mrs Ames and then gave her a curt nod. He motioned for Drake to follow him and shut the door behind them.

Drake walked into the clubhouse and headed straight for the bar and pulled a beer. He saw Shee give a report to Chance and saw Chance look in his direction. Chance ran his hand through his hair and walked in Drake's direction.

"She's Hellfire," Chance stated, a gentle tone in his voice rarely heard. Drake gave a sharp nod.

"I'm fuckin' aware she's Hellfire, you keep ramming it down our throats," he snarled, annoyed.

"You're interested brother," Chance stated, his sharp eyes searching Drake's. Drake made his face go blank, he was more than interested in Phoenix. Not just because Phoe's laugh was captivating, and she looked and smelt good. What type of woman made an entire MC curl around her? What was it that Phoenix had that made a whole MC possibly go to war over her?

"Yeah, woman's good to look at, and she's somethin' special, I'm thinking," Drake didn't bother denying it.

Chance knew him better than he did himself, he'd always looked out for him. Drake wasn't lying, even when she'd been lap hopping, he'd been interested. Thinking back now, Drake realised the lap hopping had nothing sexual in it.

Fuck, his interest had peaked when he'd watched her laughing at her staff dancing on cars. The lap hopping had infuriated him, seeing an obviously classy woman whoring herself hadn't gone down well with Drake.

He'd wanted to shove her against a wall and claim her. Drake had stifled the relief he'd experienced when Chance had explained. There was something about her, wrapped up in a tiny package, she couldn't be taller than five one, five two, in height.

Phoenix had gorgeous, long blond sun-streaked hair and laughing green eyes. Her figure was made for loving. He'd seen something lurking behind those green eyes. A pain she kept hidden from everyone, he wanted to know more. Drake wanted to lay claim to her and wipe the pain away

"She's everythin', the one thing that can rip Hellfire apart. Phoe fixed us in a way everyone felt and still feels. Phoe has so much love to give, she's our soul, the one thing we'd die for. Without her, Hellfire would be lost, Phoe healed us," Chance said into the silence that had fallen between them.

"I get it, woman's off-limits," Drake said shortly. He didn't like this conversation, was he never to have anything good in his life? He'd eaten shit, done shit, he and his brothers were clean now, it was time for something beautiful for his club.

The club they'd fought to get free of dirt. Drake wanted a woman to claim, Phoe could be it, Drake was sure she could. Her laugh had attracted him, but the woman herself brought out his baser instincts.

"More than off-limits brother. Fuck even though we'd cleaned Hellfire up, we were still splintered. Phoe strutted into our lives and healed our wounds. Hellfire needed her, fuck, we still need her," Chance muttered eyeing Drake.

"Told you, I get it. Fuck me, brother, I ain't stupid."

"Love you, Drake, like my brother, my baby brother." Chance confirmed their closeness, Drake thought unnecessarily.

"Know that."

"She's better than you or me and anyone else here. Phoe deserves the world, and we can't give her that. Can't give her all of us. Don't let…"

"I get it, brother," Drake said, cutting off Chance's warning. He tipped the beer back, swallowed and walked out and hit his bike. Drake wanted something he couldn't have, Rage could destroy a woman like Phoenix, and yet he wondered. Phoe had managed and loved Hellfire, could she manage Rage? He'd seen the way she handled Hellfire. There was a hidden strength in her, he saw and felt it. Maybe Phoenix had it in her to perform one more miracle. Drake hoped so.

Chapter Four.

I woke up to a darkened room, curled up against a warm body. Bear snored next to me. What the hell had happened? The last thing I remembered was my head killing me and stumbling towards my car, to get more medication. I guess with Bear sleeping next to me, I didn't make it. With a groan, I rolled over and felt relief at having no paralysation, I felt a slight numbness, that was all, which was good news. The pain was reduced to a dull throb in my head.

I put my feet gingerly on the ground and felt no lingering dizziness. Warily I rose to my feet and shuffled to my bathroom. Something had curled up and died in my mouth, so I vigorously scrubbed my teeth. I jumped in the shower and washed what felt like three days' worth of scum from me. Deftly wrapping a towel around me, I checked Bear was still sleeping and walked hurriedly to my walk-in closet.

Quietly, I yanked on underwear, jeans, a loose sweater and slipped on socks. Moving silently, I left my room and made my way downstairs. The smell of bacon cooking led me into the kitchen. I nodded as

I saw Shee sitting at the island while Mrs Ames cooked breakfast.

"Shee brought Bear a change of clothes," Mrs Ames, my housekeeper and good friend, said. I smiled and sniffed the air. She grinned at me, I was hungry, and Mrs Ames knew it.

"Want food?" Mrs Ames asked. I nodded, my gaze caught sight of the kitchen clock and gasped. It was midday.

"How long have I been out?"

"You hit the black around six o'clock," Shee said.

"That's eighteen hours I've been out," I stammered in dismay.

"Bear shot you another dose around three this morning honey girl. Couldn't take you whimpering in pain, so we agreed to dose you." I parked my ass on a stool and stared at Shee.

"I have a faint memory of you being there?" Shee gave me a curt nod and bit into a bacon sandwich. He swallowed and then grinned at Mrs Ames.

"Fantastic as usual, Mrs Ames," Shee said.

"Today is Thursday?" Another sharp nod from Shee and he bit into the sandwich again and chewed. His eyes scrutinised me.

"Family weekend," I muttered. Ah, two sets of annoyed eyes glowered at me, and I shook my head. "No, I let this beat me, I lose everything, this doesn't break me, he doesn't win. I'll be fine, I'll stay home today and tomorrow. Which is lousy timing as we just opened HQ, but I'll stay home and do nothing. Family weekend happens," I stated firmly.

"How did Rage get invited?" Shee asked abruptly, I looked at him in consternation.

"They did?" Shee's body tensed, as I thought hard. "I remember Drake being in my office, I must have invited Rage. Honestly, I don't remember much." Shee nodded, but he didn't look sure and then finished his sandwich.

"Tiny is on his way up, Mrs Ames making her pot roast, so he's keen for it, he'll stay tonight with Bear. Both of them will take you shopping tomorrow okay?" I nodded, and he kissed my forehead and gave Mrs Ames a cheek kiss and left.

"Good man, good men," she muttered as her husband entered the kitchen. Mr Ames's eyes narrowed on my face as he greeted his wife. With a nod, he removed his boots and sat down to eat a bacon sandwich with us. Mr Ames was as used to my migraines as his beloved wife was.

Late afternoon hit by the time Bear awoke, as he'd been up most of the night with me. Poor Bear had toast and refused anything else, saying he'd wait until the pot roast was ready. Tiny arrived, we watched movies, ate pot roast, watched more movies and then I crashed in Bear's arms.

I was up and dressed and watching from the morning room's large bay window for the first sign of my kids arriving. Dawn had just broken, but I knew they were due back any minute now. I spotted a car pulling around the corner, and I was running before they'd even parked. Micah got out with Eddie and Tony in the car with him. Carmine pulled up, carrying Cody, Jared and Aaron.

Tye parked behind with Serenity, Harley, Timmy and Scout. Jodie climbed out of Albert's car with Christian and Garret and Jake. Eddie ran towards me, her hands above her head, screaming "Mama Phoe" at the top of her lungs. Tony, her twin brother, followed at a quieter pace. I crouched and swept them both into my arms. I got hugs and kisses, and then Eddie spied Bear coming descending the stairs, and she was off. Eddie loved Bear as much as her little heart could manage. Tony followed at his slower pace.

Micah stopped and threw me a hug and kiss and then moved past me to greet Mr and Mrs Ames. Carmine approached me with a "Ma", gave me the same treatment as Micah, Tye followed their suit. Cody wrapped his arms around my waist with a "Mum" and then rushed off, Christian, Jared and Aaron, did the same.

Harley gave me a "Mom" and scarpered. Jodie gave me a grin as she and Serenity opened her trunk and I rolled my eyes at the bags in it. Two sets of twin babies were put down cooing and blowing bubbles at me. The security team pulled up in two more pick-ups stuffed full of suitcases.

The crew greeted me with chin lifts and head tilts as they unloaded their bags and the kids. Chatting they made their way over to their small set of houses set back in the trees. Tiny had his hands on Jake and Garett with whom he'd not had much time. Tiny carried their car seats into the house. Eddie was announcing at the top of her lungs her love for too's (tattoos) and nearly ripping Bears tee off to study his. The boys scattered, I peeked at Mrs Ames and rolled my eyes.

Let chaos reign.

Later that day, I managed to get to the stores to buy what I needed. I doubled the regular quantity because between Rage, Hellfire, the security team and my inner circle at HQ, there'd be over one hundred people.

Aware of how many were expected, Mrs Ames had miraculously organised on short notice, a catering service for breakfast and lunch and we'd grill on Saturday night. Sunday, the catering service would return for breakfast and cook a full Sunday lunch with a buffet for the evening.

Even so, I needed staples, I knew that the kids and Hellfire were perfectly capable of running through enough snacks to fill a store's aisle. I bought three carts full of soft drinks and placed a large order for more to be delivered on Sunday morning. I'd three carts full of what Mrs Ames and I called junk, crisps, sweets, biscuits.

Between us, we loaded up the three vehicles we'd brought with us. I'd placed a large meat order at the beginning of the week, and I darted into the butchers to double it. His eyes widened but agreed he could deliver. I paid him in full and popped to the grocers, doing the same there. Mrs Ames popped into the bakery and ordered five times what I had ordered earlier. Lord, we knew how much bikers could eat! I'd had qualms about the amounts when I'd ordered on Monday.

The Hall was amazing, we'd created lots of indoor and outdoor activities. If you weren't activity minded and wanted to relax, the other choice was one of the Adirondack loungers or hot tubs. Our home had been restored primarily with the kids in mind and then the massive family I'd acquired second.

Carmine was in the diamond hitting balls. Cody got one buck a ball for collect and return, and Cody shamelessly fleeced Carmine. Yeah, my kids had pocket money, but they weren't daft by a long shot! Tye was on the ice, he and Micah shooting pucks while Christian and Jared charged them a dollar per puck. Jodie and Serenity were on the tennis courts with Aaron and Harley running balls for a buck each too.

Tiny had remained behind with three sets of twins to watch, I stuck my head in the family lounge and checked on them. Tiny had settled any issues by sticking Disney films on which shut Eddie up at once. Eddie loved Disney films, Tony was a happy chappy as long as Eddie was happy.

Once shopping was done, Celt and Shotgun arrived with a load of pizzas, and manic chaos ensued once again. I was worn out, and grateful they'd brought pizza, we camped out in the family lounge until the younger kids fell to sleep. The elder ones disappeared into their towers and left the adults alone. I loved nights like this. Bear was taken with Garret and Jake and hated giving them over to someone else. To my amusement, he shut up whining when he got his hands on Timmy or Scout. He'd be such a wonderful dad, I sighed.

I was barely awake the next morning and was stumbling to the shower when I heard bike pipes. Eddie ran downstairs, screaming Chance's name at the top of her lungs. A groan escaped me, my youngest daughter was excitable, to say the least. Around seven o'clock that morning, I'd woken to the noise of trucks and Mrs Ames, and I had supervised the deliveries. I'd only just got the chance to shower.

Upon entering the kitchen, I discovered the catering staff were present and cooking full English breakfasts and whatever else people requested. I glanced at the clock and noticed it had just turned nine. The informal dining room off the kitchen was crowded full of kids and Hellfire.

The security team was present stuffing their mouths, many were in trunks and tees, obvious where they were heading. Liz had helped Mr Ames remove the swimming pool cover that morning. As a bonus, I allowed my staff full use of the amenities in the house. Controlled chaos landed, as Hellfire corralled the younger kids and the elder kids corralled them.

I was laughing when I heard cars arriving, and I met Stuart and the others getting out of vehicles. With a frown, I looked at my drive. I knew the kids wanted the ATV's out later and so was concerned about cars being damaged.

Those who weren't eating I got together and made them move the vehicles into the small field next to my house. The area was only a few minutes' walk to the main house. Chance banged in a sign he'd crudely drawn up saying, 'Park here,' with an arrow pointing to the field.

I cherished these times, this was why I bought the Hall. It was generous enough to take everyone I loved, including those who had invited themselves. Late last night, I'd remembered Drake's conversation in the office, but didn't say a word. Let him learn the happy chaos of my life, he may back off then. After everyone had been fed, kids and adults scattered in different directions. ATV's started up, and dirt bikes roared.

Eddie disappeared into the fun shed as she called it and ran out with hoppers. I rolled my eyes and caught Bear and Pyro looking at water guns and knew the day would descend into mayhem.

Micah, Jodie, Carmine headed into the trees on ATV's, with Tiny and Shotgun hard on their asses. Levi and Stuart were on dirt bikes chasing Harley, Serenity and Tye. Banshee, Kyle and Chatter were shooting Cody, Christian, Jared and Aaron with water guns. Happily, I relaxed on my porch swing with the baby twins at my feet turned to watch the commotion.

Diesel, North, (my Director of Public Relations) Stefan and Susan were chasing Eddie and Tony around on hoppers. It was amusing to watch a badass biker chase two four-year-olds on a hopper. Bear and Pyro flew past me on ATV's loaded with water guns and in the direction of my eldest kids. I looked up and spotted Christian, Jared and Aaron, still shooting water pistols, on the adult rope bridges. The guys now including Rooster and Celt chased them across the platforms.

The adult rope bridges were kick ass. Even I'd played on them, the bridges spanned trees and ended on platforms which then had ropes to swing across to the next one. Bridges extended in a multitude of different directions and had rope ladders and climbing nets. They were good fun.

"This is it Phoe, you achieved it," Chance said, sitting down next to me. He kicked my porch swing off with his foot, and I nodded at him. I winced as Diesel took a water balloon in the face. Diesel roared with laughter and then bounced after my terrible four-year-old drama queen.

"Guess you'd better rescue Diesel from your niece," I smirked. Chance threw me a grin and went and picked up a hopper.

Drake saw the sign for 'drive slowly, riders in the road' and cut his speed. He'd received a message from Chance telling him and Rage to arrive early. Only the brothers, no old ladies or skanks, Drake realised that Phoe was making her own point. He thanked God he'd slowed down when two ATV's with teens on, flew across the road in front of him. Chased by what suspiciously looked like, two Hellfire brothers on more ATV's.

He stopped the bike totally when dirt bikes jumped out of the woods, skidded, their riders regaining footing and charging off, whooping. Drake blinked when he recognised two more Hellfire brothers after them.

"What the fuck?" Apache asked looking up and following his brother's gaze, he observed two kids scrambling through the trees on rope bridges. Again, being chased by yeah, Hellfire members and a few of Phoenix's office staff.

"Chance mention this to you?" Ace asked frowning. Screams come from ahead, and they saw an ATV skid across the road and Pyro on one behind, standing up and firing a water gun. The girl on the ATV screamed with laughter, flipped Pyro the bird and spun the ATV and shot off with Pyro on her heels.

"Well, I'm guessing we're in the right place," Drake muttered not knowing what to expect next. They followed the sign for parking and pulled their bikes into a half-full field. Dismounting, they began strolling up the road towards the shrieks and shouts and general chaotic noise.

As they rounded the treeline, they met absolute bedlam. The ATV's were now parked up haphazardly, and water balloons were being launched from behind two piled high haystacks. Hellfire was aiming back. Drake looked across and caught Chance on a child's hopper chasing a tiny African American girl around who was giggling uncontrollably. Phoenix's office girl was piggybacking on Bear and shooting kids around her.

"Jesus Christ, what is this?" Fish muttered. Drake shrugged and looked up as he heard a piercing whistle that came from his cousin's direction. Kids froze, and Drake saw Phoenix looking a hundred times better than when he had last seen her. She rose to her feet on the wraparound porch and came to stand at steps leading to her house.

"Line up," Chance bellowed, kids and teenagers scrambled.

"They can't be all hers?" he heard Ace ask gruffly. Drake began walking forward as Hellfire began gathering up stuff. After a hasty glance, he realised they were filling water balloons and guns with stupid smiles on their faces. Phoenix came to greet them and offered everyone a welcoming smile.

"Welcome to Reading Hall," Phoe said as Chance approached and slung an arm around her.

"Thanks, didn't realise it was a street party," Drake said glancing around, he counted sixteen kids.

"It's not. Drake, Rage meet my kids. This is my eldest Micah, he's nineteen and studying to be a mechanic, he wants to open a garage in Miami and make streetcars."

"Design Mum, design," Micah said in an English accent much like his mothers.

"Sorry, design street racing cars. This is Carmine, he's eighteen and on a try-out for the Cubs."

"Yo, good to meet ya's. Ma and Chance have spoken of you, good things," Carmine said in what Drake placed to be a Maine accent. Drake frowned. Two different accents and two apparently similar in age teens. Carmine was a half African American, half-white good-looking kid.

"This is Tyelar, he hates Tyelar, so we call him Tye. He's seventeen and eleven months," she teased the boy. "Tye's aiming for the Blackhawks, a try-out promised when he reaches eighteen."

"Dudes, welcome to our home and Ma ain't no try-out, I'm a shoo-in. Gonna be right-wing." The kid was built like an outhouse and again mixed race, half white and half Mexican. Another damn good-looking kid, the teen had another Maine accent.

"My daughter Jodie who's seventeen."

"Hiya, welcome. Eddie no!" The girl moved and caught the little girl ready to make a run for it. The girl had another English accent. Drake's confusion deepened.

"My second daughter, Serenity, she's just turned sixteen."

"Welcome to our home," another Maine accent.

"My son Harley, he's fifteen."

"Nice to meet you," the boy replied. His gaze narrowing over their shoulders at Hellfire. Drake followed his gaze and saw Hellfire were sneakily re-arming themselves. Maine accent again.

"My son Cody, he's fourteen, my son Christian, who's twelve, my son Jared aged ten and my son Aaron who's nine," they said hello. Cody in what Drake thought was Colorado accent and the other three in English accents.

"My terrible daughter Eddie and her younger twin brother Tony. They're four."

"Too's!" the little girl squealed. South Dakota accent.

"No too's baby, too's later," Chance said firmly and received a pout.

"She's tattoo mad," Phoenix explained. "My babies, Timmy and Scout, ten months and Jake and Garret, six months."

"Good to meet you," Drake said, swallowing his confusion. Similar greetings followed, and then the kids scarpered.

"Shit," Fish muttered as a water bomb narrowly missed him.

"I suggest you come to the porch, it's a no-fire zone because of the babies." Phoenix bent and picked up two car seats with one set of twins. Phoe carried them to the porch swing she'd been relaxing on. She set the car seats down, turned to get the other set of twins and found Drake carrying them up the steps. Phoe placed them facing outwards and let them watch.

"Mrs Ames, would you mind the babies for a moment?" Phoe asked serenely, and the older woman that Drake had met came forward. She nodded and settled on the swing and began rocking. Phoenix turned to them.

"Have you eaten?" Phoe politely asked. Some of Rage shook their heads, and others nodded. "Follow me. I'll take through the house to the kitchen, it's safer," Phoe said and started walking into the house. "Eddie, don't you dare!" She spoke over her shoulder, and Rage looked around and discovered the little girl had crept up behind them with water balloons. Eddie gave a cheeky grin, twisted and got Chance straight in his face and ran.

Drake chuckled and followed Phoe into the house. He openly checked out the house as they walked through it, he'd guessed Phoe was from money but not this extent. What else was the woman hiding from him and Rage? Phoe led them straight into the kitchen were trays of pastries, and sandwiches were being put out. Drake couldn't fault her manners.

"Please help yourself, it's early still, so lunch will be around one o'clock. Snacks are constantly replenished, those guys are going to work up appetites." Drake watched a few of his brothers' step forward and grab paper plates. Plates piled high, they stood around chatting although it was kind of subdued Drake thought. None of them had been expecting this. Rage felt out of their depth, and he didn't like it.

"Bring your plates," Phoenix said with a smile. She stepped out of the folding kitchen doors and led the way onto the porch. Drake followed her, admiring her ass in her jeans, Phoe had a hell of an ass.

"The swimming pool is just over there," Phoe said, pointing. "If you need short's, we've new ones never worn, in the pool house, in all sizes." She carried on, walking around the side of the house. "ATV and dirt bike shed there, help yourselves to them, fun shed there, it includes water fun, balloons, guns, hoses etc. Please keep that second shed locked, it's the paintball shed, and Eddie gets carried away.

We've the adult rope bridges in that direction, the Ewok village over there. Rivendell there, and general carnage on my front drive. We've the hot tubs in that direction near the pool. Fridges with beers and soft drinks are outside the kitchen if you didn't notice them. Food is available all day, lunch is at one, and we'll start the cookout at around five."

"What's over there?" Rock asked, pointing at a few paths.

"The first leads to the Hall's formal gardens, they've been restored so have a wander if you want. The walled garden is locked at the moment. The second leads to Carmine's baseball diamond and Tye's ice rink. Want to see them?" She asked. Phoe got several nods, so she took them down the path. Drake followed behind, impressed. Fuck, he was beyond impressed. The woman had established something here.

"You had this built?" he asked.

"Carmine has a gift with a ball and bat. He continually hits it out of the park. I want my boy to succeed, and I'll give him what he needs to do that. Tye has a talent on ice that has several teams looking at him.

When I got him three and a half years ago, he couldn't skate. I took him once and witnessed a miracle. Never seen skill like Tye's, not for someone who's been skating for three and a half years. Tye's partial to the Blackhawks because I am." Phoe showed them the rink, they left after a few minutes admiring it. Drake's ears had perked up when Phoe had mentioned getting Tye a few years ago. There was a story behind Phoe and her kids.

"What's down there?" Fish asked, pointing at another path. Drake followed his arm.

"Tennis courts. Jodie and Serenity like skating and baseball but they prefer a gentler workout where their brothers are not squishing them. Although I've seen Serenity slam Tye a few times," Phoe giggled. Drake remembered the slim girls and could understand why she found it amusing.

"Over there?" Apache asked.

"Our garages, bikes and cars, ones we use daily."

"This is like a luxury hotel," Slick said.

"I hope not, this is home, it's huge, I need it huge, I've got sixteen kids. I got Hellfire, my HQ people and my staff. Obviously, we need somewhere big to meet up for weekends like this. We try to get together at least once a month. When winter kicks in, and it's too brisk, we're going to need those games rooms, cinema and bowling alley the house boasts." Phoe looked up and bit her lip and then turned and faced them. She squared her shoulders and Drake tensed.

I stared at Drake and Rage and saw varying expressions on their faces. I centred my shoulders and took a deep breath. There was no doubt they were judging me over the Hall and its excesses.

"I'm rich, one could say I'm stinking rich. I've sixteen kids, five of those kids I gave birth too, eleven I adopted over the last four years. Yeah, I got money, it's a gift. I can help those kids I adopted have a better life, and I'm damn well going to do that.

Some of my kids were on the street, some were dumped unwanted. Simply, because they were born the wrong colour to a white mother. The twins are mine because their incubator mothers abused them in the womb and force-fed them drugs and booze.

I took them on, they're mine, I'll fight and die for them. I bought an enormous house not because I wanted to be flash or shove my money in people's faces but because I've a large family. Don't care how anyone judges me, I want my family, which consists of my kids, HQ and Hellfire. I need space for them.

No one would know, but I've had it rough, eating shit for years and so did my kids. Every single one of them, I'll give them what they need to be happy, and I don't care what it costs. If building Tye an ice rink is excessive, so what? It means my boy can practise when he wants, so he gets to sign for the Blackhawks. That's what matters.

I build Carmine a diamond, so it means he gets his dream after eating years of shit, that's what I'll do. My kids are happy and well-adjusted after years of terror. Harley decides he wants to play NFL, I'll build him a damn field, so he can. You want to judge me so be it, but I'm opening my home and everything that's in it, to you. The toys here aren't just for my kids, they're for everyone." Drake stepped forward and placed his hand on my shoulder. He gently tilted my head up towards him, and I saw warmth in his eyes.

"What a woman. What a fuckin' woman," Drake whispered. I blinked. "How much love you got inside ya? How big is your heart?" Drake mumbled something else I couldn't altogether catch, it sounded like 'Do you have enough to save us too?'

"Chance told us about the charities you set up. Didn't tell us shit about your kids but if you think that is off puttin', you're wrong Phoenix. I thought you couldn't get any more amazing after finding out about what Trusts achieve.

Now I find out, you adopt eleven kids to give them a life free of shit. To make their dreams come true, you build ice rinks and baseball diamonds. Jesus Phoe," Drake said approval deep in his voice. I blinked away tears.

"This is my world, this is what family means to me."

"I guess we are gonna get a weekend we didn't expect. If my fuckin' cousin can bounce around on a child's hopper, I guess we can as well. Paintballing sounds fun with Eddie."

"Watch her, Eddie's a tattoo fiend, she'll have you stripped before you know it," I whispered back. His eyes held me mesmerised, and I knew I was weakening against him. Drake was worming his way into my good books.

"Wish Marsha was here to see this, she'd have loved it," Fish muttered.

"Your old lady?" I asked, Fish nodded.

"The old ladies are welcome, not skanks. Don't want skanks anywhere near my children. My kids have been exposed to enough ugly in their life's and from what I saw Rage skanks are freaking ugly!" I told him as Fish whipped out his phone.

"Give Silvie a call, she'll adore this," Apache said. "She's not a skank, she's an old lady but doesn't have an old man," he explained. I gave a nod, confused, but I'd take his word for it she was a good person. Although I was curious about how Rage had an old lady who didn't have a brother. It was unheard of, Rage had their own secrets!

"What's Rivendell?" Mac asked. My eyes lit up, and he gave me a smile. Slick snorted and grinned, I guess he knew what Rivendell is!

"It's the Elven village off Lord of the Rings, Eddie loves it. Come, I'll show it to you," I told him.

"Prefer the Ewok village," Texas muttered with a half manic grin.

"We can do that too." I began leading the way, not seeing Chance step out of the trees and give Drake a chin lift of approval. Drake gave him one back.

Drake had his ass on a chair and was watching a four-year-old child trace his arm tattoos with reverence. Phoenix hadn't lied about her daughter, Eddie was a total tattoo demon. She'd had half of Hellfire stripped down to the waist so she could examine their ink and the brothers hadn't flinched.

Eddie was now trying to convince him to take his tee off for her. The twin, Tony he thought was sat batting water balloons at those in the pool. Most of which seemed comprised of Phoe's security team. They'd been introduced, but it was too many names to remember.

He glanced over and noticed Apache in the treeline with Slick and Texas and a couple of Hellfire, from his distance it looked like Bear and Celt. Phoenix was lazing on a lounger by the pool, wearing cut-off jean shorts and a floaty top. She was chatting to Marsha, Silvie, Emily and two other women, he thought their names were Susan and Diana.

"Mama Phoe has too's," Eddie suddenly told him. Drake looked down and hooked her up with one arm and sat her on his lap.

"She does?" he asked his eyes sliding over to her mother.

"Yup. She got lots'a too's, she got a secret too," the little girl slyly said. He saw Phoenix look over and her eyes narrowed.

"Eddie," Phoe said with a warning in her tone, which made Drake's curiosity perk up.

"If you show me your too's, I'll get Mama Phoe to show you her secret one."

"Eddie!" Phoe hissed, and Drake was amused to see a tinge of red on her cheeks.

"Nope baby girl," he said, smiling.

"Mama Phoe has a too in a real secret place. Not even Unca Chance has seen it," Eddie coaxed, Phoe turned even redder.

"Honey, come play with Tony," Phoe said, clearly trying to distract the child. Eddie sent her a scornful look and Drake couldn't stop his chuckle escaping. This little girl was something.

"You show me yours, Mama Phoe will show you her secret one."

"Eddie, I will not!" Conversation was dying as people began listening. Drake wondered where the secret tattoo was. By the look on Phoe's face, it was somewhere private.

"Mama Phoe, he won't show me his!" Eddie shot back looking disgruntled.

"That's life sweetheart now come and play." Eddie leaned forward, and Drake wrapped his arm more firmly around her.

"He has too's!" Eddie snapped, "you show him yours, I get his." Little girl logic.

"Eddie we're not discussing my too's," Phoe replied. Eddie turned to him with huge eyes. Drake's heart melted. She was adorable, and then he recognised the glint in her eyes and changed adorable to cunning.

"Mama Phoe has a nice ass, Uncle Chance says so," the little girl shouted. Diesel choked on his beer and spat it out, luckily, he hit one of the plant pots. Chance chuckled.

"Yeah, she does," Drake warily agreed, not knowing where Eddie was going. He'd try to stop her putting his neck in a noose. Although by the glint in Eddie's eye, he wasn't going to have much success.

"Bet you want to see her too," Eddie carried on trying to bribe him. Phoe, eyes narrowed, was getting to her feet.

"Yeah, I suppose so."

"Show me yours," Eddie coaxed him one more time. Drake shook his head. Phoe gained her feet and began walking towards them.

"No," he told Eddie.

"Mama Phoe has one on her ass!" Eddie hollered at the top of her lungs as Phoe got within arm's reach. Eddie flung her arms around Drake's neck and clung to him. "No Mama Phoe, you show him your ass, he'll show me his too's." Silence. Pure silence and a completely horrified and mortified woman!

"Oh my god, Eddie!" Phoe finally exclaimed bright red.

"Get your ass out, Mama Phoe!" Eddie shrieked. Chance gave up the ghost and began laughing out loud, Diesel, Tiny, and Levi also started laughing. Fuck, even Ace broke a smile.

Drake looked to Rage and saw Gunner, Mac, Rock and Blaze laughing. Stefan and his husband were howling to one side. His mouth twitched, and Phoe's eyes shot to it and narrowed. Drake couldn't help it. His laughter broke out of him as a beautiful child glared at her mother, clearly expecting her to get her ass out.

"You don't use the word ass!" Phoe finally said, grabbing onto something desperately.

"Get your tushie out, Mama Phoe. I dop'ied you, you get your tushie out!"

"Hush," Phoe said mortification growing.

"You show him your tushie, I get too's," Eddie continued. Micah swept in and took Eddie from Drake.

"I'll show you my new one if you stop with Mum. And no, I don't have to get my ass out, Eddie," Micah sent a sly look at his mother who glared at him. Micah began walking to the pool with Eddie. She shrieked with glee and began grabbing his tee to look down it.

"My daughter, the tattoo fiend everyone," Phoe said bright red still.

"Darling, I dread to think of that child in ten years." An older man, well into his sixties, grinned.

"Albert, I'm leaving the country when she hits thirteen," Phoe said with a smile.

"And I'm coming with you," Albert agreed with a nod. Drake studied them, the children had introduced him as Grandad or Grandpa. Yet from their relationship, he'd deduced that Albert and Phoe were not blood relations. There was a story there, Drake wouldn't mind knowing what it was. In fact, Phoe had a lot of stories he'd like to listen to, the issue would be getting her to open up to him. Mr and Mrs Ames alternated between calling him, Mr Wilkes or Mr Albert.

"I not dop'ing you again, Mama Phoe, you are a *let-down*!" Eddie shrieked over Micah's shoulder.

"Fine by me," Phoe muttered.

"Dop'ing?" Slick asked approaching. Slick had a child under his arm, Aaron, Drake thought. The kid was laughing himself hysterical.

"Eddie means adopting, she can't say it properly. Eddie was one and a half when I met them. Instead of them letting them know I picked them, I let them think they picked me. Well, Eddie marched her eighteen-month-old tushie up to me and told me I was her new Mama. I had to adopt them after that. Eddie thinks she adopted me," Phoe smiled. "Over time, we've learnt with Eddie, it's best to give her lots of leeway."

"Can understand that, she's a bright kid," Texas said nodding.

"Eddie's either going to be a criminal mastermind or President one day. I'm not sure which," Phoenix laughed. Mrs Ames waved, and Phoe walked over to her. There was a gong on the patio by the door, Phoe belted it twice, and kids appeared from everywhere and shot into the kitchen.

"Two gongs mean kids come and eat, three means the adults," Chance said. "Kids always go first, even the older ones or Phoe loses her mind. Seriously loses her fuckin' mind."

Minutes later, kids reappeared with laden plates and Aaron bitching loudly he wanted cake. He was told in a don't mess with me tone, by Carmine that once everyone had eaten, then they got dessert. Aaron glared at Carmine and went to sit. From a yet another storage shed Hellfire, HQ and Rage had dragged out large fold-up tables and chairs. With the masses of patio furniture and wicker sofas and swinging hammocks, there was plenty of seating.

Drake fast came to realise that Phoe needed these weekends and did it at least once a month, if she could, twice a month. Everything he'd seen so far was about comfort and fun for her family. Drake realised that the people present needed this time together to strengthen the bonds they had created.

Hellfire was rough and ready, same as Rage but here they let it hang out. No one cared if they were snapped on a phone, on a child's hopper bouncing around. It was the most fundamental principle of both clubs, family. Drake could understand why the woman who held his interest was the heart and soul of Hellfire. Damn, he wanted that for his own guys.

The entire estate was built around the premise of family and good times. He hadn't yet seen the inside, but it would be the shit considering the outside. Drake saw Phoe laughing with a few of his brothers, Chance next to Phoe. He dropped a kiss on Phoe's head and then with a squeeze went to get some food when Mrs Ames rang the gong three times. Chance inclined his head in Drakes direction and grinned. It was shaping up to be a good day.

Chapter Five.

"Can we look around the house?" Marsha said to me two hours later. We were sitting around the swimming pool watching HQ against security in a water polo game. HQ was winning. I'm sure they were cheating, but I kept quiet.

"Of course!" I exclaimed, "you don't have to ask. Do you want a guided tour or a wander on your own?"

"Love a guided one. That way I don't stick my nose where it's not wanted," Marsha replied with a grin.

"There's not much off-limits, Silvie are you interested in a tour?" I asked the other woman who shot to her feet instantly. Silvie was everything Apache had claimed, a lovely woman.

"Where you going?" Fish asked, reaching out for his wife's hand. Romantically, I thought, he snagged it to him and kissed her knuckles. I felt my heart melt at Rage's brusque sergeant of arms. Marsha laughed and kissed her man.

"Phoe's going to give a tour of the house," she smiled.

"I'm up for that," he said getting to his feet, calling out to Texas and Axel, who joined our huddle. When I looked back, Rage stood behind me.

"Hey, wait, we haven't had a tour yet," Bear shouted from the bushes.

"Snooze you lose!" Silvie shouted back. Bear flipped her the bird, and she chuckled.

"We'll watch the kids and take a second tour," Chance called out, and I nodded.

An arm slipped around my waist, and I grinned at Silvie who was bouncing in her boots. Silvie was so sweet, I genuinely liked the woman already, she was younger than me but full of life. There was a quiet pain in her eyes when she looked at one of Drake's brothers, Apache, I wondered what the story was. But I didn't know her well enough, I ruefully admitted, to ask her outright.

I took them through the kitchen and down into the basement first, it was huge, the size of the house and then it extended further back beyond it. The entrance was done up to resemble a cinema, red carpeting and posters on the wall, hotdog machines and popcorn carts and a candy counter.

Silvie loved it, and so did Marsha and a couple of the guys made awed noises. I opened the first door to the man cave Micah had designed. The older boys had decorated it in dark tones with dark furniture. A multitude of spotlights had been put in to brighten it up if they wished. Micah and Carmine had the biggest flat-screen TV they could find, with games consoles and a soft drink fridge filled to the brim.

There was their own food fridge which Mrs Ames kept well stocked, a pool table and other paraphernalia guys think they needed. Arcade games were stacked along one wall, and large black leather sofas were spread around the TV space. Although the older teens had decorated it, all the boys had access to this room.

"Nice," Texas said with approval in his voice. Leading them out to the door opposite, it opened to the cinema which could seat one hundred and fifty people. Further on down the cinema-themed hallway was the bowling alley combined with a jungle gym for the smaller kids.

Finally, at the end was a large indoor heated swimming pool, with a sauna and hot tub. I showed them the gym the boys had insisted on having installed. There was a weight room and a dojo as Micah practised ju-jitsu holding a black belt, second dan.

We went back upstairs, and they peered into the wine cellar off the kitchen. I waved them into the informal dining room, which doors folded back to make it part of the kitchen. Next room up was the male study and then the female study and then into the first of the lounges, this one I called the family lounge. Large beckoning sofas surrounded a large fireplace, bevelled glass windows looked out over the gardens. It was the one we used the most.

Through the doors and into the formal lounge, which I used for entertaining people. Adjoining that was my Pride and Prejudice morning room, which overlooked the drive. Nerves kicked in around a few of their comments, such as 'I know she said she was rich but fuckin' hell!' All in all, though their admiration was honest, and although a couple proclaimed to be jealous, it was good-hearted comments.

Silvie began commenting on my décor, and I was nervous at first. While the family lounge was modern, the rest of the house was decorated in keeping with the age of the building, eighteenth-century regency. Soon enough, I understood Silvie's remarks were complementary, and so were the comments being uttered by everyone.

We walked across the large entrance hall that was a room in itself and held a piano and a large ornate harp. Intricately carved wooden stairs soared up both sides of the hall and met in the middle, creating a musician's parlour. The next room was a kid's toy room, neatly stacked away but filled with toys. I showed them the large room which had been converted into study cubicles for the teenagers.

Axel and Texas both fell in love with my third favourite room, the smoking room. A bar in one corner, fully stocked, a second pool table and the walls were panelled in dark wood. The room reeked of old-fashioned opulence. Next up was the music room, which I assured them, was soundproofed. Harley on the drums was loud! Christian was louder, and Cody could make a guitar scream for mercy. I led them into my pride and joy, my second most favourite room in the house. Built along the full length of the east side of the Hall was my library.

"Shit," Marsha exclaimed her mouth open in awe, "this is awesome." It was. I loved this room, it had been one of the hardest to restore but well worth it. Floor to ceiling with wooden panels and shelves covering most of the walls. Restored sliding ladders.

Decorated in dark green leather Chesterfield sofas and heavy Edwardian desks, the library offered comfort and peacefulness. Two marble fireplaces had been restored and took up a large amount of space.

There were two substantial stained-glass windows at either end of the room taking up three-quarters of their respective walls. One depicted a George and the Dragon scene and the other King Arthur, the windows were framed with heavy wooden shutters that folded back. Old-fashioned green reading lamps were dotted around on the desks and around each fireplace were three huge armchairs facing them. In the middle of the big room were intricately carved free-standing bookcases lined up in rows.

"No books?" Slick asked. With a sigh, I pointed to a far corner, and we could see a wall of boxes facing us.

"There were hardly any books here when I moved in, those that were left was tragically irreparably damaged. Preservation is important, I sent them away for restoration if possible, but a good many were just pulp. The ceiling leaked terribly in here and did so much damage," I made a disappointed moue with my mouth and continued.

"The windows underwent a major restoration as most of the glass was broken. The shutters are original on the inside, but the outside ones had fallen and rotted away. We had new ones made up in the correct style. The bonus is I get to put my choice of books in this magnificent library. Each letter of the alphabet has three columns of shelves to it. Someone loved this once." And I loved it now, that's what mattered.

"I'd move a bed in here Phoe and never move out," Slick said with a grin. He gazed upon the shelves with a large brass Z scrolled on a plaque above them. I understood his feeling.

"Don't think I could ever fill three floor to ceiling columns of shelves with authors beginning with Z," I joked. Slick rolled his eyes at me.

I led them down a hallway at the end of the library and into what I called the glass ballroom. The ballroom ran adjacent to the library and the full length of the house and cost a whack to restore. The ceiling slanted downwards in a ninety-degree angle, with stained glass panels in a variety of images. This right here was my most favourite room in the Hall.

Two enormous, original candelabrum chandeliers hung from the ceiling. The three external walls were glass and wooden beams. Big glass windows, gleaming in the sun, went from floor to ceiling. The wooden floor we'd managed to restore, and it shone in the low lighting.

"Sadly, most of this was horrendously damaged, the ballroom took a massive effort to restore." Awed silence fell, looking around, I saw stunned expressions on their faces.

"Close your eyes, I can just see ladies in their ballgowns here. This is awesome. Think it's my favourite yet." Silvie said, craning her neck and looking at the images. I grabbed her hand and dragged her to the floor and laid down on it with her. Now she got the full experience. Silvie's soft gasp let me know how much she appreciated it.

"Oh my god, Marsha get down here." Asses hit the floor and long legs covered in jeans popped into view, as most of the brothers did the same.

"Envisioning this when there's snow on the ground," Marsha whispered.

"Vandals smashed numerous panels. Luckily, we found the original designs in a folder in a sideboard. The plan for the repairs was more straightforward than you could imagine. Water damage had ruined a few designs, so I had an artist design new panels to go with the originals," I told them. My eyes on the twisted rose vine panel with its bright red flowers.

"The dragon's ace," Drake said, and I jumped as I realised he was laying by my side.

"The phoenix is out of the world," Apache said from Silvie's side.

"Love the mermaid panel," Silvie whispered.

"Can't take my eyes off the knight on his charger," Marsha said, pointing out another panel. I felt movement at my side, and Drake's hand slipped into mine and squeezed. I hesitated for a few seconds, and then I pressed back. Drake tugged on my hand and pulled me closer. I allowed him a few moments and then pushed up.

"Shall we continue with the tour or lay here dreaming?" I teased them.

"Fuckin' lay here all day watching the sun play over them," Texas replied, but got to his feet, and we left the room. I showed them three out of the four towers, I didn't intrude on Alberts realm. They loved the boy's tower, the bottom level, a living room, second-level a games room and bar (soft drinks). And the third and fourth levels their bedrooms with en-suite bathrooms.

"Who lives here?" Blaze asked.

"In here we have Micah, Carmine, Tye and Harley. They could've had bedrooms in the main part of the house, but they are older now and so deserve their own space." Blaze nodded. Jodie's and Serenity's tower were much laid out the same. But the fourth floor was a dressing room/makeup room and the girlie paraphernalia they thought they needed.

The third tower was set up as a second jungle gym for the kids on the bottom level. The first level I had my stuff set up and Marsha and Silvie gave a gasp.

"Phoe, you make candles and soaps?" Marsha asked, touching wax.

"Yeah, bath bombs and bath oils and you get the idea. I enjoy making stuff, and they're easy. Definitely, a relaxing hobby to have," I replied.

"I want to try someday," Marsha hinted. I smiled at her, she was lovely and genuine.

"Anytime you want to try, give me a shout, you'd be welcome." Marsha squealed, and Fish rolled his eyes at me and muttered, 'Here we go!" The next level made the girls go crazy as they surveyed my stained-glass making equipment.

"Did you make those panels?" Mac asked. Vigorously, I shook my head.

"No, that skill is beyond me." I denied as Mac smiled.

"Don't think much is beyond you." Grunts of agreement followed his statement. I ducked my head embarrassed. The final floor was my parlour, it was set in a nineteen-thirties style Chinese parlour. The parlour was authentically decorated, taking tea up here and looking out over the Black Hills, was a calming experience.

"Love this," Silvie said.

"When the kids are in bed, I bring a book and just sit and gaze at the scene in front of me. So relaxing," Silvie nodded in agreement.

I took them back down and showed them the boring rooms, the linen room, china room and the silver room where the tableware was kept. Everyone poked heads into a large dark room that was empty and made suggestions. I'd been researching what the room was used for when the Hall was designed. Then I showed them my display room, I hesitated before doing so, and Drake noticed. He gave me a warm smile, and I opened the door.

"Wow," Drake said. The room was filled with glass display cabinets, wall to wall. Each cabinet was filled with decorative plates of mythical creatures and fairies and elves, shelves held ornaments of mythical creatures.

"Love this dragon," Rock grunted point to a big black dragon with its wings spread aggressively.

"Lovin' this woman," Lex spoke from the corner where he was looking at my huge free-standing red dragon lamp. The lamp came up to my waist and held an orb in its jaws, which was the lamp.

"This is crazy," Silvie said, staring at my two cabinets of fairies.

"A lot is Tudor Mint and Enchantica items," I said, walking forward to my pewter dragons and figurines.

"Stunning," Marsha whispered, looking at my dark angel that crouched with obsidian wings.

"I like them," I said shrugging. No one ever saw this, I was shy about showing my collection to people.

"What's upstairs?" Texas asked.

"Bedrooms, above the library is the long portrait gallery."

"Portrait gallery?" Marsha said.

"Yeah, I got restorers in doing them. The family left them there, and I'm having them restored and researched, seems wrong to have them removed. To me it feels right to have them here and labelled up correctly, they built this home, and now I share it because of them.

Researchers discovered that the last of the family died here, leaving the lawyers to search for an heir. They found a distant one who left the Hall to go to wrack and ruin. The heir had no interest, sadly it had taken so long to find an heir, the decay had begun in earnest. The heir had no interest in restoring the Hall. So keeping the portraits feels right to me." Saying that last out loud sounded ridiculous and sentimental but Drake interrupted that.

"Called respect," Drake grunted. He stood staring at my emerald green dragon that had wings spread and claws up and its maw open.

"Can we see it?" Marsha asked, I nodded and took them up. Briefly, I showed them the bedrooms as we passed, and then I took them through the gallery. Silvie was in heaven as she took in the straw-woven flooring that I'd had repaired. The only one I'd ever seen similar was at Hardwick Hall in Derbyshire back in England.

Most of the portraits hung on walls still, but the window's shutters were closed protecting them from further damage. One corner was given over to the restorers. Their equipment was left around, and we peered at the painting of a woman wearing a huge ornate ballgown, that was being restored.

"One day, I'll know each and every history of the portraits. I have researchers working for me," I shyly said. Drake nodded.

"I'd want to know who was hanging on my walls too."

"Many of these are so old. I believe that the family who built this were direct descendants of an aristocratic English family. Lots of paintings such as these exist at historic homes in England. Researchers will track back the family ties, I think this may have belonged to a dishonoured son or a second son. Could even be an heir who left his stately home in England."

Marsha gazed at the tapestries that hung full length on the walls, and I told her they were being repaired as well. A few empty spaces were open were the most desperately damaged had been sent away for repair. Marsha commented that she'd noticed the other tapestries hanging in the hallways and downstairs on the ground floor. I told her those had been restored and preserved.

On the third floor, I gave them brief looks into the guest bedrooms. There was a second long gallery above the first-floor one that held models of old-fashioned sailing ships kept in glass cabinets. Of course, the ships were far more up the men's street than portraits and tapestries. The second gallery was more a museum with other works of art placed haphazardly.

"Private?" Silvie asked when I didn't open two doors that we passed by, and she cocked her head at me. I blushed, and eyebrows shot up.

"Ah, that kind of private," she giggled, and I heard a few manly chuckles.

"No, no! Those are my Halloween rooms and Christmas rooms." The word Halloween hadn't even left my mouth, and Silvie was through the doors. Squeals came from the room, making everyone file in behind her.

"Shit you like Halloween?" Slick asked, laughing as he looked around at my decorations.

"I go mad," I mumbled, Slick nodded, still laughing.

"Can't wait to see this place at Halloween," Apache grinned.

"Fish, Fish come see this!" Marsha called from across the hallway where she'd found the Christmas room.

"Like Christmas too?" Drake asked as he sauntered past me. The dratted man grinned at me.

"Halloween is my holiday. Christmas is the kids."

"Attic not used?" Drake asked me as we descended the stairs.

"No, it's creepy, I've only been in it twice. It's full of trunks that possibly have treasures in, but I can't go there alone."

"Can ride up next weekend and we can take a look around?" Drake offered. Unsure what to say, I paused. Drake's eyes softened, and I gave him a nod.

World War Three met us outside as the kids and security team had teamed up against Hellfire and HQ. Blasting the hell out of each other with water guns, hoses and bombs, the kids were winning. Forced to duck from a water bomb, I escaped and proceeded to show Hellfire around as Rage took their place.

The catering staff went home after cleaning up, and I gave them a bonus for a job well done. Then I watched alpha males argue over who did the grilling. The women rolled their eyes, as they argued, there were twenty large barrel grills for Pete's sake! What was there to argue over! Marsha and Diana were howling as they gave each team five grills each, Hellfire, HQ, Rage and Security.

The women let them get on with it, and I began ordering the kids to put stuff away. Micah and the elder ones stored the ATV's and dirt bikes away. The younger ones gathered up water guns and so on and put them back on their hooks in the shed.

Eddie threw a tantrum as she didn't want the hoppers put away, but one look from Chance and she did as she was told. Once everything was put away, the older kids got out the garden board games we had and commenced playing chess and snakes and ladders. The smell of the grills drifted on the air, and I listened to calls of cheat, and you can't do that from the board games.

Tony ran off carrying a pawn that was just as big as him. Eddie was trying her hardest to roll dice's that was half her size, and she ended up kicking it to make it roll. Stefan was in fits as Tony got the pawn to the pool and pushed it in drowning Bernard at the same time. Everyone was grinning as Bernard pretended to be disgruntled and Tony giggled.

"Good day," a deep voice I was beginning to know well said, as Drake sat next to me.

"Yeah, this is what family means."

"Didn't know what to expect, thought beers, talk and a grill. When Chance told us to get here early, I still didn't have a clue. Judged you wrong, woman." Drake's voice made me shiver, and I wondered if he'd seen it. I glanced at him and saw him watching me with that focussed attention I recognised from Chance.

"Yeah, you did," Drake's mouth tilted up.

"Think it's obvious why Chance got his ass here for this weekend. Chance said you don't always use catering?"

"No, usually me and Mrs Ames manage and maybe a couple of extra chefs, but with the number of people here, we decided to be lazy. Usually, start baking and cooking two days before but got to admit this was easier for us both."

"Mrs Ames been with you long?"

"Five weeks after we moved to the U.S. I bought the house in Ouray first, then Camden and with five kids, and getting things up and running I knew we needed help. I couldn't do everything and learned to lean on other people.

Before Hellfire there was only a few I trusted, Albert's one, Mr and Mrs Ames two more. Liz, my security manager, has been with me ever since…" I broke off and changed direction, but I saw Drake had caught it. "Sally, you haven't met, she's my second in command. If I'm not available, Sally is the next port of call. I used to enjoy doing meet and greets, but as the kids got older, and my family expanded, they became impossible to do. Sally does them now, she loves it."

"Albert's your dad?" Drake asked with a question in his tone. He was curious as to the man's relationship to Phoenix and the children. Drake was letting Phoe know, he was going to let her change of direction pass for now.

"No, my parents are dead. Albert comes a damn good runner-up for Dad though. The kids think of him as their grandfather, and he's family. Albert helped Micah and me before we moved here. Never seen a purer heart for love than Albert's," I explained.

"Trusts mean a shitload to you." Drake changed direction, not liking the sudden sadness that crept over her face. Phoenix lit up.

That inner light was precisely what Drake wanted to see. Phoe deserved to be lit up with happiness. Sudden doubt crossed his mind around his decision to rope her into Rage and then shrugged it away. Rage had love to give same as Hellfire did. They just didn't show it openly.

"God yes, the men and women the PT help, they risked everything so I can sit here and do this. Wounded, they come home and are thrown aside because they are broken and injured. They're real heroes not those idiots often lauded as heroes. How they are treated is so wrong. So very wrong.

The men, women and kids who use the RT, they don't deserve the abuse they suffer. Been there and done that, I've been in their position. Forced to choose whether to get my kids safe and lose them or let them watch me get beaten. I got lucky, I got incredibly lucky." Ouch, I realised what I said and immediately carried on as Drake's beautiful eyes darkened and he opened his mouth to speak.

"That doesn't mean I can sit on my pile of money and keep being lucky. That level of money comes with responsibility, and I take that seriously. Many wealthy and powerful people don't react, don't help and take the easy way out.

Look after number one and ignore those less fortunate. Not in me to do that, I won't do that. I won so much money that giving back is the least I can do. My kids have it good, my family have it good and now I help others have it good."

"Beaten?" Drake finally growled, the darkness in his eyes touching fury. I ignored him.

"Tell me, what child asks to be kidnapped, raped and tortured and sold into the sex slave trade? No, no child asks for that. These assholes steal their innocence, steal their childhood, which should be safe and beautiful.

We're looking at expanding ETs. I want to get a group of badasses together who can track these slave traders and then complete rescues. But, it's not something Trusts can advertise, but it's something I can research into paying for personally. I'll find those kids, I will!" I stared at the sun, beginning to sink low in the sky.

"Believe you. Will it make you happy?" Drake appeared genuinely interested. For a moment, he was distracted from what I'd unintentionally revealed. He was actually listening.

"Yes," I whispered.

"Then, I hope you find your rescue team."

"Me too. I've someone in mind, just need to get Artemis on board. She's done work for me before, but she had a variety of interests, but she'll go out after kids for me." I looked up as Bear approached and lifted me up off my lounger. Bear grunted as he sat and pulled me down and turned on his side and cuddled me into his. We were both facing Drake, and I knew he caught my sigh of relief, he wouldn't be able to probe over the abuse.

"Eddie is trying to get in the paintball shed," Bear told me.

"Good luck with that. I have it fingerprint locked. Eddie can try all she wants," I grinned at Drake. He gave me a faint smile back, one filled with a promise that he wasn't going to let my slip drop.

"Tell me about the kids? How did you find them?"

"It's a sad story, today is a happy time."

"Not sad Phoe, look at those kids. It would have been tragic if they hadn't found you." I took a deep breath.

"Three weeks after we moved into the house in Maine, I saw Carmine going through our bins. I made sandwiches and put them out. Carmine watched me watch him, but he snatched them up and ran with them. Next day I put out a hot meal, but he rolled it up in the bag the sandwiches were in and ran off again. I figured out pretty quick he was feeding someone else, so I made extras and waited."

"Christ," Drake bit out, and Bear's arms tightened around me.

"I put a coat, hat and scarf out until Carmine came back wearing them. Carmine had taken responsibility for three people. So each morning I put food out for four people to eat for breakfast and lunch. Cooked hot meals that I put in stay hot containers for four in the evening. This carried on for approximately six weeks. I slowly earned his trust.

We put out clothes and shoes, socks and toothbrushes and whatever else we could think of.

Then one day he didn't come, I knew something was wrong. Around three in the morning, he finally approached my door and banged on it. He said one word, 'Help.' Carmine had never spoken to me until that night. I can't explain the sick feeling that hit me, something had to have been very wrong, for Carmine to come for help.

I followed him down the streets and into back alleys, where I found Harley extremely sick. Serenity and Tye were with him, guarding him with bits of wood. Took one look, called my lawyer, called Sally and called an ambulance. Made Carmine, Tye and Serenity go to my house and followed Harley in the ambulance.

Harley had pneumonia, he was damn lucky to have survived. Steven got the ball rolling, and I'd enough clout to get what I wanted, and that was those kids. They'd been on the streets for years, and they've been mine four years. After I checked Harley would make it, I told those four they were mine, were staying mine, and the rest was history.

Carmine being the eldest, took responsibility for Tye, Harley and Serenity. I know he and Tye did shit they won't talk to me or anyone about, I don't care what they did to survive. I will never, ever judge them. They're my kids," I spat the last defensively, and my gaze challenged Drake to condemn my boys.

"Jesus Christ," Drake swore again. He gazed into Phoe's eyes and recognised the fierceness of a mama lioness protecting her cubs. Drake had a damn good idea of what Carmine and Tye may have put themselves through. The fact Phoe did as well, hit him hard in his stomach. He didn't want Phoe to know the ugliness of the streets for kids, but he knew she did. His admiration for the older two escalated.

"When we holidayed to the cabin in Colorado, Carmine began to disappear. Then one night he walked in with Cody and so I got Cody. Carmine and Tye stated Cody was going to live with us. They'd seen Cody on the street and worked for ten days with him to get him to trust us. Carmine won't leave a kid on the streets if he can help it.

Eddie and Tony, I met at an orphanage, each Christmas we buy a load of stuff and take it to our local one. On one visit, Eddie tottered up to me and looked at me with those eyes. Announced loudly, I was her new mama and weeks later I had her and Tony."

"That's cool," Drake said, he looked into my eyes. "You'd adopt them all, wouldn't you?" he meant every orphan, I gave a nod. Drake saw the soul deep inside me, he saw what I tried to do by helping everyone. Drake understood my motives, Bear's arms clenched tighter around my waist.

"I've a friend who does lots of pro-bono work for the Trusts, he works in a hospital. Timmy and Scout's incubator was a drug addict, hardcore, the twins were born at thirty weeks and born addicted. I got involved in paying for their care, and two months later, they came home with me."

"Incubator?" Drake asked me. I glared at him fiercely.

"What else would you call a drug-addled woman carrying twins? She's not a mother, doesn't deserve to be called their birth mother. No mother will harm their kids like that. She was an incubator and not a good one at that!" I sniped, and Drake held his hand up in peace.

"I agree, Phoe," he said gently. My anger faded, and he smiled kindly at me.

"Jake and Garrett have the same story, the only difference is they were born at twenty-four weeks. They were borderline survival, even with the best prenatal care. That they didn't have until I came along. Spent several weeks at the hospital willing and praying for them to pull through.

The four have severe medical problems, but I'm hoping time, love, and the best damn medical care money can buy will fix that. If not, they're going to grow up in a house full of love and when I die their brothers and sisters will see to their care. They'll not ever be put into a home, because I've raised my kids right and Micah will annihilate anyone who gets in his way."

"Lot of love in those kids," Bear said. I nodded in his arms. "Micah, being the eldest will literally take anyone down in his way, he's real protective of them. Phoe has a point of view that blood doesn't matter, a family is what you make it. Blood means shit to these guys. Love does."

"We try, wherever we live to find the local orphanages or child centres. Once we do, I find out information on the kids there, their birthdays, etcetera. Make my kids go out and buy them presents for their birthdays, Easter, Christmas. My kids got lucky, each one of them, I don't want them to take money for granted, they will work, and they will earn their own money. Doesn't mean to say I haven't secured their futures. I have. I want them to remember there are children with less than them and that what they have means something."

"What's Micah, Jodie, Christian, Jared and Aaron's story?" Bear's arm got tighter, and I felt him give Drake a warning glare. I clammed up.

"Life is shit until you make it not shit," I told Drake as an answer. Men began putting plates of food down, distracting me. "Looks like food is ready," I said and got to my feet, the conversation ended.

The night was a good one, drink and chat flowed. Kids had fun, and adults did too. I mingled with everyone staying away from Drake and his penetrating eyes. I felt them on me and knew he wanted more answers, I'd given him all I intended too.

Chance didn't need to warn me that Drake was interested in me, I was picking that up loud and clear. The difference was as much as I felt an attraction to Drake, I couldn't act on it. The monster had done such a number on me and my self-confidence that I doubted every man that showed a genuine interest in me.

The party continued until late, and I put sleepy babies and tired children to bed with Chance and Bear helping me. I put on their intercoms and carried the receivers around with me.

Chance finally wound the party up and told everyone that breakfast was at nine if they wanted to come. People began getting in their cars and on their bikes and leaving. I saw Drake hovering, but he realised that Hellfire was staying the night and so he left too. Completely missed Chance watching me, watching Drake, as the dratted man tried to get past my defences. I had tonight to shore them back up!

Pipes sounded in a loud roar, and I pulled my pillow over my head and moaned. I looked at my clock and nearly threw it across the room. With a groan, I opened my eyes and saw Timmy sleeping curled up and surrounded by pillows to stop him from rolling off, on my bed. He'd had a rough night, a real nasty night, and I'd been up most of it with him. Poor baby finally fell to sleep two hours ago.

I got up and walked to the shower as I heard a noise from downstairs. Jodie came in as I was dressing, with a plate of food, checked Timmy and curled up next to him. Resembling a zombie, I made my way down, snarling good mornings at people and heading straight towards the coffee. Typically, I wasn't a huge coffee drinker, but today I needed it. Rudely, I grabbed a bacon sandwich and walking past everyone, I curled up on my porch swing with it.

"Christ babe," an amused voice said, and I raised bleary eyes to Chance.

"Timmy had a terrible night," I muttered.

"How bad?" he asked, crouching next to my swing.

"Bad."

"Go back to bed, Mum, I got him," Jodie said, carrying a smiling Timmy. I narrowed my eyes at the baby and wondered how he could be so cheerful. Timmy blew bubbles at me, and I collapsed on my side in my swing and pulled cushions over my head and closed my eyes.

"Funny bed," Chance said, amused. I flipped him a finger and dragged the blanket off the back of the swing and wrapped it around myself. Chance put my cup and sandwich on the floor and let me be. Snuggled up and swinging gently, I fell back to sleep.

"Die evil storm trooper!" a voice yelled from the trees. I opened my eyes and saw Aaron belting Slick and Celt with a paintball gun. Oh, hell no! In horror, I looked at the paintball shed and saw it wide open and empty. Adults and kids were darting amongst the trees. Christian and Jared were up on a platform shooting at anyone's heads who popped up.

I looked up and saw Liz (head of security) and her second in command, Matthias shooting from behind haystacks that had been pulled around, they were damn good shots! Chance popped up and shot what looked like Slick in his ass to a huge roar, and then Mac shot Chance in the chest five times. Slick shook his head and began making his way in our direction.

"Bedlam," I muttered and heard a chuckle. Drake and Tiny sat in front of my swing and fed Jake and Garrett.

"Feel better?" Tiny asked.

"How long have I been asleep?" I asked.

"Three or so hours."

"Yeah, I feel better. Not up for paintballing though." I grinned as I saw Pyro launch out of a tree and crash down on top of Levi and Shotgun. "That never gets old."

"Think they'd learn," Tiny agreed. Jake pushed his bottle out, and Tiny threw a burpee over his shoulder and began whacking Jake on his back. Jake let out a tremendous burp and looked shocked.

"There's my tiny biker dude," Tiny rumbled.

"Watch out for…" I was too late as Garrett scrunched his face up, burped and threw up over Drake's chest. Drake's nose wrinkled and Garrett let out a second burp. "Sorry, he does that," Tiny smirked. Drake shrugged and laying Garrett back in his rocker, whipped his top off, and my mouth went dry.

His skin was smooth and tanned with a light sprinkling of hair, his chest well-formed and his abs were rock hard, and he had a six-pack. A really lickable sick pack! Tattoo's covered his back and chest, and he had full sleeves. Oh boy, did I look at his tattoo's or his body?

Why did Drake affect me so differently from Chance? Both men were nearly identical, yet Chance didn't make me heat up the way Drake did. Drake met my eyes and whatever he saw in mine made his flare, and I looked away.

Slick sat in front of me and chucked Garrett under his chin. He looked uncomfortable, and I looked at him curiously. I expected him to say that Eddie had got him too. He checked with Drake before glancing at me, whatever he wanted to ask me, Drake silently approved.

"Your library," Slick stated. I frowned puzzled.

"Yeah?"

"I like readin'. Your boy, Tye, he said you have those boxes in the library and loads more in the attic and in the garage on a mezzanine level. Was wonderin' if you wanted help to shelve them?"

"That would be grand," I said. Slick broke into a shy smile. I blinked, he was hot.

"Like readin', figure I help you stack them, you wouldn't mind me borrowing or coming and readin'." I laughed and gave him a nod.

"Welcome whenever you want Slick." Drake gave his brother a dirty stare, and I laughed again. I don't think Drake expected my offer to Slick and warmth filled me at his disgruntlement.

"Ouch, the fucker gonna feel that," Tiny commented on a headshot from Chatter on Ace. Ace popped back up and shot Chatter in the balls.

"That's fighting dirty," I laughed as Chatter hit the ground groaning. "I'm guessing you alpha men didn't use groin pads again."

"Some did after we learned that's as high as Eddie can shoot." Tiny winced, and I knew he'd been on the end of some of Eddie's shots. I caught Drakes wince as well.

"My girl got both of you," I said to two sharp nods.

"That's when we decided to feed the kids to get away from her. Ever thought of taking her sniper training? That child's lethal," Drake rumbled. I laughed.

"She's small so aims at what she can see."

"My dick needs a week to recover," Tiny groaned. And I laughed again as there was a startled yelp from the trees and Apache came running out with my little terror behind him.

"Which idiot gave her that?" I asked as I looked at the automatic paintball gun she was carrying.

"Chance," Drake and Tiny said together. Apache hit the ground laughing and grabbed her and spun her up. Aghast I watched as Apache handed Eddie ten bucks and sent her in a different direction.

"Did he just bribe her?" I asked, stunned.

"Woman she has over one hundred and fifty bucks so far," Tiny laughed, and I narrowed my eyes. That child!

"Yeah and she's working out who'll pay her," Slick said with a shit-eating grin. I looked at him. "Twenty bucks."

"Oh my god," I exclaimed.

"Leave her, she's having fun. Not as if those she's fleecing can't afford it," Micah said, sitting on the step in front of me.

"Micah, she's fleecing people!"

"Yeah, think that's why she begged Chance for the automatic," he agreed. My gaze drifted to the tree line where people darted around. My eyes grew wide when I saw Eddie swinging from a rope wrapped around her waist and arm. And as my tiny terror turned, Eddie took aim and started firing the automatic.

"Shit!" Micah exclaimed and jumped to his feet.

"Ah leave her, Micah, she's having fun," I glared at him. He began racing in the direction of the trees when Eddie got her feet to a tree trunk and pushed off swinging outwards and still firing.

Heads popped up as adults jumped to their feet to grab my holy horror and then get shot. Eddie was screaming like Tarzan as she pushed off the tree again and kept shooting.

Drake sat up straight when he first heard it and his eyes and Apache's shot in the direction of Ace. Slick mirrored their actions. I frowned and followed their gaze. Ace, the brother who never smiled, had managed to get out of the firing line. He was standing watching Eddie as she repeated Tarzan, his hands on his hips and head thrown back, he was out and out laughing.

Apache moved out of the treeline his eyes on his son, and Drake pushed to his feet. Both men looked at Ace in disbelief, then Drake looked straight at me. There was something potent in his eyes, but I didn't know what, I know my breath caught in my throat. His eyes moved to Chance, who was also staring at the laughing Rage V.P, and Chance began moving in Drake's direction.

"Told you, brother, she heals."

Chapter Six.

Two days later, on Tuesday, I sat at my desk and frowned. Kyle, Diana, Charlie and Abigail sat in front of me. None of us was happy. Abigail's investigator had sent a troubling email, California was missing over three million dollars. I buzzed my desk and got Emily.

"Call Jon in California please Emily. Inform Jon it's a conference call with Diana, Abigail, Kyle, Charlie and myself." I asked and cut the intercom.

"This is dangerous for the Trusts," Kyle said, tapping his fingers on his knee.

"Could be an accounting problem, mislaid donations, could be anything," Charlie said. But the worried tone in his voice was unmistakable.

"The situation needs investigating by the book," I said. The phone rang, I picked it up and greeted Jon. As Jon finished the report, my door opened, Drake stood there with Apache. They caught the call and began backing out, and I waved them to come in and pointed to the sofas. Curious glances were aimed at them, but no one commented.

"Okay, Jon, thanks. Sally is on a flight to Cali, she'll arrive within an hour. This gets done by the book. Three million dollars is missing, I don't need to repeat how serious this situation is," I told Jon. Drake's eyebrows shot up, and he glanced at Apache.

"Keep this small Jon, only those on this call know. No one else for now, Sally has Anna with her to take notes," Diana said. Diana pursed her lips and leaning forward on her elbows, she rubbed her brow in stress.

"Jon, sit Saffron in a private office, offer a rep, she wants someone, let her choose who. Saffron declines, carry the meeting forward. Inform her three million dollars is missing, ask if she can explain. Whatever Saffron says gets documented. Then whether or not she explains, suspend her with pay for three days and set a time for another meeting," I spoke into the phone.

"Even if Saffron can explain?" Jon asked, interrupting me.

"Yeah, because as F.M (Fundraising Manager) Saffron should have brought an error to Charlie's attention, maybe she needs more training." Diana snorted, and I looked at her but continued. "From that suspension, we'll dig further, the investigating team will need to be on the ball. Diana can't get involved, and neither can I, as appeals will come to Diana first and then myself.

Once Saffron's suspended, escort her from the building. Explain her rights, Sally knows them off by heart as she helped draw up the policies. As soon as Saffron has left, there's an accounting team ready to rip their records apart and track everything back."

"I think it's an error Phoe, Saffron has tracked the donations, but they aren't showing in the banking," Jon said.

"Doesn't matter, she should have contacted Charlie. If this implodes, the Trusts appear inept. Trusts don't need accusations hitting us, not when we're pushing to open in three more states in a fortnight. Plans are in place for PT, and RT's and one of those states is having an ET. Under the radar but by the book," I told Jon. Diana nodded an agreement.

"Okay boss," Jon said. Diana gave a few more instructions, and we cut the call. I glanced at Diana.

"Saffron doesn't need more training Phoe, she's been with us from the start," Diana said annoyed.

"We have to consider that, Diana." I looked across at Kyle. "How are we doing with those three states?"

"Well on target and in two, we're over the target. Won't be an issue," Kyle said and rose to his feet. Troubled, they left the office, and I turned to Drake and Apache.

"Sorry. What can I do for you?"

"You okay?" Drake asked, and I realised I was rubbing my temples. I dropped my hand and smiled.

"Yeah, just tension, not a migraine. With the deadline in two weeks, Trusts don't need a scandal right now. Talk about poor timing."

"Think the money's stolen?" Apache asked, sitting forward.

"No, I believe it's an accounting error, looking at what Kyle and Jon have put together, it's likely to be that. The fact remains, though, Saffron should have brought this straight to Charlie's attention. She shouldn't have let Charlie discover this."

"Get that. Don't have to ask for our silence." I loved that I didn't have to ask. Drake continued. "Slick wants to come up sometime soon, brothers got a hard-on for your library."

"Sure, that's no problem." Leaning over my desk, I pulled a gold-embossed card from a cardholder. Apache took the card from me. He looked at it and then the different coloured ones held in silver card stacks on the desk.

"Different colours mean somethin'?" Apache asked.

"I'm anal-retentive," I laughed. "Gold card means you've my direct email, cell and home phone number. Red means it's the emergency phone which the Directors take turns at carrying. Lilac means you get my direct office phone and email. Silver means you get Emily's phone and email and black gives you the reception downstairs." Apache nodded.

"Saves being bothered by asshole's all the time," Apache mused.

"Good idea," Drake agreed.

"So that was it? Slick wanting to come up and steal the library?"

"Got a hog roast going this Saturday, wanna come?" Apache asked as Drake opened his mouth. Drake shot Apache a frustrated glare, I bit back a giggle.

"Got the kids, remember," I replied, feeling them out.

"Get two hogs, feed the kids too," Drake grinned, I smiled back. "I'll come up during the day, check your attic with you. Slick can hunt through boxes and then we'll come back for hogs."

"Sure, okay that's great, I'll look forward to it." I jotted it down, and when I turned back, Apache's long legs were disappearing out of my office. I raised an eyebrow at Drake.

"Wanna know what you do with your week. Want to be nosey," Drake explained.

"I run three national charities."

"Phoe, wanna understand what you do."

"Well Emily plans most of my days, so maybe it's her you should talk to?" I teased him. Drake's mouth twitched.

"Okay, okay!" I put my hands up in surrender. "I got an hour free, so I'll take you through my day. We've twenty states with PT's, RT and five states include ET's. Each building has a manager that manages everything. The Trusts have a fundraising team in each state with another manager. Each manager reports to an SM, State Manager, that's based here in HQ.

SMs get reports each week, and they compile those reports and bring them to me once a week, and we go through them. I allocate each SM an hour a week. Plenty of time to study reports and fix anything that needs fixing. Usually, meetings only take half an hour. If everything's okay, I file the report, and they go on their way.

The reports contain items such as fundraising figures, who has donated and how much. That is meticulously tracked. The reports consist of catering bills, electric bills etcetera, numbers around the intake, people we've found on the streets or people we've been requested to find.

The reports state how long clients have left in safe houses and if Property need to purchase homes. The SM does the liaisons on those. But I get an overall look at what's happening. Everything is discussed once a week in a meeting."

"So, you lose twenty hours a week going through those meetings. Detailed ain't they?" Drake nodded, showing understanding.

"Yeah. It's why my day starts at eight in the morning and finishes at five at night. I work fulltime."

"The other twenty hours?" Drake asked smirking. I poked my tongue out, and his gaze dropped to my mouth.

"Take other meetings, my director's get half an hour a week, I got fifteen Directors out there. Take phone calls, manage problems that turn up. Hold meet and greets from large donators, plot our next state to open buildings. Make sure the teams are doing what they need to be doing and oversee properties that may interest us.

Sally will do the legwork, I'll pick from a few that interest me and Sally will go check them out. I make sure Diana knows what state we're opening. Diana will send out a recruitment team to interview and wheedle out people who won't fit or who doesn't understand the Trusts vision. She'll spend two weeks in the state completing the final interviews."

"Diana enjoy travel?"

"She likes to travel but likes a home base too, this way Diana gets the best of both worlds. Once Diana has an SM in the state, they take over the bulk of the work, they'll liaise with the architects and volunteers. The SM will be on final interviews for Property Managers and other staff. Sally and I try to promote within the Trusts, we try internal first and then externally. I get the overview. In the beginning, I was in on everything, but considering the kids, I take a back seat and supervise."

"You don't work past five?" Drake asked.

"No, I have kids. None of my staff works past their shift end unless it's a fundraising push. Most of my team have kids or family lives, and my staff expect to clock off dead on time.

A few might work an extra ten minutes to finish a call or something they'd started. But they bank overtime with the HR and get to take it back as time in lieu. A skeleton staff works nights, two G.SMs who each work five shifts each, and a third one that does Saturday and Sunday."

"You leave here at five?" Drake repeated.

"Yeah, go home, eat dinner with the kids, spend family time together and then put little ones to bed, spend time with older ones. And then read any reports I didn't get time to, in bed and it's lights out by ten as I get up at six every weekday."

"HQ closes at weekends?" he frowned. That didn't feel right, after everything Phoe had put into making the Trusts work, shutting at weekends was irresponsible. Drake wanted to know the ins and outs of everything Phoe did. He was interested in her work.

"No, there's staff and GSMs who prefer Monday and Tuesday off, so they work Saturday and Sunday. It works for us, not quite a skeleton staff but not a full staff level by far. Typically around fifty members of staff here at the weekend. SMs get two days off a week, and a daytime GSM covers any issues that may arise while they're off. The Directors take turns working one out of three weekends, so there's always five Directors on at the weekend."

"You've made it work. You work one in three?" Drake said, looking around outside my glass walls. I nodded an agreement, I did indeed.

"Yeah, I look after my staff, I want loyalty, need them to believe in what we're doing. Staff get an automatic four-week paid holiday a year. Each year they're with us they gain an extra day until they hit the maximum of six weeks. Staff get a full paid six-month sick policy, a company-paid dental plan, and a discounted medical insurance.

The team get federal holidays or public holidays as a paid day off. A minimum three days over Christmas and each year that alternates between the three days and a maximum five days. Half the staff will get three days and the other half five days. The emergency phone covers those three days, the following year they swap. Easter Sunday, they get off, and there's always a huge New Year Eve party.

Trust staff know if they've got issues at home, a sick child, a sick parent, maybe financial trouble they can come to Diana if they are HQ. Or their PM, who will bring it to Diana's attention and we'll help. I have money put aside from my fortune that is used to help them with a loan or pay medical bills. My investment brokers grow that each year for me, so it never shrinks luckily enough."

"Jesus babe that's a hell of a staff package you offer. Don't know many companies out there offer shit like that. Overly generous?" Drake wondered if Phoe was being taken advantage of. Sure as hell bosses were few and far between who'd put a package like that together for their staff. Drake was dubious around this, he'd already seen Phoe was generous at heart.

"Well yeah. These people gave everything up to move here and support the Trusts. Happy staff are more productive, got to support them back." I wondered if Drake picked up on the unspoken 'duh' in my voice.

"Add to that Chance said that you paid for everyone to move from Norfolk. Helped them buy their houses cash so no mortgage, you paid their moving costs and helped partners find jobs if they needed one. All that out of your own cake," Drake interrupted a strange tone in his voice.

"They showed loyalty and came with me. Of course, I'd help them."

"Baby, back in Norfolk they had mortgages," Drake pushed harder.

"Yeah, but I asked them to move across states and come here. Took them from what they know and were used too, many left family and friends, there's displaced and unhappy kids. Look after the staff, and they'll look after my dream," I argued. Drake shook his head.

"You're not just loaded, your fuckin' loaded," Drake stated, and I nodded. That's something Drake needed to understand.

"Just under an official billionaire. In fact, at the end of this year, I should hit official billionaire status," Drake's eyes widened in shock.

"Fuckin' hell," he muttered.

"Yup," I agreed, nodding. Drake let that shock sink in for a few minutes. The fact Drake struggled with that was visible, Chance had too. Drake raised his head and gave me a smile.

"When do you date?"

"Don't date," I instantly said. Drake didn't like that answer.

"You don't date?"

"Nope."

"Why the fuck not?" he asked. He wanted to date her, fuck, what was wrong with him? Drake didn't date!

"I had a good marriage, married young and was widowed before Aaron was born. Micah was born when I was just sixteen. Justin and I weren't stupid, but it ripped, and we got caught. We married fast and built a good life.

Justin, same as me, had no family, our friends helped, we finished school and Justin got a good job working construction. Had eleven years together. Married for ten of them before it got ripped away. A crane collapsed with Justin on it," I paused as a familiar pain hit me.

"Pregnant and with four young kids, I went into survival mode and made a friend. Friend became a husband when Aaron was one. Left him four years ago, dreadful marriage. Turns out it wasn't even a real marriage, he was a bigamist." I saw Drake working out the math.

"You were with him for five years? Marriage went south that quick? Woah, wait, asshole was a bigamist? That's the one who beat you?" he asked anger in his voice.

"Marriage went wrong on the wedding night. I don't discuss it, don't talk about the monster. I won the euro millions and won a hell of a lot of money, that money bought us an escape. I built this, this was a dream, I lost one dream, my Justin. Found a second dream, this, never thought I'd see it come to fruition. I don't date because a man wouldn't like sharing his life with my vision.

Wouldn't like taking on someone else's kids except for a dubious reason. No man will take on sixteen kids. Not into casual sex, only had sex with two men and I married them both. Yeah, I miss sex, but I have this," bluntly, I told him. I had to make Drake understand that there won't be an *us,* if that what he was hinting. I spread my arms out. "I have my kids and family, which I built. Show me a man who will be happy to share with everything else in my life."

"Chance will," Drake replied, I tilted my head. "Any of Hellfire will."

"Chance deserves a life filled with love, and he deserves someone who can give him everything. I can't do that, I love Chance as much as possible, but I'm not his. Chance will always hold something back from me, and I can't handle that. I'd need every bit of him.

Make no mistake Drake, I'd lay down and die for him to live. But we aren't soul mates, we aren't fated to be together, Chance knows this." Narrowing my eyes at Drake, I wondered where this was going. Perhaps my gut was wrong, and Drake wasn't interested in me. My tummy quivered, and I ruthlessly pushed it away. Chance would never have sent Drake in to ask around a possibility of him, and I, both of us knew we couldn't work.

"Other men out there might," Drake mused.

"Okay, let me explain a few things. I don't date, but I've had fundraising dinner dates with whom I've been paired. Politely, they ask what I do, ask if I've any kids. Once they're aware of how many children I have, it's in their eyes. Easy, that many kids, that's what I am. Never ask if I adopted them, men hear the figure and then think I spread my legs easy.

Dates aren't interested when I don't, they aren't interested in me as a woman or as a success. That interest gets lost easily, but they are interested in me as a quick lay. I'm thirty-five, not saying I don't miss a sex life, but I'm not an easy lay. One-night stands hold no interest. I'm surrounded by hot sexy men most of the time, HQ and Hellfire, and I can't have them. It's shit, it sucks, but it's life."

"Can't or won't?"

"Won't."

"Men who see an easy lay are dicks baby. Total dicks." Nodding an agreement, I ignored how my heart leapt at his 'baby'.

"Agreed, so I don't date. Having kids, means they come first. Jake and Garrett, I've only had a few months, they don't know any different, but being a mum means being there for your kids. Simple as that." I sat on the desk and faced him. Drake studied me for a few minutes.

"Got to say, babe, you strutted your ass into Rage, didn't like it, didn't understand. Saw you in laps thought high class, high maintenance and gave it out easy." I gave him a sharp nod, I expected that, I knew it had crossed his mind. Drake didn't know me.

"Yeah, I saw you think that," I replied. His gaze got intense, and he stopped sprawling on my sofa and sat forward.

"Thought it, went outta my head the minute I saw you with Hellfire at your home. Shit, it left my head when Chance and Hellfire told me what you did for a living. Dunno what others think, I saw greatness, generosity, strength. Met your kid's babe, love Eddie down to her toes, rest of 'em are great kids. Do you credit. Proper saw them, no judgement, opening, welcoming, loving, yeah, I saw what you'd created babe.

Gotta tell ya, only got a weekend, left me wanting more. Got a taste of what you're capable of, what you can create, what love you got inside of ya. Tellin' ya, I want more. Ain't Chance. Rage ain't Hellfire, we've got same principles, but we're different. Clubs both tied tight," Drake paused.

"I saw that." Drake's eyes didn't leave mine.

"Yeah, I know you did," he replied. "That's why despite welcome you got on Rage, you still gave us everything. High class, high maintenance, the complete package, yet you curl up on a hammock, flip Chance the finger and go to sleep. Not a care who's judging you.

Got a pain in you we can taste, got a soft spot we want to protect. I want more babe. Tellin' ya straight, want more of you, want more of your kids, definitely want more family weekends." Drake rose to his feet and stalked towards me. I shifted backwards until my knees hit the desk and I'd nowhere to go. He got in my space and leant into me.

"Eyes through to the soul," Drake said bizarrely.

"I don't date," I whispered.

"You date me," he whispered back. "And I don't date Phoe, never dated. My idea of a date is a beer and then hittin' the sack. Gonna do you right, treat you like the lady you are."

"Want sixteen kids, Drake? Want to be a dad to sixteen kids?" I threw at him still whispering.

"Want that and everythin' you got to give. Don't know the future babe, know I like a fuck load what I'm seeing. Know I want a shot at havin' sixteen kids, and a baby throw up on my favourite tee. Want to see kids shooting my brothers in the ass with paint pellets. Want huge grill outs and letting it hang out, my cousin bouncing on a kid's hopper.

Saw you, first day here on that Sunday, you were laughin' at them, crazy-ass dancing on their vehicles. Heard you laugh, and that laugh passed through me and then I fucked up, treated you like easy pussy. Then my brother sets me right, gives me the truth of you. Yeah, I want that laughter, want that light in my life. See it in Chance's, and I want a shot.

Club's about family, 'cept we ain't got no kids. Marsha and Fish can't have 'em. Lost a kid we took into the club. Broke Ace. Never healed. Swore if I saw my shot at goodness, I'd take it with both hands." Drake's hands slid up my arms, and he pushed between my legs. "I'm taking my shot baby," Drake said, and his mouth hit mine.

I hadn't been kissed in over nine years, once married my second husband didn't bother kissing me, just took what he wanted. Drake's mouth was gentle but firm, he slanted my head, and his tongue touched my lips, and I opened. Heat slammed between my legs as the kiss went wild.

My hands moved to his head and clenched in his hair as Drake controlled the kiss and racked the heat up. Our tongue's duelled, his commanded and demanded. I gave him what he wanted, and the kiss grew deeper. Drake pulled away, and I looked at him with dazed eyes.

"Fuck me, wanna see more of that look too," Drake muttered. His mouth crushed mine again, and I moaned. Arms slipped around me and cupped my ass, dragging me closer to him, and I felt him pressing between my legs. The first kiss was hot, the second sent me straight to the fires of hell. I grabbed fistfuls of his tee and pulled him closer, pressing against his groin.

Drake broke off a second time took a step back. I gazed at him from another world, I had bypassed dazed and hit zoned out. My breasts felt heavy and achy, and I knew that for the first time in years, I was wet between my legs. Drake was feeling the effects of the kiss too, my eyes dropped to his groin, he was hard, and it was obvious! Drake was big all over! His eyes searched my face.

"Fuck me, liking that look on you baby," he whispered, I whimpered, and his eyes flared again. There was movement outside my windows, and I looked over and saw Stefan and Emily stood there with Diana behind them. All three open-mouthed. Drake followed my gaze and then chuckled.

"Yeah can't continue with your windows," he muttered. Drake stepped closer to me and tilted my head to gaze at him.

"Date night tonight," he said firmly. I opened my mouth to argue, and he put a finger to my lips. "Call

Mrs Ames, tell her dinners being delivered tonight, I'll be at yours at six." Drake removed his finger and gave me a gentle but no less sexy kiss and then strode out. I was still sitting on my desk trying to gather my thoughts when Emily, Stefan and Diana raced into the office.

"Oh my god!" Diana gasped.

"That was hot!" Emily chirped gleefully bouncing on the spot. Clearly, Drake was forgiven as far as Emily was concerned.

"What happened?" Stefan asked, taking in my face and grinning.

"Think I have a date," I told them and then was surrounded by gossiping people.

I paced my bedroom. What did Drake mean by date night? And bringing dinner? For all of us? Just me and him? What on earth did I wear to a date night? Panic was hitting Defcon three when my door opened, and Micah lounged there, hip against the doorjamb.

"Mum," Micah said.

"Son?" I asked. His eyes looked me up and down. And then at the jumble of clothes on my bed and his lips twitched. Good god, my baby boy had the soon to be a mega badass look going on.

"You look great," Micah said calmingly. I glanced down, I had on blue jeans, a vee necked floaty blouse, that was controlled by a wide leather belt around my waist. A white tank underneath it as my blouse was see-through and the blouse came to mid-thigh.

I'd left my hair loose, and it fell to below my waist. I'd brushed it until it shone and then put frizz ease in to keep it smooth. Fawn coloured ankle boots with a broad strap over the foot part were on my feet. And I had on a chunky silver choker, silver bangles on my wrist and silver hoop earrings.

"I don't know, think I need to change," I whispered, and Micah grinned as he looked over his shoulder at the huge picture window above our front door. Opposite the landing where he was standing.

"Bit late Mum, a black SUV just pulled up, guessing it's him." Panic made me hit level two, not good, in my world, I was nearing Defcon one. "Carmine, Tye, think Drake needs a hand," Micah hollered at his brothers, who were somewhere downstairs. I crept over to my bedroom window that looked at the front-drive and peered through it.

Drake was swinging out of the SUV wearing jeans and a black tee that stretched tight across his muscles and his cut. He walked around to the passenger side of the SUV. I watched as Drake leaned in and pulled out a box which he handed to Carmine as Carmine reached him. Tye received another large box, and he handed Harley a six-pack of beer.

Cody was next in line, and my boy got six large boxes of pizza. Christian was hovering shyly, he was the wariest of my boys. Drake winked at him and then Christian was given four of his own boxes. Jared and Aaron received a further four smaller boxes each. Drake was chuckling as he then reached in and pulled out four large-sized grocery bags and kicked the SUV's door shut.

I heard voices downstairs and Eddie screaming 'Drake too's', and I sighed. Micah grabbed my hand and led me downstairs. The entrance hall was deserted, and we found everyone in the family lounge. Drake had put the boxes on a table, and I saw Serenity coming back with plates and cutlery.

"Pizza, Mama Phoe!" Eddie screamed at the top of her lungs. I shot her a stern stare and turned to Drake. He was standing by the table and checked me out head to toe. Drake broke into a small smile while his eyes showed pleasure at my appearance.

"Pizza sweet baby," he said to Eddie as she pushed up against him. Drake rubbed his hand over her head and crouched next to her.

"Eddie stand back," Micah told her, she glared but backed away. I walked over to help Drake feed the masses.

"Got pizza's, didn't know who ate what so got meat feast, pineapple and ham. Pepperoni, plain cheese and barbeque chicken. Bought extra-large, plenty to share. Salad, chicken wings, cheese garlic bread, plain garlic bread, onion rings, cheese sticks and dips.

Fries are in a bag. Figured there'd be something for everyone. Boxes got soft drinks in for kids, and bags got dessert," he said, grinning at me. My mouth dropped open, dear god, the man had brought a feast. Talk about a great first impression on our first date!

"Okay," I said as I didn't know what else to say.

"Where's Albert, Mr and Mrs Ames, got shit for them too," he said, looking around. I heard a stampede of footsteps and saw Cody, Christian, Jared and Aaron running out the room to get them. Eddie was hopping from one foot to the other while Tony was hovering and sniffing the food boxes.

Jodie and I grabbed plates and began serving the little ones who got their plates filled and grabbed a seat in front of the TV. Carmine fed the four boys when they got back and then stood back and let the rest of the kids serve themselves.

"Kids first always," Drake muttered in my ear, and I turned my head and saw the warmth in his eyes. Once the kids were settled, the adults fed themselves. Tony was trying to put a DVD in the player when Drake stopped him. He looked up huge-eyed as Drake reached into a bag and pulled out two DVDs.

"Kids were sayin' they loved the Avengers Movie, so brought that and heard mention Sleeping Beauty was a favoured Disney around here. Figured we could watch it here or watch it in your home cinema." It was that moment I knew I was falling for a guy who thought of my kids before himself. Drake hadn't brought stuff for just him and me, he'd brought choices for everyone. My eyes gave something away as I saw the warmth in Drake's eyes rachet up a notch.

Micah took the Disney and shoved it into the DVD player and hit play. The younger children stopped fussing and began watching while they were eating. Kids scattered over the couches facing the TV and Mr and Mrs Ames and Albert were on another. Albert had a plate balanced on the arm of the sofa and Eddie in his lap with her plate.

Drake lounged next to me one arm slung across the back of the sofa and the other lifting food to his mouth. He was close but not close enough to alarm the kids. Timmy and Scout were for once eating nicely and not throwing food around.

Cody and Jared were ploughing their way through the salad, and everyone appeared happy and content, which made me happy and satisfied. Drake stated halfway through Sleeping Beauty that dessert could be eaten after the film, and as soon as the Avengers started.

A little hand placed itself on Drake's knee, and he looked and saw Tony standing there gazing at him with solemn eyes. Drake moved the arm he had behind me and hooked up my little boy and settled him between us. He wrapped that arm around Tony's shoulders and drew him close. My heart melted even more.

By the time Sleeping Beauty finished, the food had been demolished. I should have warned Drake that teenage boys can eat a pizza on their own. The final onion ring was chewed and swallowed, and Eddie was drowsily looking at dessert bags.

Micah pushed in Avengers and Drake pulled out boxes upon boxes of doughnuts. Drake had brought different kinds, and the kids went wired. Luckily, he'd bought twenty-one of each doughnut, so there were no fights.

"Got brothers, adults or not I know it gets messy when one wants a doughnut the other has. Don't ever fight Gunner for a vanilla one," he whispered in my ear. And I giggled at the image of badass bikers fighting over a custard doughnut. A few swapsies later, everyone had the doughnuts they wanted.

"Next time remind me teens eat a shitload," Drake said as he watched Micah, Carmine, Tye on their fourth doughnut. "Thought you might have leftovers for breakfast, guessed wrong." I laughed amused. Yeah, teens ate a load! Mrs Ames despaired at the food bills.

Forty minutes into the film, Eddie and Tony crashed, and the babies followed suit. Drake and I carried Timmy and Scout up. Micah hit pause and carried up Eddie, and Carmine got Tony, Jodie and Serenity had Jake and Garrett. Timmy and Scout shared a bedroom until they got older, and we placed them in their cots after I checked their diapers.

"I usually bathe the kids, but it's a special night," I told Drake as I gazed at my sleeping babies. Drake came to stand behind me and wrapped an arm around my waist and rested his chin on my shoulder.

"Don't think one night will hurt," he gently said. Jodie poked her head in and said Jake and Garret were down and she had their baby-monitor. Micah and Carmine did the same. I gave them nods, and they left Drake and me alone.

"Thank you," I whispered.

"For?" Drake smirked, knowing why I was thanking him. He just wanted me to say it out loud the infuriating man!

"For being you. Thinking of my kids first and me and you second. Thank you for including Albert and Mr and Mrs Ames."

"They're your family too, babe," Drake whispered back. Scout snorted in his sleep and wriggled around and then settled. Drake turned me into him and traced a finger down my face.

"Thanks, angel for a great night. Loved this. Fuckin' great night," he whispered. My eyes dropped to his mouth, and he tipped his head, and his lips took mine. It started gentle and then grew wild like it did in the office. Christ, Drake knew how to kiss. He wrapped himself around me, and I lost myself in him.

A wheeze from Timmy made me break the kiss, and I looked over at my baby. Timmy settled and rolled over and shoved his diapered tushie in the air. Drake grinned as I came back to his face.

"Yeah babe, fuckin' love this," he whispered and then taking my hand led me out of the babies' room. We joined the older kids, and no one blinked as Drake draped an arm around me. Only one who gave him a stare was Micah. Drake held his gaze for a few seconds, and something passed between them, and they went back to watching the film.

At the end of the film, Mr and Mrs Ames excused themselves and strolled to their cottage. Albert chivvied up the younger teenagers (including Jared and Aaron) and made them go to bed. The older teenagers needed no chivvying and took themselves off.

That left Drake and me alone. The five eldest kids had cleaned up, and we were left in the dimly lit room curled on a couch together. Drake was content to sit in silence, playing with my hair, and I was snuggled into his side with my hands on his chest. It was nice and relaxed, with no pressure on either of us.

Drake's hand dipped lower and then swept up and cupped the back of my neck, and his mouth was on mine. He bent me backwards, swinging my legs up and leaned his weight onto me. My hands slid to the back of his tee and pulled it up. Drake nibbled, licked and kissed me, and I cupped his ass, loving the feel of him pressing against me.

He lifted and shifted us, resettling between my legs and my hands stroked his back and then slid back to his ass. With his weight pressed into me, there was no doubt in my mind how much he was aroused. I was wet between my legs and lightly panting when he lifted his head and his mouth locked onto my nipple through my blouse.

I bit my lip and moaned softly, and he tugged gently, and I pushed upwards with my hips. He raised his head and watched my face as he thumb swiped my nipple. My eyes closed, I pressed against Drake again. His mouth came back on mine, and his hand kept caressing my breast.

He shifted his weight and balanced on his forearm, and his other hand cupped my other breast. Drake was merciless, teasing, arousing me until I was a hot wet mess. Still kissing me, his hand undid my belt and slipped up my blouse to caress my stomach. Louder, I moaned into his mouth, and his hand slipped up my blouse, and he touched a breast.

I tensed, and he lifted his head and looked into my eyes, looking for permission. I blinked, and he smiled, his head dipping to my breast. Pulling my bra to one side, his mouth kissed the soft skin around my nipple before taking it into his mouth. Drake made a noise of pure male satisfaction. My legs clamped around his waist, and I pushed upwards, harder, desperate to feel him.

"Christ, baby," he whispered. "You're gonna make me come in my pants and I ain't done that since I was a teen." I pulled his head back to my breast and arched upwards. My hands pulled his tee upwards, and I communicated I wanted skin against skin, and he gave me what I wanted.

I pushed him back and straddled him and began kissing my way down his chest. Drake held my hips, grinding slowly into me through our jeans as I explored his chest with my mouth. His own breathing was unsteady, and I found he liked his nipples being kissed and licked. I kissed my way down his throat and then trailed back up again, using my tongue, and he gave me a hard thrust.

"Baby, we got to stop. I'm seconds away from takin' you, and we got kids upstairs," Drake muttered. His fingers twisted into my hair, and he pulled my head back, exposing my throat. He growled, and his mouth kissed me there. I shivered under his touch, and he growled again and then with great effort, he put me away from him.

I stared at him dazed, couldn't remember a time I had been so aroused. Not for a long bloody time. Not even for Justin, had I ignited like this and we'd had a fantastic sex life. Drake's face was intense and focussed, and that made me wetter if possible.

"Shit, I just want to sink deep inside you," Drake grated.

"I think I need that," I whispered. He gave a half-grin and leaning forward, kissed my forehead.

"Yeah, need it too, but I'm going to do right by you, babe. Gonna court you and then take you and when I do, you'll know you're mine and no one else's. Going to burn me into you, babe," he told me cupping my face. Who knew bikers could be romantic?

"You know when you do, I, um, I'm adventurous," I whispered my face beginning to burn.

"Oh yeah?" he asked curiously.

"I like being tied up, blindfolded and having headphones. It's called sensory deprivation," I whispered as my face burned hotter. Drake closed his eyes, and I bit my lip. "Drake?" I whispered. Was he turned off? Oh god, what if I'd disgusted him?

"Shhh babe, I'm enjoying the image in my head," he told me, and I relaxed against him. Drake held me tight and then let me go.

"I better go, you got work tomorrow," he said. I nodded and straightened my clothing. Drake dragged me to my feet somewhat unsteadily as he rose above me. Drake stepped into my space and wrapped one arm around my waist and raised his other and ran his fingers across my cheek.

"We'll do this again, Phoe," he muttered, and then he walked out with me following behind. He climbed in the SUV and drove away. I waited until his lights disappeared and then shut the door and set the alarm. I turned and to my surprise saw Micah sitting at the piano in the entrance hall.

"Son?"

"Be careful, Mum, he's not Chance," Micah replied. I stiffened.

"I know, Micah."

"No one deserves happiness more than you, I'd hoped for a long time it would be you and Chance. Maybe it's not meant to be, but Mum be careful of him. There's a darkness in him," Micah warned and then got to his feet and went to bed.

Chapter Seven.

I was sitting in my office Friday, going through paperwork when my phone pinged with a message from Drake saying he was bringing lunch. Two weeks had passed since our first date, and Drake had kept his word. He was wooing me, we'd been out for several dinners, and he'd come to the Hall often, bringing food for everyone.

Drake brought me lunch every day since our first date. We'd had the hog roast, and it had been fun watching them in their own environment. We hadn't yet managed to get into my attic, which was frustrating! Things kept cropping up and distracting us.

Drake sent me a wink emoji, and I smiled. Sent him an okay and received one back saying he'd be here in half an hour. We were getting closer to each other, and I was enjoying learning about him. I liked having lunch with Drake a whole lot. Lunch included heavy petting behind my blinds. I'd got used to smug smirks from the Directors when the blinds closed, and Stefan had begun singing immature songs. 'Drake and Phoe sitting in a tree!' Childish, I know.

Although we'd reached second and third base several times, Drake never let it go any further. Sexually I was extremely frustrated! Much more and

I'd be ripping his clothes off and pinning him to the bed. I'd just finished a meeting, wrapping up what had happened in California. It was an error and not theft thankfully. Saffron had hired a cousin who'd mixed the accounts and receipts up. To say I wasn't amused was an understatement, and both women had reprimands on file now.

Sally had disciplined Saffron and clarified that this should have been brought to me straight away, and we could have resolved it sooner. The cousin had been placing the funds in the PT account and not fundraising. Kyle had a simple task of transferring them. At the end of the day, Saffron's performance was under par, not acceptable from one of my long-term managers.

My office door was open when I heard phones start ringing in a chorus and looked up as Directors began scrabbling. Curiously, I watched Kyle flying out of his office and jogging down the stairs. As he didn't call me, I turned my attention back to the file in front of me. A loud bang on my window, ten minutes later, made me leap out of my chair.

With a frown, I walked out of my office, and Stefan scurried past me. He headed for the stairs, and I called out his name, and Stefan turned and shouted at me to hurry to the first floor. I chased after him and jumped as Stuart raced to the stairs. Stuart grabbed my hand and tugged me to move quicker, picking up the urgency I hurried behind him. I noticed that there wasn't a single director or assistant on our floor and wondered what the hell was happening.

The first floor was manic, people shouting and phones ringing off the hook. Stuart let go of my hand

and hurried to an empty desk with a phone ringing insistently. Not even when we were fundraising, did the lines get this manic. Confused, I looked for someone to explain it to me.

"What on earth is happening?" I asked, finally catching Kyle, who ended a call.

"Phoe, you're not going to believe this!" Kyle exclaimed in excitement, practically bouncing in his seat.

"What!" Kyle's excitement was catching, but it would be nice to know why.

"Texas, it started in Texas! Those beautiful cowboys! A billionaire donated twenty-five million to build a PT in the state." I jolted upright. Texas was one state we weren't in, and we certainly needed to open in.

"You're joking?" I whispered, disbelief colouring my voice.

"No. Straight up, twenty-five mill. Didn't need to fundraise, the guy just up and donated this morning. The guy's nephew was Navy and came back messed up, PT found his nephew a few months ago. The nephew was situated at Norfolk PT, got straight, and his uncle wanted to say thanks.

Not to be outdone the guy's business rival, who the guy phoned to boast too, donated another twenty-five million for an RT. The nephew's father, also not to be outdone, donated another twenty-five million for an ET, this happened in an hour!"

"Oh my god," I said, starting to bounce on my heels, excited.

"A donation war!" Kyle trilled. I glanced around and saw my directors sat on phones speaking to people.

"Donation war?" I asked, somewhat dumbly, I didn't fully believe what I was hearing. Usually, it took a few months when we planned to open in a state for momentum to kick in.

"The Texans bragged on social media and sent out a few challenges. Further donations are flooding in from Texas. People are goading one another on social media, and we're at two hundred million. They've been at it for three hours now. Texas has gone insane, it's a frenzy, everyone trying to outdo one another. Those big badass Texan oil barons!

The phones are ringing off the hook, a SM rang upstairs for help. Business rivals are daring each other to donate and bragging what they have donated. Wealthy families are trying to out donate each other. It's not just gone freaking mental in Texas, the frenzy has spilt over to other states."

"No way?" I said as I sank into a chair in stunned shock. Two admin staff rushed by waving paperwork at Stuart.

"Arkansas has started their own bidding war, the last check it was at a fifty million." I put my hand to my head, staggered. "Millionaires and billionaires are donating left, right and centre. Ego is playing a huge part of it, but the Texan Three as the media are calling them are challenging people across the country."

"Emily run to reception, make sure she's not being drowned," Diana ordered putting down her phone. Emily dashed past me, and Diana looked at me. "Oregon's hit forty million."

"No!" I breathed.

"Turn on the TV," someone shouted. The TV flashed on, and a reporter was standing outside a well-known NFL ground. The chairman's name was flashing across the screen, and we caught the end of his speech.

"To sum up what I was saying, the team has always taken part in the annual charity match. Our aim has been to raise money for these worthwhile causes, ever since the Trusts opened. But today we as a team are donating ten million dollars to the Phoenix, Rebirth and Eternal Trusts. The teams' challenge is for other NFL teams to donate at least two million each to these worthy charities. Our own players are donating sums from one hundred thousand dollars of their personal money too." The chairman's name was called, and he looked over his shoulder, "excuse me." The chairman walked away and came back to the camera, smiling.

"Our quarterback wants it known, he's just donated his fee for his latest set of advertising. Four-point five million dollars. If our quarterback can donate a fee, who else can? Let's raise some money and show those oil barons in Texas, it's not just them who can kick butt!" The chairman finished on a holler and cheers sounded behind him from where his team gathered, and my eyes shot across as people sat back stunned.

"The phones will go nuts," Abigail exclaimed.

"Redirect every phone to log into the donation line, accounting, admin, everywhere. Susan get on the phones to anyone at home, get them here. Call in my family, get anyone in who can answer a phone, we're going to need a load of help. Emily print up hundreds of donations sheets, the pitch is on there, and they can follow the sheets. It's easy enough with the sheets," I ordered spinning in a circle.

My eyes caught Drake standing by the door. He dumped a bag on a nearby desk, flipped his phone and left. I felt hurt and then puzzled for a minute as I pondered his actions. Drake hadn't even spoken to me, not even smiled or acknowledged me. Was Drake that petty that this interfered with his lunch plans, he was angry? I didn't understand, I thought I understood Drake. Then a chorus of shouts and cheers rose from a corner and distracted me.

"Vermont just hit thirty million to Trusts in their state!" Ignoring what I perceived as Drake's hurtful actions, I turned back to organising HQ.

"We need trackers. Get wipe boards up, flip boards, something we can write on." Admin staff not on phones bustled past, heading to the supply closets to get what I'd asked. The door opened, and Bernard walked in, following him were a few of our SMs.

"Thought you might need reinforcements. The Trusts have taken over the media," Bernard said with a chuckle before I could speak.

"I love you," I told him, "get them to the second floor. We need to open it." Diana hustled as I grinned at Bernard. Two admin staff came racing back in with flip charts. They began writing on them with state names and pinning them to walls.

"Yo!" Kyle bellowed, following up with a loud whistle. "Donation sheets are being given out. Use them, if you don't have any yet, write details on a piece of paper and someone will come around and collect them up. Make sure you write the state, name, address, contact number, bank/card details and amount of donation."

I grabbed a phone that was ringing and was halfway through the call when I blinked. Rage, every single brother, their office girl, their mechanics and old ladies (the two of them) walked into the room. Diana spoke briefly to Drake and sent them upstairs, Drake gave me a wink and left me to my call. I was lost for words as I realised what Drake had done.

He'd seen me calling for help and getting extra people in. Drake had marched across to Rage and shut their business, just to give me additional people we desperately needed. My throat clenched with tears, and I swallowed hard. To think I'd worried Drake may not understand or maybe get jealous over the Trusts, he'd just proved me very wrong.

How could I possibly have doubted Drake? Despite our rough start, he'd taken time to prove he was serious about the kids and me. Drake was inserting himself into every aspect of my life and proving himself true time and time again. I needed to stop doubting him and stop doubting my own self-worth.

As soon as my call ended, I passed the phone an SM, who'd just arrived. Running upstairs to the second floor where three SMs were explaining what to do, I slammed into a chair next to Drake. Drake gave me a shit-eating grin, and I huffed at him. Still grinning, Drake grabbed the back of my neck and dragged me across for a kiss and then carried on listening.

"Think I'd let you down, Phoe?" Drake growled as the SMs finished speaking.

"I was worried when you walked out."

"Will always have your back woman, trust me on that," Drake growled and kissed me.

Asses hit chairs, and I phoned downstairs and spoke to Emily, who sounded frazzled. The second-floor phones were re-routed to our donation line, and the phones began ringing instantly. Admin staffed bustled around and started pinning up flip charts. An hour later, my heart leapt a second time as I saw Hellfire arrive and hit a desk. Chance sent me a look and Bear grinned.

I wondered if Drake had called them or if they'd seen the media coverage. Drake reached over to me, holding Chance's eyes and tucked me under his shoulder. A claiming sign, Chance narrowed his eyes and then took a call.

Stuart locked our work cell phones into the network. This freed up the desk phones for people coming in, and the Directors and SMs could perch on someone's desk. Drake snagged me around the waist, and I was sat next to him, hip to hip on a desk. I felt eyes from Hellfire and Rage watching, Rage in approval, Hellfire warning.

Husbands, wives and older teenagers came in, the families of those working. Every phone on every floor had a person answering it. Enough volunteers arrived that there was two per call. As a call ended, the volunteer not answering the phone grabbed the paperwork and tracked the correct chart. They wrote the figure on it, and we finally had a rudimentary tracking system going.

Donations kept coming. The three Texans who had started this were being interviewed snug as bugs on several news channels. The MLB, NHL and NBA not to be outdone by the NFL had kicked in with their own challenges. There was a big interview in Nashville, where famous music artists were donating money and challenging other performers to do the same.

Even states which had Trusts' had people who were calling in adding extra to their states pot. I took several calls on the emergency phone telling me that Trusts properties in established states were getting lots of calls. PMs were calling in extra staff of their own. The whole country literally seemed to be on a donation bend.

Antony and Andrew gave interviews, other interviews played on the news with Phoenix Trust Heroes. My heart was in my throat and tears in my eyes as I saw Rebirth Trust Survivors and Eternal Trust Fighters on the news. Everyone giving their own interviews, telling their stories and praising our virtue for everything they were worth.

Drake watched with me as poignant stories were played out for millions of people to watch. Several times I wiped tears from my eyes, and I thought Drake did the same at one point. Men, women and children bared their souls on TV for people to understand what the Trusts did. After a particularly sad story, Drake hauled me into his lap and buried his face in my hair. My man had a big heart.

Ordinary people got involved, donations for five dollars, ten dollars, one hundred dollars, the everyday Joe deciding that they weren't being left out. A few hours later, I stretched my shoulders and rolled my head around and caught Chance's eye.

His eyes looked deep into me, and I saw him scribble on a piece of paper and pass to Bear. Bear had just ended his call, and his head snapped my way, and he strolled in my direction. Drake on a call, watched the big man lumber our way.

"Phoe?" Bear asked, crouching by my feet.

"I'm okay, just stiff," I replied. Bear nodded, left the floor, and a few minutes later reappeared with a coffee and sub.

"Local delis have been sending food," Bear said, and I snatched the sub from his hand and bit into it. A moan of pleasure escaped me, I was starved. Drake lifted an eyebrow and then dropped his phone and called for a spare volunteer.

He began massaging my shoulders while Bear walked back to his desk. Drake's concern was plain to see, his dark gaze kept people away for ten minutes. Bliss, sheer bliss. Diana came over, suit jacket off, sleeves rolled up and blouse unbuttoned to a low neckline. No shoes on her feet and her usually impeccable hair was scraped up in a ponytail. Drake gazed at her for a few seconds before giving her permission to talk. I snickered internally, Drake was showing his overprotective side.

"Calls are slowing somewhat, but every time someone ends one, there's another call on the line. Good news is that no one is queueing for over fifteen minutes. Call waiting is down to around ten minutes. The internet site was up fast, so donations are coming in using that too."

"Any idea of how much raised?" I asked yawning.

"No, but we are well over nine hundred million raised so far. Everyone's involved. The entire country! The press is reporting it as a donation frenzy. Monied folk on TV sending personal challenges to rivals. Sports teams buying in and posting their own challenges. Broadway, Hollywood, Nashville.

Big businesses are donating and sending their own challenges to business rivals. More oil barons and media owners are donating big bucks. Four actual properties have been donated, and five people have granted acres of land for an ET to be built."

"Christ," I said in shock, not even on our best day, had we ever raised figures near to this sum. Drake squeezed my shoulders, and I reached up and grabbed his hand.

"Someone has told the media about the auctions, and we have holidays, cars, yachts being donated. Tiffany's have promised a ten-thousand-dollar voucher, and other jewellers and retail stores are offering vouchers.

Hotel chains are offering all-inclusive weekends away, to a two-week all-inclusive paid for vacation. Manolo Blahniks have offered a five-thousand-dollar voucher, I think you're getting the drift." I nodded. A noise made me glance up, and North the Director of Public Relations came into view.

"The CEO of Ford is crowing on live TV that his company was the first to donate a top of the range car. Chevrolet is on TV too, giving an interview and they've donated. The media are going crackers with the stories, making a real big performance of this.

Sally is giving Skype interviews constantly to the press, and she's on a flight coming here. She has a team with her answering questions, but Sally's the face of the Trusts. Press are camped outside and the RCPD (police), have put up a cordon to keep them back." North looked across at Drake and Chance and showed awkwardness.

"Sorry, but the press saw Hellfire MC pull in, and someone has mentioned both MCs are here. Both MCs have hit the news as well for operating the phones, Sally is taking questions on the MCs being here. Don't know if you wanted the MC's in the media, is free publicity good for you guys?

Sally's driving what good MC's you are to the media, shutting your own businesses to man the phones to raise money for the Trusts. Sally's even flirting that callers may just get a hot biker at the end of the line. Your own builds are featuring in the press." I bit my lip and looked at the two MC Presidents. Chance nodded, and Drake shrugged.

"Good press for the MC's will help drive our builds," Apache said, ending his phone call and clicking on another one.

"Staff are flying in from Fundraising teams and from Trusts, and we are putting them together as a night team," North said.

"Get their ticket details. I'll pay for them," I said, rubbing the back of my neck.

"No need, the airlines are giving them free tickets, great publicity for them," North said with a shark's grin. Damn, North was good, I knew he'd swung that.

"Wonderful," I breathed, and North gave me a grin.

"There are calls for you to give an interview." Drake felt me stiffen and clasped my hand. The one thing I loathed was being in the public's eye, I far preferred being behind the scenes. "Sally is bypassing them and giving her own, so, don't worry. We've released information on the sum of money raised so far in each state, which has driven a few states into a bigger frenzy.

Rival states won't allow the other to outbid them, so it's frantic and hot, we update every hour, my team is on that. Computerised tracking is working now. I sent half of our staff who came in as extras home to sleep, and they'll come back tonight to take the night shift."

"Okay," I said as my mind whirled with a thousand things to do.

"Trust us, you trained us well, we have this," Diana said, putting her hand on my shoulder.

"I know, I just need to be into everything," I sniped ruefully. Drake laughed and cupped the back of my neck. Drake was giving me as much support as he could, it was plain he was struggling to control his bossy side. And as much as he wanted to order me to rest, he didn't.

"We know," North said and laughed with Diana.

"Have the kids eaten?" Drake asked.

"Pizzas were delivered, and every kid in the building has eaten. Several local restaurants and take out's have called on asking how many people are here and are promising to provide hot meals when we call. The younger children are upstairs in the day centre, and the older ones are taking calls.

They're cool. Day-care reports the children have spilt out into the lounge. But they've called in extra staff and have organised night staff. Honest Phoe everything is fine," Diana said. I nodded and picked up my cell as it rang again. Drake dragged my chair over to his and slung his arm around my shoulder. Drake winked at me and sitting together, we took calls for tens, hundreds, thousands, millions of dollars of donations.

At ten o'clock, the night staff kicked in and the day staff five hours after they should have finished began making their way home. Diana had got everyone's names who had turned up to help. The husbands and wives of my staff, sons and daughters even friends they'd made. I watched as night staff approached those who operated phones and then when they ended a phone call, they took over the phone, so the day people could leave.

Eleven o'clock had gone when I got up to leave. Hellfire was staying at my home, and Mr and Mrs Ames and Albert had taken my kids back several hours ago. Rage was passing their phones over, and most of Hellfire had left. Rage disappeared to their clubhouse, and I was left with Chance, Bear, Drake, Apache and Ace. Drake wrapped his arms around my waist, looking stunned but happy.

"Never could imagine what your job entailed until now. Being part of the excitement...not got the words. Those people you've helped, no words. So fuckin' proud of you angel, can't say how proud I am of ya," Drake muttered into my hair.

"Never seen the like. Now I understand the value of what the Trusts achieve," Chance finally said, looking at me with something akin to awe in his face.

"Was cool being part of today," Apache chipped in a grin.

"Callers were funny on the phone, they asked a few times if I was a biker," Bear said grinning. "When I said yeah, the donation doubled," he laughed, and we (apart from Ace) joined him.

"Yeah, I had a few ask that too," Ace grunted.

"Hot, sexy biker men? Maybe I should do a bachelor auction with you lot," I giggled. "Or publish a calendar, we could make a fortune on that, half-naked bikers leaning or sitting on their bikes." Alpha males growled back a denial, and we began making our way down the stairs together.

Chance saw how tired I was and snatched the keys out of my hands to drive me home. Drake gave me a look, a kiss on my forehead, and I watched his fine ass stroll across Rage's forecourt.

"Can't believe today. Chance we've raised one point three billion dollars, it's crazy. Sheer crazy, the generosity of people is unbelievable. Such large sums being donated, I've never seen the like of."

"Everyone knows who we owe Phoe, those guys are heroes, the women and children victims. No one wants to see them shit on. As Sally explained over a hundred times, even five bucks can make a change. Yeah, it's overwhelming how many of the rich donated, movie stars, music stars. Not donating the usual few thousand or whatever but donating mega big bucks. Plus how many will claim tax breaks on their donations?" Chance, cynical as ever!

"Did you hear that the actor Lan Whist donated his entire fee for his latest film? Sixty million dollars. I mean, Christ!" I shook my head and yawned. "He said he wasn't going to be outdone by a quarterback," I snickered.

"Bed darlin'?" Chance murmured, putting his arm around my shoulders. By the time we got home, I was sound asleep.

The next day, I parked in the underground car park and used the internal stairs to avoid the press. Dressed casually as it was the weekend, I opened the door and stopped in amazement. It was Saturday, most of my guys should be off, but I faced nearly all of my weekday staff sitting by phones taking more calls. Tears came to my eyes, and I wandered upstairs and saw more volunteers on calls and more of my team.

I was greeted with chin lifts, smiles and cheers. I let my tears fall and then turned on my heel and walked to my floor. Makeshift desks had been set up, and Rage and Hellfire had taken over the conference table. Directors and lots of other people were jammed into our offices all on phones.

My office was occupied by Drake and Chance. I dropped my bag before logging my cell into the donation line and began taking calls again. Around mid-morning, I stopped when Stefan came to get me. Drake and I went to the second floor and watched a TV interview with Antony and Sally outside HQ. The media presence was even more substantial today.

"I'm calling this Thank a Hero weekend," Antony said. "These three charities are so important to our country, they should be embedded into our national holidays. That's for the President to decide." Sally chuckled beside him.

"I'm asking everyone to dig deep and donate something, five bucks makes a difference. What these charities do is look after our fallen heroes. Look after our vulnerable people who need aid, help children so vilely abused we can't stand to imagine it.

Every single day, they dedicate themselves to bettering someone's life. They walk the street and speak to countless people in attempts to find our fallen heroes. The Trusts visit every soup kitchen, every shelter, they look in alleys and parking lots and under train bridges. They don't stop, and I believe they'll never stop. Every single one of us has been touched by a hero, a cop, a soldier, sailor, EMT.

When circumstances go wrong, these amazing angels, right here, step in and make everything better. I've been informed today that you can visit any Trust property near you to hand a donation over, but please don't intrude on the residents' privacy. Banks are open and taking donations across the country and will stay open till eight o'clock tonight. Many retail chains have collection buckets and are showing signs that they will take donations for the three Trusts." Antony stopped talking and looked at Sally.

"This was one woman's dream, a dream to help those less fortunate. Phoenix started these three charities nearly four years ago. Thanks to our dedicated staff and the generosity of donators, we have a PT and RT Property in twenty states. We have five ET Properties. Phoenix's dream is to open one of each in every state, you can't understand how much they are needed.

To do this, we need you, need your money, your time. The Trusts need professional help, doctors, counsellors, dentists, for example. If you can donate time, please contact us. Most of our Trusts are staffed by retirees who give one set day a week.

So many thank you's, starting with our Texan friends for beginning this. The sports team who started an even bigger ball rolling. Hollywood, Nashville and Broadway, who started their own challenges to raise money. Everyone who is donating money, time and gifts to be auctioned or raffled off again thank you, it means so much you can't understand how much.

Phoenix is operating the phones at headquarters. With her are dedicated staff and their family and friends. A huge thank you to them for giving up their weekend. To Rage and Hellfire MC's, a massive thanks for closing their businesses yesterday and today. For donating their time in operating the phones.

Lastly, a massive thank you to the local cafes, deli's, restaurants and take-outs who have fed and watered our people since yesterday. It means so much you thought of our staff and volunteers and sent help in the way of food and drink."

"Time for me to man a phone," Antony said with a wink at the camera, and I saw him turn towards the building and enter. The screen flashed to the reporters who were standing by the cordon. A reporter began talking about the Trusts, and I turned away from the TV and hugged Sally as she walked towards me.

"I've been watching the donations online, we're rocking it Phoe!" Sally chirped.

"The country is united as one," Antony said, "the Trusts are on every news channel. A few local channels are running the hourly updates for their state and perhaps a rival one. The President's happy and intending to make a comment on it later this evening."

"The President?" Slick asked near to me.

"President's not daft, he's up for a second term. The country is full of good spirits, this is great for him to support." Sally smiled eyeing Slick up. Slick returned her interest.

"President allowed to get behind charities?" Lex asked.

"He's meant to stay impartial, but he'd be a fool to ignore what this can bring to his second term. He'll use it," Antony replied, "it'll be great publicity for him, he'll get points supporting the Trusts."

"Can anyone honestly believe this? I keep waiting to wake up. We have charity days, but I've never seen a country go as insane as this. This doesn't seem real, it's as if I'm in a dream or a story. An alternative reality maybe," I said breathlessly.

"As Antony said, everyone knows or has been touched by a cop or EMT or someone that the Trusts help. Lots of negative feeling sometimes in our country, but what's going on is making people feel good. People are high on that," Drake said, hugging me. He dropped a kiss on my head.

"Andrew's on his way with his staff," Stefan shouted across the room at us. And I nodded. Staff looked wired, but they looked tired too.

"Uh, oh," Antony said, laughing and sat as a phone began to ring. I noticed there were far more strangers in HQ than yesterday. Worried about security, I saw the police and my team at the door and relaxed. The press was still outside interviewing, and most of Sally's time was spent giving them.

North was deftly organising media for individual states. North and his team were giving interviews praising those who had donated items in those states.

Between North and Sally, they made sure each news outlet got at least ten minutes with one of them. Which did lots of good for our public relations.

Yet again, my team managed to keep track of the donations. So as Sally and North were interviewed by local and out-of-state media, they had up to date figures. Yesterday had been manic, after a slower start this morning it picked up again around midday. The President had given a statement mid-afternoon instead of that evening, and that went in our favour.

There were Facebook challenges and Twitter comments, social media was overwhelmed at the posts! The phones were again queueing, and the donation site crashed twice overwhelmed by the number of people clicking on it. Kyle had pulled his hair out for a full half an hour until it came back up the first time and fell into a raging tantrum the second time. Stuart took him out of the building for a drive while technicians worked on getting the site back up.

Luckily for us, the website didn't crash on Sunday, and everyone was there again. The kids, HQ staff, people who had flown in, Rage and Hellfire. Kyle was much calmer on Sunday than Saturday! Come Monday, everyone was tired, including me. While it had finally slowed into a more manageable pace of work, it was still busy but a much gentler pace. Rage and Hellfire both spent the entire weekend on phones.

As I entered the offices Monday, I saw Rage had opened their bay shutters, and there were lots of people on the forecourt. The two days they'd shut had doubtless cost them time and money, but Drake hadn't mentioned it once. Nor had Chance or Hellfire who'd left last night. Then again, judging by the number of people on their forecourt maybe it hadn't cost them money. The two MCs had got loads of free publicity.

Diana had gathered long lists and left them on my desk. Detailed information of those who had come in on their own time and supported us. I plan to organise thank you gifts for every single person. She'd guessed this and pre-empted me by getting the lists. Diana was finding me a company that could deliver thank-you hampers to the people that helped.

I leaned back in my chair and looked at the pile of mail sitting at my desk. With a sigh, I began to open them one at a time and started creating piles. Many were cheques and donations again, a couple were offers for properties. Others were standard mail and a final letter that made me frown. It was a badly typed envelope, and it had been hand-delivered.

Warily I opened it, slipped out a piece of paper and then read it with stunned eyes. With a cry, I dropped it with a gasp. I pushed back in my chair away from it and ran my fingers through my hair. Stefan entered and stopped as he saw the pallor of my face.

"Jesus Phoe what is it?" Stefan asked, rushing across my room to crouch near me. Shakily, I pointed at the letter, and he went to pick it up.

"Don't touch it!" I shrieked, and his hands froze. Worried Stefan bent over and read it, and his face turned angry.

"What the ever-living fuck?" Stefan hissed. He turned back to me and grabbed my hands, which were shaking.

"It was hand-delivered, he was in my office!" I whispered, staring at the vile letter in front of me.

"I get Abigail to pull footage," Stefan replied. "Don't touch it, we'll need to call security and get the police involved." I nodded eyeing the letter hatefully.

Stefan shouted for Emily and crouched back beside me. He held me in a tight hug he looked up as Emily rushed into my office. In curt tones, Stefan told her to call Abigail, Liz and the police. Emily paled but hurried out, and minutes later Abigail joined us.

Abigail picked up the letter in a pair of tweezers and read it and then put it back. Liz came in a few minutes later, having been in the building and she repeated Abigail's actions and then got on the phone.

I vaguely heard her snapping orders around the children and their safety. To find my children and lock them safely in the Hall. I stared at the letter again and saw the blood-red letters jumping off the page at me.

'Everyone thinks that you're so great, but you and I know the truth. We know what you are, the whore, the bitch and backstabbing cunt that you are. Last night's sleep was the last peaceful sleep you'll ever have, you thought you'd done with me. I'm coming for you, not even death can keep us apart. You thought I made you bleed before, prepare to lose every last drop.
But your kids first, I'll break them, cut them, bleed them, then slit their fucking throats while I fuck them into oblivion. You can't protect yourself, you can't protect them. Before you die, you will know all the pain you gave me you stupid fucking bitch. I'm coming for you, I swore until death do us part, I meant it.'

Gasping out loud and bent over clutching my stomach, I re-read it. I knew, I freaking knew who it was, but I didn't understand how. How could it be him? Jesus please it can't be him.

"Call Chance," I whispered. Stefan gave a sharp order to Emily, and I heard her leave the room. Fifteen minutes later, two police officers in uniform came through the door. They looked at the note, and one stepped away and radioed someone.

"We've called for a detective," the other said speaking to me. "Can someone get her a drink, please?" he asked those in the room.

Liz was on her phone checking the status of the kids, Micah, Carmine and Tye were not at the Hall but being escorted there now. Liz informed me my smaller kids were accounted for and downstairs in the basement, which doubled as a panic room. The door was bombproof and once dead-bolted, and a criminal needed a miracle to get through it.

For the moment, the door was open and heavily guarded by ninety percent of the security team. Liz kept me up to date as one by one, my kids had been taken there and secured. I relaxed when she told me the kids were accounted for and in the basement, which was secure. Liz was constantly on the phone to Matthias and was keeping me updated. Best place for my kids was a bomb-proof panic room.

The door opened, and an officer moved to block Drake, who was striding in looking worried. He squared up against the officer, and I felt the vibes coming off him. Drake was pissed at being kept from me, and he was about to act on it. I rose shakily to my feet, and then I was in his arms. They closed around me, and I swallowed a sob back. I felt the officer's eyes on us, but I didn't look up, I burrowed into a muscular chest and clung to him for dear life.

"What the fuck is going on?" Drake asked Stefan, tucking me under his chin, his hand at the back of my head.

"Death threat," Stefan replied shortly. Drake tensed and, if possible, his arms got tighter around me. He glanced over at an officer who wore gloves on and was putting the letter into a bag.

"What the fuck?" Drake whispered.

"Phoe and the kids," Abigail replied. She covered the phone and then carried on her conversation in low tones. Drake saw the bag in the policeman's hands and snatched it from him and began reading it over my shoulder.

Emily came back in carrying a tray of coffee mugs. She kicked the door shut on people beginning to gather outside, but I knew my inner core wouldn't be kept out for long. Vibes hit the room from Drake, dark, angry and dangerous. Drake gave the letter back to the officer and walked me over to my sofa and sat, pulling me into his lap. He wrapped his arms back around me and tucked me back into his throat and spoke over my head.

"Who has the kids?" In that moment, I fell irrevocably in love with him. Drake thought of my kids, put them first.

"My team," Liz replied. She was in the corner speaking to Matthias from the corner where she was back to the wall, watching the main floors coming and goings.

"They safe?" Drake kept on snarling.

"In lockdown."

"Are they fuckin' safe?" Drake shouted, losing control. His large hand cupped the back of my head, his heart thumping through his chest.

"The basement doubles as a panic room, the children are locked down. Only Phoe, Matthias and I have the codes, not even the Ames, Albert or Micah have the codes. They are *locked* down." Drake shuffled, and he lifted his hip. He pulled his phone from his pocket and finger, dialled someone.

"Get those who can to Phoe's home and get a patrol on the perimeter. Don't enter the house without identifying yourself," he snapped into the phone and ended the call.

"They're safe," Liz reassured us both.

"Feel better if Rage is on-site just in case," Drake told her.

"I'll let my people know not to shoot Rage," Liz replied sternly. Drake just raised an eyebrow at her.

"Chance is on the road," Emily said, sitting beside us. She held my hand for a few minutes and squeezed it. Then leaning forward, she gave my cheek a kiss and left the room to make sure we weren't disturbed. I stared as a man walked into my office, and my eyes widened. Despite this horrific drama, I couldn't help myself.

The man was gorgeous, tall, over six-foot, black wavy hair that was just a tad too long. Beautiful Mexican olive tanned skin, brown soft, gentle eyes. He was lean hipped and long-legged and wide-shouldered, not as broad as Drake or Chance. But he'd be able to hold his own. He wore blue jeans, a plain navy buttoned shirt and a sports jacket, on his feet were worn and comfortable cowboy boots.

"Detective Antonio Ramirez, Rapid City PD," the man said, and a shiver ran through me. His voice was like silk, and I felt Drake's arms twitch, and I looked up to see his eyes laughing at me.

"Phoenix," I replied. Detective Ramirez looked around the room, and the others introduced themselves and their positions. There was a commotion outside the door, and a police officer who had been guarding it flew backwards and Chance, Bear and Chatter stormed into the office. Chance didn't hesitate but strode across the room and ripped me from Drake's arms and swept me up.

"The kids?" Chance bit out. Anger plain in his voice, his whole body gave off stay away vibes as he held me tight, I clung tightly to him, soaking up his strength.

"Safe. Lockdown," Liz replied. Chance nodded.

"Go," he said over his shoulder to Celt, Tiny, Pyro and Levi, who was just entering my office. They spun on their heels after checking I was alright and left the room.

Drake growled and made to take me back in his arms. But I saw the look Chance shot him and Drake stopped moving, no one took on Chance when this mood rode him. Although for a few seconds I thought Drake just might. Drake instead tilted his head, giving Chance what he needed at that moment.

"You a cop?" Chance spat at Detective Ramirez, who nodded, "what you are doing about it?"

"Just got here a minute before your grand entrance. If you don't mind, I'd like to begin," Detective

Ramirez snapped back, and my gaze shot to him. He looked pissed, was the detective judging me for knowing two MC's?

"Get on with it," Chance said, and I knew he was just holding on by his fingertips. I think Drake and Ramirez had realised this.

"Can you tell me what happened Miss Phoenix?" Detective Ramirez said, dragging a chair over to me as Chance sat with me on his lap.

"Call me, Phoe," I invited and then ran him through the letter and what had led up to it. The detective walked me through my morning and through the manic last few days. Ramirez looked to Abigail who was no longer on the phone, and she informed him that she was gathering footage from the cameras. Gently he asked a few more questions and then finally looked at me, Drake and Chance.

"This person knows you Phoe. Knows you well, do you have any ideas?" he asked me gently.

"It sounds like my ex-husband, but it can't be," I bit my lip and swallowed. I didn't dare look at Chance.

"Can't be?" Ramirez asked me.

"He's in prison in England. Locked up for the next ten years," I whispered. Chance's arms twitched, and I buried my head in his throat, we both knew otherwise.

"Are you sure he's behind bars?" I nodded. God no, I knew he wasn't behind bars. "For what?"

"Bigamy, domestic violence, fraud, child abuse, battery, rape. You name it, the asshole committed it," Chance replied to Ramirez when I couldn't speak.

Drake's body stiffened, and then he jumped to his feet and stormed from the room. An aura of violence went with him but didn't lessen as Chance, and the others remained in the room. Ramirez straightened and with a visible effort, turned his now angry look into gentle. The detectives' own vibe was dangerous as well.

"Do you need to talk alone?" he asked me, I shook my head. There was no way in hell Chance was letting anyone else hold me. I couldn't let him go either, I needed him, his strength, his love, just needed him. Chance already knew.

"They all knew, apart from Drake," I whispered.

"Take your time Phoe and tell me what you can." I began speaking hesitantly and then switched off and began telling it factually. Chance kept a tight grip on me as I spoke.

It was the only way I could cope with talking about my story. I did this from the haven of Chance's arms, focussed on his tattoo of a Phoenix that curled around the lower of his left arm. I didn't see or hear Drake come back, it wasn't until I'd finished that I lifted my head and saw him, his eyes burning into mine.

Drake moved forward, and I found myself yet again dragged from someone's lap and dragged into someone's arms. Chance let go, but I could tell he wasn't happy too. He sent his cousin another look, but Drake closed his around me and buried his head into my neck.

"Never again, never again my angel, I swear on my life. You'll always be safe, I swear it on my cut," Drake whispered. I blinked, that was huge, I understood what that meant. To swear on their cut was something so extreme it rarely happened. I wrapped my arms around him and held him as tight as he held me.

"He'll have to get through me and all of Rage before he breathes your air again. I promise you're going to be safe." I clenched my fists in his back and bit back a sob. I knew the monster wouldn't breathe my air again, and I looked across at Chance who held my eyes.

"I'll have to contact the United Kingdom police, check his status," Ramirez said, watching us. "Can you think of anyone else? Someone you may have turned away? A disgruntled ex of a client?"

"Lots of those," I whispered.

"I have letters sent previously, we keep them and track them. Our own security team access the threats, and if deemed viable, they are turned over to the local police in the relevant state. We've never had a death threat aimed at the children before, though. Lots of violent promises but nothing in this category. HQ is secure. This weekend was ideal for someone to breach security," Abigail said, looking at her shoes.

"Abigail, you couldn't have prevented this," I told her. She glanced at me, and I saw it in her face she thought she'd let me down.

"Tell me about this weekend. Could someone be after money? A threat and then a possible demand for payment? I need to know everything," Ramirez said. Drake held me tight as my team talked to Ramirez and answered his questions. During which time my eyes held Chance's, well aware of the secret between us.

Chapter Eight.

I sat curled in Drake's arms, the police had left taking the letter away. Detective Ramirez promised to let me know what the U.K reported back. I gave him a tired nod. Liz had left to sort out security for the kids, and Abigail went to consider further protection for the building. Rumours were running riot outside my office, but the inner circle was squishing them for now.

After the weekend and the high, the guys were on, I didn't want an upset bringing everyone low. Drake looked at Chance. A question on his face that hadn't been vocalised when Ramirez was present. Chance gave a single headshake, then clenched his jaw and turned away.

"Definitely not the ex-husband," Drake muttered.

"No," I whispered and guessed Drake had sorted part of the puzzle out.

"Not gonna ask. Can it be tracked?" Chance turned back and shook his head, eyes burning.

"Need to lock Phoe down until we catch this sick fuck," Chance grunted, and I shook my head.

"You can't! The Trusts need me to be visible. What happens if I disappear? The gossip?"

"What will it say if a sick fuck gets a'hold you or the kids?" Chance shot back, and I trembled in Drake's arms.

"People are dying out there, Chance," I whispered.

"And someone fuckin' could kill you! I'm worried about you. Fuck Phoe, I can't lose you!" Chance roared, his body towering over mine. I shrank back feeling his anger.

"No one will lose her, Phoe's gotta have someone on her all the time. Rage, Hellfire, cops. Put in a call to Dylan Hawthorne. Hawthorne's the best in Rapid City, best in South Dakota. Man owes Rage a couple of markers." Chance's eyes flashed to Drake, who funny enough was being the voice of reason.

"Call Hawthorne. Both of ya's been at opposite ends several times but need the best on Phoe," Chance agreed. He looked at me. "Gonna surround you, Phoe, no matter where you are ya don't move without four people beside you. One Rage, one Hellfire, one Hawthorne and one Liz's. Don't move without those four, no thinkin' that okay, there's three of them. Want front, back and sides Phoe. Understand me?" I nodded.

"Kids," Drake said.

"Same with kids, gonna curtail their shit but they'll understand. The younger kids do not leave that house, I want the Hall on total lockdown. No one gets in or out," Chance decided before I could say a word. The door opened, and Liz entered.

"Teams are coming in, enough for two guards per child. The younger kids will stay home with patrols guarding them. Motion sensors, cameras, every security measure installed at the Hall, went live as of half an hour ago. Matthias released the teens into the Hall. Not the grounds, not till a freaking army gets there to protect the kids." A phone began buzzing, it was mine and Micah was calling. Hitting answer, I spoke to my boy.

Micah sounded calmer than one may have thought as I told him the full truth. Micah agreed with the security measures and agreed to get the older kids to keep the younger ones inside the Hall. At the end of the call, a sudden thought hit, which caused me to pale and shake harder.

"Christ Phoe," Drake said, wrapping his arms tight around me.

"That asshole was here, my children were in danger." Fear crawled up my throat. Drake and Chance's faces said that they'd considered this. The grimness in their eyes said everything.

"Going to be okay angel," Drake whispered. I hadn't tasted fear this strong for years, and yet terror crawled back under my skin like an old friend.

"My kids Drake." Without a doubt, I could give everything else up, money, the Trusts, the houses, but never my kids. No two ways about it, I couldn't live without them. Drake drew me close and held on tight.

"No asshole's getting' near the kids' Phoe. Swear it," Chance rumbled, he kissed my head and left.

"I need to go home," I told Drake and pushed against him. Drake let go, and I reached for my bag. Drake followed me from the room, quietly explaining to Stefan, and we left the building. Eyes followed us and concern stifled the air, Drake guided me to my car, opening the door I got in the driver's side.

"Rage got shit to finish, do that, and then I'll be at the Hall, I'll bring food. Tell Mrs Ames not to cook," Drake said and bent to give me a long kiss.

I drove home fast, seeing a security team in the car behind but not paying conscious attention. Cameras tracked the vehicle from the trees as I approached the Hall. Security walked the grounds to my gratification, Celt and Tiny guarded the front door.

Pyro and Levi came running down the steps and met me from the car and escorted me into the house. Inside were Apache and Ace, Rooster and Shee. The older kids were talking in the morning room. I cocked my head not hearing the younger ones.

"Babies are in the basement with Slick and Lex," Ace said abruptly. He looked over his shoulder as the older teens came out. Micah was pale, Carmine, Tye and Jodie looked scared and Serenity, Harley and Christian looked worried.

"Mum?" Christian asked, walking towards me. I opened my arms, and my boy flew into them.

"Is it that bastard?" Micah snapped.

"No, son, never going to be him," I assured. Micah gazed across at Pyro and Tiny with a question in his eyes. Pyro gave him a sharp nod, and Micah relaxed.

"Fair do. So any leads?" Carmine asked. I shook my head and ran my hand over Christian's hair. My son let go and wandered back to Micah.

Christian idolised Micah, constantly seeking out his bother for love and comfort. Micah was the default for Christian when he needed reassurance. Christian slipped under Micah's arm and burrowed into him. After the escape, Micah had taken on the role of surrogate father to the kids and becoming far older than his years.

"Drake's comin' up with Chinese. If ya want somethin' special, gimme orders now," Ace said curtly.

I gave him food orders for the little kids, and then the older ones gave their own. Pyro spoke to the kids, and everyone disappeared in different directions. I remained standing in the entrance hall and then walked upstairs to get changed.

Drake arrived two hours later, and everyone crammed into the lounge and ate. Even at home, I was on edge and tried to hide my nerves, Rage and Hellfire both picked up on the tenseness. At seven o'clock it was a relief to put the babies down, followed by Eddie and Tony.

The middle kids would go to bed at their given times, and older teens were old enough to sort themselves out. I sat staring at the fire that Pyro had started an hour earlier before Hellfire left. Pyro had to be reassured by Chance that I was covered tonight before he left. Tomorrow Shotgun was the guard from Hellfire, riding up tomorrow morning before work.

Blaze, a prospect from Rage was meeting me at HQ tomorrow. I'd several meetings that couldn't just be ignored or rescheduled. It was imperative I went to work tomorrow, it couldn't be avoided. Luckily, the kids were on a school break, and so I didn't have to worry. The kids were registered at well recommended local schools and kindergartens. Now I wondered if I needed to send them to private ones.

In such a small space of time, I'd been hit by a multitude of events, leaving me reeling. In dealing with the aftermath of the huge donation weekend, the death threat, Rage's arrival in my life, I was overwhelmed. Chance wasn't happy that someone had breached HQ. Add to everything else there was the growing attraction between myself and Drake. Yeah, my life had a lot going on lately.

Most of it could be tackled quickly, the team would manage the donations and sort out what needed doing there. Property would investigate the land and buildings that had been donated. Kyle was busy ensuring that the donations were going to the correct states.

Rage threw me for a loop, not because they were an MC. That meant nothing, MC's had a rough rep, but Hellfire and Rage were good ones. Rage and Hellfire's past may be murky, but both clubs were now clean. How Rage fitted into my life was a worry when Hellfire took priority. Hell would freeze over before I'd cut Hellfire out because of Rage, a balance needed to be found. This was the first chance I'd had, to consider the implications of both MCs.

Chance being unhappy, was because of Rage and Drake. Chance possibly felt threatened, although there was no need. The question was how to reassure the man I loved so dearly. The man meant everything to me, and when Chance was upset, I was affected too. Chance had been there ever since our infamous jail time together. He'd never called me weak for the past nor ever judged me. Chance accepted who and what I was and loved me. I'd known Chance had warned Drake off and Drake had pushed it this weekend.

The death threat didn't worry me, security or the police, Hellfire or Rage would get to the bottom of that. So while scared and worried, at the end of the day, I knew I'd be safe. As safe as I could be. Chance would burn the city before harm came to the kids or me. I should be reassured, but the fear was still present.

The attraction between Drake and myself, that was a huge problem. Was I ready to risk another chance on a man? Could I risk the kids again and their safety and happiness? Instinctively, I knew that Drake would never physically harm me. Like Chance, Drake wouldn't dream of raising a hand to a woman or child. But what happened if Drake got close and then ran? Maybe finding everything too much, with my kids and Trusts.

Yeah, the weekend just gone by, proved that Drake supported the Trusts, but long term? How could that play out? I glanced across at where he sat, face lit by the flames of the fire. Yes, I'd fallen in love with Drake over the last two weeks. The strength of my feelings was not a joking matter. I needed Drake, but I'd the children to consider. No man, no matter how much I loved him, would come between my children and me or the Trusts.

Slick sat next to Drake, talking to Chance who sat next to them. Chance's tense body a good sign of the anger he was struggling to contain, Drake's body was as tense. Drake was a protector, he felt deep. I'd never been attracted to Chance after our first meeting, but Drake knocked my socks off. Something was building between us.

Let the chips fall where they fell, I decided. No point in trying to fool myself into believing I wasn't in love with the man. When Drake touched me, I lit up like a heat-seeking missile, not just sexual attraction, I was deeply attracted to Drake on every level. This was intense, a relationship that was worth fighting for. I'd the intuition that once Drake was in, he gave his woman everything.

Drake made me laugh, was kind and caring although at the same time grumpy. We cared about the same things, Drake made sure I'd get what I wanted. Okay, honestly, maybe Drake some did things to guarantee he'd get what he wanted too.

Drake looked over, and I don't know what was in my face, but his body relaxed, and he sent a shit-eating grin at me. My thoughts must have been evident because his eyes lit with wicked glee and satisfaction. I held his gaze and announced it was time for a bath to relax. The guys sent chin lifts and nods and carried on talking.

The next day after midday, Emily opened the office door. A tall, handsome man strode in, following swiftly behind him, was Drake. Drake appeared mad, and the other man pissed. Warily, I watched as they both approached my desk, and both men glared.

"You'd consulted Hawthorne's?" Drake spat out slamming hands on my desk.

"What was the point of having my top security expert go over HQ, if you only implemented half the measures Davies suggested?" Dylan Hawthorne snarled. Uh oh, here comes trouble.

"Imagine my fuckin' surprise, when I contact Hawthorne, only to find you previously were a client!" Drake spat again.

"Davies suggested cameras in private offices. Where are they?" Dylan snapped. Okay, these two were tag-teaming me. Enough!

"Okay, both of you stop right now. Yes, Drake, I know Dylan Hawthorne, Dylan consulted with Abigail on security for HQ. Davies oversaw the installation of most of the security features." I pointed at Drake and swapped to pointing at Dylan.

"Yes Dylan, Abigail did only carry out half of the suggestions. Neither one of us liked being watched while in private offices. It seemed like I was spying on the staff too. Yes, I made a mistake, we will correct that." If I expected to mollify the men, I was wrong. Both sent me dark stares.

"Davies is coming later today. He'll meet with Abigail and go back over the original plans and make changes. HQ will be more secure than Fort Knox. Whatever suggestions are made, I don't expect an argument, get me?" Dylan pointed at me this time.

"I get you, but don't talk to me like I'm a child." I snapped back.

"This is my business Phoenix, you understand? Hawthorne's doesn't make a recommendation for shits and giggles, we make one because it's needed. A fuckhead got through your security and left a death threat for you and the kids. Until HQ is secure to Davies's standards, you're working from home, starting from now. I'm putting a four-man rotating shift on you. Twelve hours each."

"Think…"

"Don't care what you fuckin' think Phoe. Listen to the man, or I'll lock you down on Rage!" Drake snarled. A quick glance at Dylan told me I'd get no support there, and I gave a graceful shrug. I picked my battles, and this was one I wasn't going to win. I bent and picked up my bag.

"Finished for the day."

"Good," Drake snarled. I sighed.

Sat in the library a few days later surrounded by boxes, I threw an empty box at Slick. Slick was sat on the floor next to me emptying boxes. We'd argued how to unload the boxes as there was so many of them. Finally, we'd created piles of books in front of their relevant bookcase. This led to further arguments as I'd many series' in which different authors wrote in, such as Dragonlance and Star Wars. In the end, an agreement was reached. The books would be shelved according to series and then shelved by the author.

Slick had dived straight into the books and began flipping through and piling them. He put a few books on a table which I guessed he meant to read. He'd also mercilessly teased me over the Dragonlance and Forgotten Realms books. The bugger nearly ripped my hand off when he saw me unearthing the entire collection of Clive Cussler.

Sneakily, Slick had repacked the Raymond Feist books, saying that he was keeping them as a gift. Come on, Feist is a god! Drake, laughing, had to stop us wrestling over the box. I now leaned back against his chest as we continued unloading boxes. Bear had arrived and was helping too. The four of us concentrated on getting books to the right shelves for now. By the way, I won the Feist fight. Those books were mine!

There were many sarcastic comments on the number of books. Drake had asked where the children's books were. Jodie explained that shelves were being fitted in the spare room, turning it into a children's library. Sweaty, Jodie and Serenity stopped by and helped after their tennis game.

The teens were playing a game in the ballpark. The little ones were in the jungle gym with Pyro and Tiny, it was a good day. By five o'clock, most of the boxes were unpacked, leaving plenty of time to eat dinner with the kids. Mrs Ames had cooked tacos, and they disappeared like lightning. Albert had planned a grandfather evening with the younger kids, and everyone scurried to the cinema for films and popcorn.

"Want to continue?" Slick asked, looking at his watch. Time was just approaching half-past six.

"Sure maybe start shelving them?" I asked the others. Despite nods, half an hour later Bear, was curled up with a Terry Brooks book. Slick bopped Bear on the head with a book. Bear growled and then settled back in the chair.

At nine I put the babies down, smiling because we'd had a good day. Slick said he'd return the next day, and I offered him a room for the night, Hellfire was already staying. Slick's eyes slid to Drake for approval before he agreed and took the offer of a spare room. Drake watched me expectantly, and I grinned at him.

"Ten'ish okay for you to come back?" I teased. Drake took two strides, and his mouth crushed mine. A minute later, he lifted his head and gave me a lazy grin.

"Ten'ish?"

"Huh?" I asked stupidly.

"To come back Phoe," Drake smugly said.

"You think you can kiss me like that and leave me hanging, you can think again," I said, snottily. Drake gave me that lazy grin again and then scooped me up into his arms.

"Know exactly what I got coming," Drake grinned and carried me to my bedroom.

Once inside, he kicked the door shut and plastered me against the door. His mouth dropped back to mine, and we kissed wildly. Both panting by the time the kiss ended, Drake grabbed my wrists. Lifting them above my head, Drake pinned mine there with one hand.

Drake's other hand cupped my face and tilted my head, and he kissed me again. I struggled against the hold, wanting to run my hands over that hard body. Featherlight fingers were running over my body, but Drake held my arms up, denying reciprocation. Drake let go and dragged his mouth from mine.

"Move those hands angel, and there'll be trouble," he growled. A hand slipped to my jeans' waistband and dragged my tee free. Impatient, Drake ripped it off and stood gazing at my breasts covered by a black lacy bra. I winced. Yeah, giving birth to five kids left stretch marks, and I wasn't twenty-one anymore. Drake appeared not to notice as he teased my nipples.

I gasped and lifting his head, Drake looked into my eyes. Real need, reflected in his eyes, made me squirm under the hot gaze. His lips touched my throat, and I moaned. Drake began licking and sucking as his hands cupped and stroked my breasts, setting every nerve on fire.

I struggled to keep my hands up, and he unsnapped my jeans and sank to his knees. I dropped my hands and clenched them in his hair as he kissed his way down my stomach. Drake stopped kissing me and looked up, and I went weak at the look on his face. Drake rose to his feet and shoved my arms up again, and his other hand slid down my jeans and cupped me.

One finger began making lazy circles on my clit, and I cried out. Eyes watched me intently, as that finger began stoking the fire he was building, and I began panting shamelessly. The nasty tease moved the finger away, and I cried out a denial, and a wicked look crossed Drake's face. His groin pushed against me, and I thrust against his hardness.

"Punishment," Drake whispered, and that finger slid inside my wet core and thrust. My legs were barely holding me up and moving frantically against his hand, I rubbed against him. An orgasm was building and dropping my head, I bit his shoulder. My body began to shake in release, and then Drake stopped and withdrew his hand.

Shocked and in disbelief, I looked at Drake. Still wearing a dirty look, he carried me to the bed. Reverently, he placed me on it before pulling my jeans and panties off completely. He parted my legs and sank between them.

"Keep hands above your head, baby." I glared, wet and wild and needing him, then nodded as he took me in his mouth.

Oh my god, I've never had this! Drake was skilled beyond belief. The fire banked and rose again, and for the second time, my hands clenched in his hair. I held his head there as I ground myself against his mouth, and Drake pulled away, denying my release a second time. No!

"Naughty girl," he said harshly, fighting for control and he took my mouth. A hand slid between our bodies, and Drake tugged his belt free. Deftly my hands were tied together and then tied to the bed.

"Drake! I need you!" I begged. He smiled, and it made between my legs tingle.

Drake ripped his tee off, and my mouth went dry at the sight of his chest. Outlined muscles and a smattering of dark hair Drake was a picture of masculinity. He stood and kicked off his boots and pulled his jeans down. Naked, Drake stood in front of me, and I squirmed. He took his cock in hand and began stroking up and down, my mouth watered.

"Drake!"

"What do you want, angel?" Intently watching me squirm, Drake was getting an intense male satisfaction from it.

"You, I need you." Suddenly his body covered me.

"Greedy girl," Drake whispered in my ear as his cock poked at me. I wriggled trying to get him inside, and he held off. One hand ran over my body, cupping my breasts and bringing them to his mouth. He suckled and nipped, sharing his attention equally.

I was a hot panting mess, and Drake revelled it. Drake's jaw was locked hard with self-control as he slid gradually inside me. Greedily, I tried to move my hips to make him sink deeper, but he held me down, and I could only lay there and take him.

"Drake," I nearly wailed.

Drake's mouth covered mine, and then with a hard thrust, he was seated in me. Huge and throbbing, he stretched and filled me, and I clenched around him. Now it was his to groan deep, and I clenched harder around his cock. In return, Drake nipped my lip and began to move. Supporting his weight on one arm as he looked at me. Crushing me to him, he set a frantic pace, thrusting hard. Primed to go off, I exploded.

I cried out into his mouth. Drake was battling for control as I came back to earth. His hand was still between us, and I was sensitive. With a wicked glint, he began playing with me again, as he thrust inside me. Drake removed his hand and slid it around to cup my ass.

"Christ Phoe," he muttered and then began thrusting harder. I met him with every thrust, and I felt an orgasm build again. With a cry, I came a second time, and a few seconds later, he did. Drake collapsed on top of me, both of us sweaty and hot.

"Want more," I whispered to him, trying to regain my breath. He chuckled against me.

"Need a few minutes, I've not blown like that since I was a teen." Instead of being annoyed at his crude words, I chuckled too.

"You were amazing," I whispered, my hands still tied above my head. I ached to touch him.

"Beyond that angel. Never had a woman go so wild for me," Drake told me and propped himself up on one arm and snagged me around the middle. He turned us both on our sides while remaining inside of me.

"Don't think I've ever felt like that before," I told him truthfully. Drake's hand clenched on my hip, telling me how he felt.

"Good," he muttered. He opened his eyes and looked at me. "Phoenix, you're mine, understand?" I frowned thinking I understood what he meant, but I wasn't sure.

"Yours?" I asked.

"You're it for me. You're mine." Was Drake telling me what I thought he was telling me?

"We're dating?" Uncertainty in my voice. Drake let out another chuckle.

"No angel, way past dating."

"Then what?" I asked. Drake lifted himself up and withdrew from me, a moue of disappointment escaped as he left me and untied me.

Vigorously, Drake rubbed my wrists and dragged me onto his lap, facing him. Without hesitation, I wrapped my legs around his waist as he dragged us up against the headboard.

"Going to give you one chance. Just one Phoe, if you take the out, I'll leave, even though you're the only woman for me. You chose not to take it, you're mine for life. Understand?" Although I still didn't get it, I nodded.

"Give it to you straight, Rage was shit. For years the club was rotten, I got it clean just seven years ago. Asshole President had us runnin' illegal shit. He ran

Rage like that for years until I took control back. We ran protection, drugs, guns, sold women and were enforcers. Bulldog the President back then, took the club my Da built and destroyed it.

Too young, when Da died to do shit about Rage, but I stayed in, always intending to get Da's club back. Did the shit Bulldog wanted, asshole loved givin' me the shitty jobs. I ate it and slept it, was no better than scum. Participated in illegal shit, Phoe, I don't have a fuckin' record, it's a miracle I don't. Half of Bulldogs people had records, Apache and I began looking for people to bring into Rage. Those I recruited, kept them away from a record, but we ate the same shit day in and day out.

Searched for brothers who wanted a clean, legal club that had morals and put family first. Focus of Rage is family. Before I brought them in, I made sure they knew they'd have to eat shit. Until the legitimate ways of earning money and getting the club clean, kicked in. Brothers did it, Lowrider, Ezra, Manny, Gunner, we ate that shit to get club clean, and we got Rage fuckin' clean.

Blood was split woman. Bulldog didn't go easy, brothers took some bad hurts. Ace lost a woman, girl ran away from the shit the club was in. Apache nearly took one to the head, Manny took two to the back. Did things Phoe that I can't expect you to understand. A brother took out Bulldog, but I put the asshole and others in the ground. My brothers and I took out those who preferred the illegal shit, better than the legal. Worked our asses off making sure the Rage Shop, parts store, garage and the bar brought in money.

We've been clean seven years Phoe, but bodies can still pile up. We keep shit away from the club, sometimes a quiet word works, sometimes we gotta do more than have a word. Rage ain't afraid of gettin' our hands dirty even now, but life is good. Brothers didn't take a hit when we cut the illegal shit out. We keep Rage and the area around it clean. Vigilantes, if you wanna call us that.

Made sure my brothers got the money they liked and did that the hard way. But no lyin' baby, I did shit and have shit in my past that ain't fuckin' pretty. So I'm tellin' ya I never hurt a woman, I never raised a hand to one or a kid. Sold pussy, hated it, didn't like it but could make sure those women that sold their pussy were safe.

Didn't do drugs, occasional pot now and then but Bulldog and his cronies liked hard shit. That's part of reason club got so rotten, ain't done pot for years. Don't need it, nothing can give me a high like the one I get when I see a brother receive some bounty or goodness. Nothing beats that feelin'.

Clubs clean, I swear it, angel, we're clean, but we don't back away. Paid for Rage with blood, we bought Rage with blood and Rage blood was spilt on those streets. I'll let ya go, I can do it, Phoe, you don't want this, can let you go.

But you always gonna be mine, even if you aren't with me. You pick up the phone and call I'll drop everything and be there. No matter what I'll always belong to you." The last words Drake spoke were desperate. As he'd given me his speech, I'd watched the open emotions on his face, shame, hate, pride, sorrow, a whirlwind of emotions had passed through Drake. I gazed into his face.

"Say somethin', woman," Drake said hoarsely.

"Like what? Do you think you told me something I didn't know?"

"Huh?" It was Drake's turn to be confused, I ran my hand down his face. Poor love didn't know that I knew.

"I'm Hellfire Drake. *A sister.* Honestly, do you think I don't know what Chance did to get Hellfire clean? You don't think I know what Chance suffered and how Rage and Hellfire are tied? Yeah, Chance kept me away from Rage because he and the boys are selfish. Of course, I *know* what you guys did to get clean."

"You know?" Drake asked. At once, I realised what he was thinking, that Chance had told me about Rage.

"I know what Hellfire did, I know your club was in as much shit as Hellfire was. I know what Chance did to get Hellfire clean, and I tell ya Drake, there're recent bodies in Hellfire. More recent than seven years."

"How do you handle that?" Drake asked, genuinely curious.

"How can I not? I love Chance, love Bearbear, I love them, even Chatter. I never claimed to be an angel Drake, someone held a gun to one of Hellfire, and I'd a weapon, I wouldn't hesitate to fire it.

They're mine as much as I am theirs. Bodies being buried are bad guys, justice didn't do right with them, there's justice, and then therc's justice. Do I believe Chance ever put an innocent man in the ground? No. I don't think you have either or you wouldn't be in my bed," I kept my eyes on him as I spoke.

"I haven't," Drake was quick to assure me. I gave him a smirk. I sighed.

"Drake, I lunch with Senators and Congressmen and then hunt under train bridges for lost souls. Don't you understand? I am who I am, and I can accept the dark with the light. You bring me light, bring me happiness and love. I don't care what you do, as long as its moral, just and right. All you got to promise me is to come home to me at night," I said. Drake's arms tightened around me.

"How did I ever earn you?" he asked.

"Don't know," I giggled. "I know sometimes lines are crossed, as long as an innocent doesn't suffer, I'm okay with that. I'm not daft, a woman doesn't get a say in what brothers do in an MC. I think I'm a rarity as a sister in a band of brothers. But even while I may sit in Hellfire's church, I'm fully aware that they have some meetings, I don't attend. Don't you see? I'm as much as a club member as you are, I understand Drake, all of it."

"Fuck you undo me Phoe," he muttered.

"You're going to have to share me with Hellfire. You may be Rage, but I'm Hellfire. I will cuddle, snuggle and love them. Now you have to decide, can you handle knowing I may curl up in Bear's or Chatter's lap. But it's feelings of a sibling relationship for each other?

I won't stop being me, and I won't ask Hellfire to obey your directives. You're a man, you don't like to share. If you can't handle the fact that they're my brothers, you're the one who needs to walk Drake," I told him firmly. I knew I wouldn't let him drive a wedge between Hellfire and me. Nothing would make me give up Hellfire.

Drake moved like lightning, and I was flat on my back before I knew it. He pressed between my legs which had opened as he threw me backwards. His body lay on mine, and he cupped my face.

"You gonna come home to our bed at the end of the night, and share that pussy with me and me alone?" Drake asked.

"Of course, I am." Drake gave me that infuriating smirk of his and I glared at him. He laughed and wrapped his arms around me, gathering me in tight to his body.

"You had your chance angel, you're mine," he said and then kissed me deeply. Then he proceeded to make very sure I knew I was his.

A week later, I was going insane from being locked up in my house or in my office. Detective Ramirez had no leads and no further information. Security hadn't found a lead, and I was going insane from being isolated. Pathetically I'd began begging Drake and Chance shamelessly for a night out. Didn't care where I just needed to get out.

Micah and the older kids felt the same, so Chance had taken the teens back to Hellfire's clubhouse yesterday. That had only increased my sulking. The little ones were fine as they had everything they needed at their fingertips.

Sat on my bed still sulking I glared as Drake came in and grunted at me. He took one look at my face and walked into my closet. A few minutes later carrying a red dress I'd never worn, he walked towards me. He slung the dress on the bed.

"Get dressed angel," Drake muttered. I perked up and sat up straight.

"We're going out?" I asked, letting hope into my voice.

"Going to the bar, brothers meeting us there. Don't go anywhere with anyone who is not Rage. Don't leave our sight not even to go to the ladies. You go to the ladies, take Silvie and Marsha and tell my brothers so we can guard the door. Get me?" Drake demanded his mouth tight. I bounced on the bed in glee and slung my arms around his neck.

"Yes!" I squealed, and he rolled his eyes.

"Get dressed, saw that in your closet the other day, wanna see you in it," Drake muttered. He stripped off his tee and walked towards my bathroom, my eyes followed him as my mouth watered. Drake turned and looked at me, and he smiled, making my tummy flip.

"Phoe."

"Uh-huh," I replied my eyes devouring his front. I loved his body.

"If you don't move woman, then I'm gonna fuck you hard and then you'll miss this chance at going out." I paused for a few seconds, which meant more, him fucking me or a night out? Drake's eyes blazed, and then he laughed.

"Get dressed angel." He said and took that mouth-watering body out of my sight. I was dressed and brushing my hair when he came back out with a towel wrapped around his waist. Not playing fair, he hadn't dried off, and I moaned at the water dripping down his chest. I put my hairbrush down and spun on my stool to look at him.

"Can we be late?" I asked. Before he replied, I'd dropped to my knees and ripped the towel away. His cock came into sight, and he was already hard.

"Can be late," he growled as I took his cock in my mouth and gave him a blow job that blew his mind. We were an hour late.

I was dancing with Silvie and Marsha when the first incident happened. Drake and Rage had taken up two booths and tables and kept their eyes on us. I'd had a few drinks. Drake discovered my love of Southern Comfort, and as he was driving, I'd indulged in two of them so far. Because of the kids I rarely drank, but tonight Drake was ensuring I was going to have a good time.

Marsha had handed us three leather cuts with the Rage patch focussed on the back and front. They had no designation such as prospect or V.P, but they labelled us three women as belonging to Rage. At first, I'd baulked, as a Hellfire sister, I couldn't wear another club's cut.

Marsha looked upset, she'd forgotten to consider my affiliation. But when Silvie explained they'd prevent creeps hitting on us, I agreed. I'd felt so guilty at upsetting Marsha, I said one night wouldn't hurt. Those important to me knew I was Hellfire.

Silvie and I had discovered two poles to the left of the dance floor, and while we remained in full sight of Rage, we'd indulged together. I was tossing my hair back laughing while I grabbed hold on Silvie's hips and ground against her. Drake had nearly combusted when Silvie had done this to me, and now I was reciprocating. I was amused when I saw Apache keeping an awfully close eye on Silvie. I knew he had the hots for my girl!

Still laughing and dancing, my trouble monitor perked up, when three women crossed our paths. They sneered in our direction, and Silvie stiffened, I stopped laughing and looked at them. A brunette led the pack

"What the fuck do you want?" Silvie snapped before anyone else could say a word. I glanced at her and saw her relaxed stance was now aggressive.

"Just looking at the latest piece of ass to cross Rage. The one who's claiming to be Drakes old lady," the middle woman said, and my eyes narrowed.

"Who you calling a piece of ass? No claiming about it, she's Drake's old lady," Silvie snapped back.

"Well, it's politer than what I was going to call you both, Rage whores." I gasped in shock and stepped level with Silvie.

"Which makes you what? How many months did you hang around Rage trying to get into Drake's pants?" Silvie sneered. The brunette sneered back.

"Who says I never got in them?"

"I say," Silvie replied, "Drake had more class than to fuck you. You stank of desperation. Look at his old lady compared to you." Silvie landed a brutal blow. The brunette turned with her mouth open and stared at me. Then she threw her head back and laughed.

"That's his old lady? Who are you trying to fool? No way would Drake fuck that. Maybe I wander over and tell Drake some old bitch is claiming to be his old lady." I began to see red, I wasn't that old.

"As we are the ones wearing Rage, why don't you get the fuck out of here? Dumb bitches not wanted," I finally said something.

"Yeah. You know what Phoe? They hang around Rage reeking of desperation, half the brothers used to take bets on who'd fuck them. No chance of being old ladies, shame, they were just club whores," Silvie said bitchily.

"Not the one sweetie, pathetically offering it to a man on a platter and being constantly turned away by him, that's you, isn't it? Drake just needs to see this again to remember what he likes in bed," she ran her hands down her body. I felt the hit land on Silvie, and then I took in the second half of her sentence. Before anyone could say anything else, I slapped the brunette straight across the face. She staggered back, stunned and one of the other women stepped up to slap me.

Before anyone could blink, Silvie and I were fighting them. The three bitches scratched and clawed, Silvie and I punched and kicked. Within seconds, before it got going, Silvie was hauled away by a furious Apache and Drake had me around the middle. Mac, Lex and Gunner had the three bitches, the brunette turned on the tears, and I sneered.

"Get her the fuck out of here," I snarled and looking startled the brothers glanced across to Drake.

"You heard my old lady," Drake said. Firmly he still held me back as I tried to slip out of his arms and punch the brunette again.

"They insulted Rage, the cut and Drake. Get those bitches out of here before I kick their scrawny wannabe asses from here to kingdom come." Mac's lips twitched in amusement and Lex was out and out grinning. They began dragging the three women towards the doors.

"Phoe?" Silvie asked as I glared after the women.

"You ever set foot on Rage again, and the old ladies will kick the ever-loving shit out of you. Drake's off-limits pass the word. I won't be so nice to the next bitch that thinks she can fuck my man," I yelled at them. The brunette stared back fear on her face, I was so sick of these stupid women.

Overjoyed to see she had a bruise on her cheek coming up and her lip was bleeding, I high fived Slick. When I turned back, the guys, Marsha and Silvie were collapsed in laughter. Drake was looking down at me, amused wearing a satisfied glint in his eye.

"You done?" he asked, pulling me closer to nuzzle my neck.

"Yeah, if I'm your old lady, then you're my old man. Which means I can kick the shit out of anyone who thinks otherwise," I told him mulishly. Drake threw his head back and roared with laughter and kissed me. I loved his mouth; it made me tingle in my lady parts. I was ready to climb him when he ended the kiss.

"Too fuckin' right," he said and strolled back to our table. Silvie and I joined Marsha there for shots a few minutes later. The next incident happened two hours later, it wasn't my fault! Silvie, Marsha and I were back at the pole dancing suggestively with each other.

Although Marsha kept her eyes firmly on Fish and mine were locked on Drake. Who'd yet to take his eyes off me. We were more than tipsy, several rounds of Southern Comfort and many shots later, I was well on my way to being hammered.

The song ended, and we slung our arms around each other, and I turned to the guys sitting at the table frowning and gave Drake a saucy wink. His glower didn't faze me at all. I felt hands slide on my hips and I wriggled them, thinking Silvie had grabbed me again. I was shocked when those hands tightened on me, and I was dragged back against a male groin. Don't ask how I knew it was male. I twisted angrily breaking the grip on my hips and glared into a stranger's face. He was leering at me, and his eyes were firmly locked on my breasts.

"Let me go!" I bellowed.

"Hey babe, you know you want this." The slimy man thrust his groin and hard-on against me. I struggled against him and kicked his shin. He let me go, and I was picked up and moved out of the way as my old man came roaring past me and laid him out flat. I looked up and saw Manny had hold of me, and Apache had Silvie in a tight grip. Drake was leant over the man and was dragging him up by his shirt.

"She's on Rage, wearing Rage and you put hands to her?" Drake roared. Uh oh. Drake's fist shot forward again.

"How was I to know?" the douchebag spluttered spitting blood.

"The fuckin' cut gives it away. You that fuckin' blind?" Drake hit him again. He let go of the man and kicked him hard in the ribs.

"Get the bastard out of here," Ace demanded and Jett and Hunter both stepped forward and dragged the man out. I looked at Drake in all my drunken glory and launched myself at him. He caught me, but I could sense the fury running through his body.

"No more pole dancing ever," Drake bit out. And leaning down, he hoisted me up, and I wrapped my legs around his waist. He carried me through the bar while I snuggled into him. He'd proved me right, no matter what, I'd always be safe with him.

Chapter Nine.

A week later I sat in an armchair in the Rage clubhouse, laughing at Mac shooting the crap out of Lex on an action game on the Xbox. It was funny as hell as Lex slammed his console down and stormed off and Mac did a victory dance. Two weeks had passed since the death threat, and there had been no further ones. Half my kids surrounded Mac, egging him on to greater things. The teens were scattered around, talking to the brothers.

The police still had no leads, and neither had my security team or either MC. It was a Saturday afternoon, and Drake had planned a cookout for later. Hellfire was at the clubhouse, something had happened with the bar. Although curious, I didn't ask and wasn't told. Chance, Bear and Big Al were here, although Big Al had been locked up most of the day with Texas.

Out loud, I wondered if the bar was in trouble and several dirty looks were aimed at me, so I shut my mouth. Okay, the bar wasn't in trouble. Apache came and sat with me as I watched Manny challenge Rock next.

"No money trouble, honey, but drugs were found by Mac. Texas and Big Al are looking to increase security and keep that shit out. Wanna try to track it back." I looked up at the gorgeous man sat next to me.

"That's fine, Apache," I told him, I felt icy eyes and saw Ace watching us.

Out of Rage, Ace was the one I couldn't crack. Even the monosyllabic Rock and Gunner acknowledged me. Ace acted as if I didn't exist, as far as Ace was concerned, I wasn't part of Rage's circle. The only time I'd seen Ace react to something was when I'd once approached Drake and hugged him tightly. Ace's expression had softened at whatever look had been on Drake's face.

Bear was funning with Slick, both men fencing with pool cues. A few of the brothers were egging them on laughing. My phone rang as I was chuckling at Bear.

"Hello?" I said, still trying to control my mirth. Bear pulled a face at me.

"Laugh it up cunt, while you can," a voice snarled down the phone. I stopped laughing at once, I knew that voice, I hadn't heard it for three years, but I knew it, that clipped English accent couldn't be faked. My breath choked in my throat, and I paled. The blood literally drained from my face.

"What?" I stuttered. I didn't see Chance and Bear go alert, didn't see Drake moving swiftly in my direction. I couldn't see past *his* face.

"Laugh it up Marie, I'm coming for you. No fucking biker gang will keep me from what's mine. It's time for your lesson, baby," I screamed and threw the phone as hard as I could from me. I didn't see Micah moving in with Jodie by his side. Instead, I saw the monster with his face twisted in hatred and his fist coming at my cheek.

The blow landed, and my head snapped to the side, my hand flew to my face, and I cried out. Voices surrounded me, but I couldn't separate them. The monster over-rode everyone else's, that face twisted in revulsion and I backed up a step.

"Mum!" someone called. Oh god, the kids were here, the bastard might hurt them, I carried on backing away. Blindly searching for them.

"You won't hurt them," I gasped as I continued scrabbling backwards. The monster's fist slammed into my stomach, pain forced me to bend over wheezing. One arm wrapped around my stomach, I carried on stumbling backwards. My other hand remained at my red-hot cheek.

"Ma!" another voice shouted full of fear and confusion. My eyes blindly sought the voice out, but I couldn't find him. Couldn't find my boy to protect him. The blackness swelled and what remained was a nightmare. Stalking, ready to strike, the nightmare paced after me, hands raised to wield another blow. Blow after blow hit my body. I sped up, moving backwards, stumbling as I did. The further I moved, the further from my kids he was.

"Holy fuck Phoenix," a voice thundered near my ear. I flinched away and shifted in the opposite direction.

"Drake back off. Back the fuck off," another man thundered. Someone who grabbed my arms and tried to draw me close. I kicked out, if someone got between us, they'd pay. I had to protect everyone, protect the kids, I could do that. Surrender to protect the kids, I began dragging at the collar of my shirt.

"Take me," I pleaded, "don't hurt my kids." I tried dragging the shirt off, but hands stopped me. No, no, don't stop me, the girls are here. The thought vocalised, and the air snapped red hot, I stumbled over something and fell on my knees. Peering up, he gloated over me. The monster's hand grasped my hair and yanked my head backwards.

Raping my mouth was the monsters favourite thing, I began to gag. Not wanting this, and I fought silently, I felt pressure on my jaw, and it popped open. A wail escaped loud and long.

"Jesus fucking Christ. Get the kids out of here!" the first voice thundered. "Bear let me the fuck go."

"Phoenix come back, woman, you're not there, you're safe. Come the fuck back to me," a voice kept insisting. I tried to talk but couldn't as his horrible cock shoved in my mouth. I gagged and choked my hands rising to my throat.

"Mum!" a distant voice cried, and the pressure lifted. Freed, I scrambled back on my heels. I drew my knees up and sitting on my ass, bent my head to them and covered my ears and face. There was a hand at my head, soft, soothing, but it was battling the hands dragging my hair backwards. A voice spoke to me drowning out the evil one, the voice of salvation.

"Woman look at me. Fuckin' open your eyes and see me." I searched for the voice. For a hazy minute the monsters face blurred, and another took its place, a face with bright stunning green eyes.

"Cunt, can't even have dinner ready," my head rocked at the force of the slap.

"Beat him back Phoe, look at me, woman look at me."

"Bear get the fuck off me!" that second voice shouted.

"Phoenix, your name is Phoenix, you're Hellfire, you're Rage. Look at me, woman," the second voice kept on, soothing. A girl was crying, and I gazed in that direction, Jodie and Serenity, oh god Jodie and Serenity. He'd caught the girls! I began to fight, the monster could do what he wanted to me but not the girls. Not my babies.

My body jerked one way and then another as I fought him. Punches and kicks fell in a flurry, I felt every blow, every kick but I couldn't let the girls get hurt. Screeched this at him, he couldn't have them! I'd never let him have them, repeatedly, my body bent and rose with each thud. With terror smothering me, I began fighting and trying to tear his face to shreds with my nails.

There were thuds and the sound of a body hitting the floor. A different face from the last two filled my vision. But those eyes, I knew those eyes. Burned through my terror, with a fury and passion that shocked me. Strong arms grabbed hold, and I was dragged up into a lap and forced to meet a concerned gaze.

A gaze with expressive green eyes that held a world of fear. A face that imposed itself over him, I knew and loved that face. It wavered, and the monster reappeared, but that face wasn't letting him have me. Strong arms held me tight, trying to beat back my demons, and then a second set of arms surrounded me. I heard words, lyrical words. Words that meant something. Someone was singing.

A song that gave hope and a lifeline out of this madness, I latched onto those words. My hands rose and twisted in a tee I knew would be black. They moved sideways, and I felt his cut with the patch I loved. The nightmare faded, and then I gasped and my back arched. Green eyes held me captive, and I was back, I was safe, was loved, and I wasn't alone. The monster couldn't get to me. Those eyes belonged to a man who'd walk through fire, who had walked through fire for me.

"Chance," his name broke from a throat raw from sobs and cries. "Don't let go. Don't let him get me."

Tattooed arms wrapped tight around me, a second set shoved at him, and I got pulled into Drake's. I stiffened and tried to crawl back to Chance, Drake's arms tightened, and his eyes held those same emotions as Chance. Fury and passion but fear too, a load of anxiety. He squeezed once and at whatever he saw in my eyes, he let me go. I scurried back to Chance and folded into him. One arm wrapped around my waist and the other around my chest. Drake got to his knees next to me and stroked my hair. Calmness came over me, making the black go away.

"Make it go away, Drake," I muttered, "light up the dark." Audibly, he swallowed and kept stroking. Chance just held me tight.

"Got ya Phoe, I always got you, never lettin' ya go, angel," Chance began crooning those words again. I loved those words, Unstoppable by Rascal Flatts, Chance had sung them before to me.

"Want to explain what the fuck just happened?"

Drake asked in a low voice, I sensed he wasn't asking me but Chance.

"Later brother," Chance replied.

Drake wanted to reply but kept soothing me. One hand touching my face trying to wipe away the horror etched on it. I'd shoved my head into Chance, his other hand remained on my hair. A sob echoed, and my eyes met Serenity's. Bear had folded her in his arms, holding her tight as she sobbed into his shoulder. Micah and Carmine were pale.

Marsha had Carmine, who was paler than I'd ever seen him. My boy held Marsha and his long frame wrapped in her tight loving arms. She was rubbing his back, but his eyes were on me, Micah was held in Apache's arms. Apache held my boy loosely with an arm around his shoulder. He was giving my boy the support he needed but allowing Micah to remain a man. Micah stared into my eyes, and I saw the hate and violence in them.

Then I realised where I was, and I shuddered. The bloody common room at Rage. Everyone was there, Hellfire and Rage alike, brothers, prospects, old ladies and skanks. Brothers looked shocked, and in most cases, like they wanted to beat the crap out of someone, that was Rage.

Hellfire wanted blood, they'd seen, they understood, they wanted more blood. Old ladies looked horrified for the most part, Marsha was pale, and Silvie had tears streaming down her face. Marsha met my eyes and held them. Silently, she tried telling me something, but I didn't understand.

Skanks looked a variety of things. Some nice and others not so nice. Misty was smirking at me and at the nightmare I'd suffered. Ace's eyes cut to me and then followed my gaze. His face usually expressionless hardened and he grabbed Misty by the arm, hard.

"Get the fuck out," Ace whispered harshly. Misty's mouth opened, and he cut her off. "Get the fuck out," he repeated, "you're not a brother, ain't Rage and ain't Hellfire. Get your whore ass out. This is a family matter." He forced Misty to the door, and his gaze cut to the other skanks.

"Get out, all of you," Ezra said herding skanks towards the door.

I buried my head back in Chance's chest, they'd all seen, everyone witnessed my shame, horror, my nightmare. Both clubs were judging me, I'd finally cracked, and now they realised how weak, frightened and pathetic I was. At last, he'd won. I let out a low sob as I realised, I was saying that out loud and Chance still holding me, got to his feet.

Chance carried me out of the common room and down the hallway to Drake's room. A hard kick opened the door, and Chance walked in and laid on me on the bed. Immediately I turned from him and curled in a ball and faced the wall.

Chance swore and lay on the bed and dragged me into his arms, he sang to me until I slept. I didn't see Drake's eyes burning into us. I was unaware of the living fury coiled inside him and burning to get out, all I could see was my shame, humiliation and in the end, darkness.

Micah pulled loose from Apache and letting out a

wordless yell Micah grabbed a chair and swung it at the bar. It smashed into pieces, and he grabbed a second, Apache stepped back as he swung that, smashing it too. Panting and needing to hurt someone Micah turned to Bear. Carmine stood mutely.

"Son," Drake said.

"Not your fucking son," Micah exploded. Micah turned and launched himself at Drake. Drake held him as he struggled and punched and kicked it out of him. Jodie cried out, and Bear moved her and Serenity out of the way. Micah stopped, his anger spent and a massive wave of grief rolled out, it hit the room, and everyone flinched.

"I didn't know Mum thought the girls were at risk. I didn't fucking know!" he screamed at Drake. Drake held him, pinning him against the wall, Micah slammed his head back into the wall.

"I didn't fucking know about the girls. When that asshole found us here, Mum gave in to him straight away. She did it to protect them, I didn't understand and thought Mum was weak. I fucking judged my *mother* for being a weak ass bitch, when she was stronger than I ever knew," Micah whispered. Drake searched his face and decided it was safe to let him go. Micah moved instantly dragging his sisters out of Bears arms.

"Tell me," Micah snapped, "tell me he didn't."

"Of course not, Ma didn't let him. Chance and everyone got to him first," Serenity wept in his arms.

"He'd have used anything against Mum," Micah snapped.

"Yeah, but you saw," Jodie's voice faded out.

"I didn't get you out in time. Didn't do enough."

"That's enough, son," Chance snapped from behind, exiting the hallway. "You were fuckin' fifteen, not a man, not a child. You did what you could and what you did allowed you all to escape.

It allowed eleven other kids to have a life they wouldn't have had. Asshole would have beaten you to death, Phoe wouldn't have recovered from that. You did what you fuckin' could, a boy of fifteen with no money, no course of action. No one to turn too, cops turning a blind eye 'cause 'a who he was, cops ignoring the bruises."

"I..." Micah tried.

"There's no I. Escaped to shelters, he found you, ran away, and he found you, contacted cops, and they fuckin' turned a blind eye. Do you get me, son? Everyone legal turned their backs 'cause 'a who the asshole was, the only thing you would'a done is died. You gave her those three bucks, and by doin' that you saved her. Saved your brothers and sister and you saved your other siblings. Micah, only you did that."

"She's broken," Micah whispered. Chance slid his hand around the back of Micah's neck and held him close.

"No, she ain't son, Phoe ain't broken, woman's fractured. If Phoe was broken, she wouldn't be doin' what she's doin' or bein' who she's bein', understand me? If he'd broken her totally, she'd not be Phoenix. She's Phoenix.

She's Ma to sixteen kids. Phoe's survived. She got fractures, we can glue 'em, we can fix 'em, we can fuckin' fill them, 'cause ya gotta know son, fractures can be repaired. We gonna fix them and fix her. Fill her up with love and then make her overflow," Chance raised his eyes to Drake, who stood silently.

"See him?" Chance pointed at Drake. "I'm knowin' ya don't like him. I'm knowin' you fear he'll bring nothin' but more pain to your ma.

But Drake ain't gonna. Man's going to be the one that fills those fractures, but you gotta let him. Drake don't know the shit that went down 'cause Phoe's protecting you. Stop and man up Micah, let him do what he gotta do." Micah studied Drake and then studied Chance.

"I was hoping it would be you," Micah replied.

"Love your ma until the day I die, son. She'll always own a piece of me. But I ain't the one who can spark her light. I hate fuckin' sayin' it, but Drake is. He sparks her in more ways than I can dream of. Drake fucks up, I'll be waitin', and I'll be in there, but your ma, she deserves to be everythin' to a man and that man is him."

"Still wanted it to be you," Micah muttered stubbornly. Chance grinned at him.

"Always be mine, Micah. Not ever going to change that, you need to ride son. Axel," he ordered, and Axel came forward. Axel slung an arm around Micah's neck and dragged him out. Carmine scuffed his toe on the floor, Tye by his side.

"Son," Chance said. Carmine looked up.

"Not leavin' her Chance," he said, Chance nodded.

"Go out to the shop. I'm sure Ezra has somethin' you can beat the shit out of." Ezra nodded, Tye and Carmine left. Chance turned to Jodie and Serenity.

"I don't need to ride or beat the shit out of something," Jodie said, tilting her head up at Chance.

He grinned at her, and she held his gaze, Serenity shook her head too, standing near to her big sister.

"Then sit with the old ladies and get your shit sorted girls," Drake said. She nodded in his direction.

"Will of steel those girls," Chance muttered. "Not every day you find your ma took a beatin' to save your ass and kept on taking that beating." Drake turned to Chance as the old ladies led Jodie and Serenity towards Fish and Marsha's room. Bear moved towards the back where Phoenix lay sleeping.

"I'll wait with her," Bear said and left. Drake's eyes followed him.

"Man's angry Drake, loves that woman with his heart, know we're on Rage but let Bear do what he needs." Drake inclined his head at Chance, acknowledging his words.

"Start talkin'."

"Not sure that woman wants every brother here to know," Chance denied, shaking his head.

"My woman just had a complete meltdown on Rage. Hellfire know, Rage claimed her, start talking," Drake shot back. Chance nodded at Big Al, who brought a brown file over. Big Al handed it to Chance gave it to Drake. Drake went to open it, and Chance stopped him.

"Before you read brother, make sure you're locked tight, it's Phoe's file. Got a copy from Liz. Contains everything, every little incident, everything he did, every time she looked for help and didn't get it. There are x-rays and medical shit in there. Make sure you're locked up tight," Chance stressed. Drake nodded and then sat and began to read.

"Tell us what the file don't," Drake muttered an hour later. Fury burned deep inside him, it was locked tight, but it burned. Now he wanted answers, the file gave him everything up until she left the UK. But it didn't tell him everything, it was cold and lacking the human factor, Drake wanted everything.

Chance told Rage of the abuse Phoe had suffered for five years, this time using her words, not the black and white of cop reports. How the five children she'd birthed got treated. The mental, emotional and physical abuse, how Micah had been working in secret to save money so he could get them away. Chance told Rage of how she'd taken such a severe beating one night, Micah thought she'd die. Then realised they'd the winning lottery ticket.

Chance told his raging cousin how Micah had got her, Jodie and the little three to Albert. How Albert and Sally had worked to protect the family. That Sally had insisted outside police be brought in, as Phoe's ex-husband had been an influential solicitor. That the police charged him with multiple counts and he went down for it.

Big Al spoke to Rage of how Phoe's ex-husband had escaped from jail and found her here, in the US. Asshole attacked her in a rented home in Sturgis, Phoe got the girls to safety and then let him beat her. She hadn't tried to protect herself, instead, she concentrated on the two girls. Jodie had called Chance frantically, and they'd got there within minutes. During that time, he'd beaten the hell out of her and was attempting to rape Phoe when they arrived.

Chance confirmed the body was buried in a grave in the Black Hills, on the Montana side. Drake understood Phoe's words that Hellfire had killed more recently than seven years. Drake wished he hadn't asked, but he had to know. It killed him to know the woman he was falling deeply in love with had such pain and horror in her past.

Big Al spoke of the migraines, the panic attacks that faded over the last few years. Talked of the constant fear Phoe carried, that Hellfire might get found out. Chance sadly informed his cousin of how Phoe had flipped and regressed four times in his presence. How she physically relived what he had done to her, how Phoe battled that and tried to shine love around.

When Chance and Big Al finished, the room was wired. Rage had a black past, Rage had a past dark with blood and bodies, but Rage didn't raise a hand to a woman. The club dealt with women if they needed it, but they didn't raise a hand to a woman.

Rage fucked, drank and lived as they wanted, no one judged, they were brothers. Cut them, and they bled Rage, Phoe's story was horrific, and it rocked Rage. No one doubted Phoe had a gentle and generous heart. The strength Phoe showed when she escaped from her abusive ex, who hadn't even been married to her. Rage understood her fleeing the trauma of her past, which led to Sturgis. Fury that the asshole had escaped from jail and found his way over to the States.

The brothers listened intently as Phoe's story was told to them. How by the time Chance crossed Phoe's path, she'd just adopted Carmine, Tye, Serenity and

Harley. They tasted Phoe's fear that her ex might harm her four adopted kids, as well as her birth children. Rage felt respect for a woman who'd sacrifice herself, to protect her kids. Rage harboured anger that a woman, they were fast becoming to respect and care for, suffered.

In Rage, if a woman caused trouble, his brothers would resolve the issue, if the brother who claimed her didn't. That didn't mean harming a woman. Threats usually worked against women, and knowing the history of Rage, threats were often effective.

There was a code between them, an unspoken one but every brother in Rage knew it. Beat a woman, a weaker person than you, get beaten on, the room between Rage and Hellfire was electrified. Drake heard Chance say that Hellfire had dealt with Phoenix's ex-husband. That the asshole was dead and buried, didn't mean Rage didn't want a piece of him. That Rage wanted his blood, they couldn't have it, but they wanted it.

Brothers looked sickened. Fish, Apache, Texas, had once had an old lady and Fish still had Marsha. The others had loved their old ladies, for a vulnerable woman to undergo what Phoe had, they were sickened.

Others, Slick, Gunner, Lex and Mac just looked pissed. Women are meant to be looked after, brothers had women in their families. The club would go balls to the wall to protect women linked to a brother. This anger they felt while red hot, was bonding the club tighter. Rage used pussy as it came available, but good women, women like Marsha and Silvie were respected and cherished.

Minor disagreements in the club faded. Fact was they wanted the blood of a man who'd terrorised and beaten Phoe. Scum who used the threat of beating and raping her daughters to control her. Rage had united under a woman's pain and sacrifice.

"Now I see why Phoe's a sister. Didn't get it but do now. Saw part of Phoe's attraction at her family weekend," Drake muttered at his cousin.

"Do ya? Do you honestly see that?"

"See Rage united. Can see what joy she brings." Chance nodded his agreement at his cousin's words.

"Hellfire received that bounty three and a half years ago. Phoe strutted her ass into our life. Curled up on my lap in a cell with her head on my cut. Phoe's somethin'."

"Yeah, mine," Drake stated.

"I know. Hellfire knows, but you gotta respect Phoe's ours too, she's got so much love in her; she overflows with it. Rage can take primary, but the woman will always be our sister and our girl too. You'll never cut Hellfire out of her, Phoe picks up the phone, Hellfire will ride. Ain't nothing we won't do. Includin' bleed." Drake nodded.

"We need time to be alone."

"I'll get Bear out, he'll stay overnight somewhere. Bear won't leave Phoe until he knows she is good."

"Be a time before she's good."

"Yeah, but he'll stay tonight, Bear had a sister once," Chance shared. Drake caught his eyes and muttered, "Fuck me."

"Yeah, life is fucked up, but there's magic in it, and Bear found it again," Chance said carefully. Leaning over the bar, he snagged a beer.

"I think Rage is gonna get some magic," Drake said. "That's life, brother. That's life."

I came awake curled in Drake's arms and looked at him hazily. Drake's eyes were worried and scared, and he watched me like one would a wild cat. Then what happened hit me, and I paled as I realised everyone had seen it.

"Don't," Drake said harshly.

"I ruined the cookout," I whispered, my mind latching onto something innocuous.

"Nope, brothers and Hellfire got the kids rounded up, they're in the yard. Micah's calmed down, Axel took him for a ride, kids are okay."

"I heard his voice. Yet he's dead, I don't understand," I whispered, thinking back to the phone call.

"Sure, it was him?" Chance asked from the shadows of Drake's room. I thought hard and then nodded.

"He was buried, how is he alive?" I asked Chance confused, scared and uncertain.

"Gonna find out, Big Al left to speak to Roadkill. Either Roadkill fucked up or someone's fuckin' playin' sick games." I nodded gingerly, my head pounding.

"It was his voice, Chance. He called me Marie," I insisted.

"Your real name?" Drake asked.

"My real name is Phoenix, I changed it by deed poll, Marie is long in the past."

"Okay baby, we'll deal. Need painkillers?" Chance frowned at my frown. I nodded, he left the room and left me in Drake's arms.

"I understand if you want to take a break from me," I told Drake. He frowned now and looked pissed at me.

"Think I'm going to walk because you got flashback issues? What do you fuckin' think I am Phoe? That I'm the guy who'd walk 'cause you got PTSD?" Drake snarled, I'd just pissed him off. Wonderful.

"I'm giving you a get out of jail card," I whispered to him wishing my temples weren't pounding so much.

"Don't fuckin' want one, nor did I ask for one!" Drake snapped and wrapped me up tight. "What type of man you think I am Phoe? Someone that just wants to fuck ya? No offence babe, your pussy ain't that golden. I want you, all of you, you understand that?" I felt shamed. Subconsciously, I'd tried pushing Drake away. Instead of leaning on Drake like he offered. I'd gone into defence mode.

"Phoe you need help angel, can't break like that again in front of kids. Lucky Manny got the younger ones out, but the teens saw it. Promise me you'll get help baby. Gotta get you a therapist." I agreed, totally agreed.

"Yeah, I know."

"Baby, listen to me, what you're dealin' with, the shit you been through. It can break a person, even one as strong as you. Chance said he's seen you have these before. Can't be doin' that angel, need to get that poison out of your system so we can have a good life. Ain't going to lose you now I found you. Get me?" I nodded. I'd no idea where the flashback came from, and I thought I'd dealt with my issues. But I clearly hadn't, I couldn't afford a breakdown like that again in front of the kids. Drake was right.

What if an attack happened during a meeting, at work, walking across the street? That was a terrifying thought. I'd not had therapy to help me get over my ex-husband, but the kids had. When he found me just after I'd met Hellfire, I'd been lucky enough that Hellfire had been on hand. While the monster kicked my door in, Jodie phoned Chance for help.

He'd beaten me but not for long because Hellfire barrelled through the door and given him a beat down. I'd got the kid's therapy again after that, Chance dragged him out of my house with murder in his eyes. Handed him over to Roadkill to deal with, and the monster had barely been breathing.

Chance and Hellfire had beaten him nearly to death. Roadkill had been volunteered to dispatch my ex so he could never be found alive again. Drake's mouth twitched, and I realised I'd been speaking my thoughts out loud. I was horrified. What was happening with me, I'd never been loose-lipped before.

"Behave Phoe, won't say a word," Drake drawled. "Makes sense that Chance would be sure he's dead though. Chance told us this anyway babe, you're not sayin' anythin' Chance hasn't just told us. Big Al will find shit out. If he's buried, then we have someone close enough to know to play these fuckin' games with you."

"It was his voice," I insisted. Chance came back in,

holding a glass of water and two pills. I shoved them in my mouth and swallowed with a gulp of water.

"Big Al's on it Phoe, sleep for an hour. Brothers are playin' ball with kids. Get rid of that shit in your head," he ordered, with a glance at Drake, Chance left the room. Drake held me until I slept, and when I woke up, he'd gone.

Chapter Ten.

The chill woke me up, and I realised I was alone. Noise from outside faintly filtered through the door. With a yawn, I climbed out of bed. The cookout sounded as if it was in full flow, and I was missing the fun. I took a few moments to compose myself and took a calming breath. Part of me wanted to run, hide, everyone had seen my breakdown. I felt open and raw.

The fighting part told me to strut my stuff and screw everyone else. The one thing I wasn't, was a quitter, no one came to check me, so I headed to Drakes bathroom. I rummaged through cupboards and found a new toothbrush and vigorously brushed my teeth and then brushed my hair.

Makeup had smeared around my eyes, so I wiped my face clean, while brushing I realised I'd torn my shirt. Disgusted, I pulled off the remainder of the flashback and threw it in Drakes bin. Without regard for Drake's privacy, I searched through his drawers for a top.

A Walking Dead tee was clean, so I pulled it on, the tee looked wrong against my pencil skirt, but I was decent. With a deep breath, I left the safety of

Drakes room and walked to the common room. Two skanks sat at the bar, who looked in my direction and sneered.

With a glare, I held my head high, floated past and heard the snickers. I jumped as someone slammed a bottle on the bar. Behind me, Ace stood at the other end of the bar, Hunter and Jett behind it. Ace's eyes were on the skanks, and they were so bleak, I felt the chill from where I stood.

"Judging an old lady?" Ace rumbled. I stopped where I was, not wanting Ace's angry attention.

"What?" Skank one said, her name was Krystal or something similar.

"Said, are you judging a fuckin' old lady?" Ace rumbled louder this time and Jett and Hunter both come to attention.

"She's an old lady?" Skank two said surprised, Ace's brow furrowed, and he glared.

"Phoe in Drake's bed?" Ace asked Hunter. Hunter nodded, a blush began at my cheeks.

"Woman on the back of the Prez's bike?" Ace asked Jett, Jett nodded. It was true, several times Drake had taken me out on his bike. I'd been on the back of Chance's and Bears, but there was something sexual riding with Drake. The unwritten rule in both Hellfire and Rage was only old ladies rode the back of a brother's bike. A brother's bike was an extension of himself.

"Last time I saw, Phoenix was," Jett rumbled back.

"Makes Phoe the Prez's old lady," Ace said, turning the attention back to the skanks.

"Just coz she's fucking him, don't mean she's Drake's old lady," One skank said, thrusting her hip out. Sudden recognition hit, she was the skank who had been with Misty, when Misty had confronted me over the bikes.

"No bitch goes on the back of a Rage bike unless she carries old lady status," Ace sneered. Ace drove home the point that neither of them had been on the back of a bike.

"Drake just has a taste for a high-class pussy," Krystal said, and my eyes narrowed.

"When Drake's done, he'll want a taste of me again," Skank two said. Drake had slept with that? Seriously? Krystal caught me wrinkling my nose in distaste.

"What's up, bitch?"

"Number one, Hellfire member, which means you owe respect, whether or not you want to. Number two, I've old lady status, which means this bitch outranks skanks. And number three, Drake must have been desperate or drunk to have fucked you," I snapped my temper flaring.

"Drake's feeling sorry to fuck you, heard what happened earlier. Gotta be a sympathy fuck," Krystal sneered.

"Yup," I cheerfully agreed, Krystal looked shocked. "But it's this bitch Drake's fucking. It's me, Drake claimed!" Ace's presence was strong at my back. "It's okay Ace, that skank has nothing on me."

Intent on walking past, I wasn't ready when Krystal's hand shot out and grabbed my hair. The bitch yanked me back around and slapped hard across my face. That was the only shot I let Krystal have, I reached up and outwards breaking her grip. My other hand let out a right hook that knocked Krystal backwards.

At the same time, I turned my body, and as Krystal bent from the force of the blow, my knee came up and smashed into Krystal's face. The woman let out a blood-curdling shriek, and her hands came to her nose. There was a movement at my back and spinning, my leg kicked out and knocked the other skank on her ass, the slit up the back of my skirt ripped to mid-thigh. That made me mad, I loved this skirt.

Furious, I turned back to Krystal, who was straightening and let out a quick round of punches to her torso and ribs. Krystal went down and stayed down, moaning in pain. Skank two jumped at my back, and I staggered and then dropped a shoulder and threw her. She landed in a heap and stayed there, I felt a gaze on me and looked at Ace. His face was it's usual impassive, but Ace's eyes showed approval.

"Didn't expect that, Phoe," Jett said from behind Ace and me.

"Hellfire and Liz made sure I can fight," Ace nodded in approval. I felt more eyes and saw Drake standing in the clubhouse doorway. Drake's eyes held his own approval and something else. I realised I'd aroused Drake, I gave him a slow grin.

"Hey," I whispered, wrapping my arms around him. Drake grinned as he looked at me and hauled me against his body. Drake dropped his mouth to mine and gave me a long wet kiss. When it ended, I glanced over my shoulder at the two skanks and smirked, Drake, sidestepped but kept me tight to his side.

"Twice you've gone at Phoe. Know you're dumb, but how fuckin' dumb are you?" Drake growled looking at them. Krystal paled, but skank two thrust her breasts out in Drakes direction even while she tried to stop a nosebleed. Honestly!

"Snotty bitch started it," Krystal sniped.

"Snotty bitch is the Prez's, old lady. Outranks every other fuckin' female in or on Rage! Snotty bitch is a sister in Rage's brother MC," Drake roared.

"Bullshit, Phoe didn't start shit," Ace said. The skanks looked at him. "Fucks sake Drake, everyone's dipped in their cunts that wanted too, why they here? Won't get old lady status, who's gonna want a pussy every brother has fucked before him? Get fuckin' rid of the trash," Drake nodded.

"Only kept them around coz they were easy pussy," Drake agreed. "Any brother that needed to get laid had it on tap. Easy pussy is easy to find. Get off Rage." I winced at the harsh words. The skanks began shrieking and Ace not buying it, grabbed one around the arm and hauled her out. Hunter followed with the second.

"Easy pussy?" I asked Drake.

"Never went there. I don't wanna be dipping into a brothers cum," Drake said crudely. My eyes grew wide, and my mouth opened in shock. I'd never heard Drake be so crude.

"Drake!" I muttered. Drake's gaze dropped to me.

"Weren't no angel Phoe. Had plenty of pussy, plenty of skanks but I never dropped my standards to that sort of skank. Got a past, told you that, said you could accept it. Get your head around it," Drake said harshly, and my mouth opened and shut and then repeated those actions.

"I wasn't even insinuating that! Christ give me a break. Don't you think I've been through enough today?" Stunned, I gazed at Drake.

"Don't play that card baby, was right there by your side when you broke," Drake snarled back.

"I'm not saying you weren't! Why are you picking a fight?"

"Not me runnin' my mouth, woman." I stared at Drake, astounded. This was not the Drake I fell to sleep with earlier. What had happened during my nap? Had Drake changed his mind? Why was he being so damn mean?

"I don't know you at all, do I?" I'd no idea why Drake had turned on me. I ran our conversation back over and couldn't see where I'd gone wrong.

"You know me, Phoe," Drake growled. I shook my head at him, no, I didn't know this version of Drake. I'd no idea, Drake could turn like this. Yeah, men in an MC rarely respected the women who hung around. Usually, the only women who got respect were old ladies. I'd not seen Drake act this way before, and it was a shock, especially coming on top of my breakdown.

"No. The man I love wouldn't dream of speaking to me like I'm trash. Not asking for special favours but give me a chance to get my breath," I replied, shocked at how this was escalating. For God's sake a few hours ago I'd had a severe flashback and panic attack and now Drake was attacking me!

"Phoe they're just short of unpaid whores. Got to have seen them around Hellfire, women who screw any brother hoping to be on the back of his bike. Shit don't work. Going to open your legs easy, not gonna get a brother by the balls. Don't lead me around by my balls woman," Drake said, and my eyes opened wide. Was he suggesting I'd given in to him too easy? Was Drake saying I was no better than them? I concentrated on his last few words pushing the others to one side.

"Wasn't leading you around by your balls," I told him indignantly.

"Don't," Drake ordered. I bristled angrily. How this had resulted in an argument between us? I wasn't sure, but I wasn't taking his shit, with Drake, I was safe from physical harm. Emotional harm was a different story, I may have broken, but I was still strong enough to defend myself.

"I didn't do anything except take out two smack-talking skanks. By the way skank two says when you've finished with the high-class pussy, you can go back when you want. Said you liked what she gave you." I wrenched myself away from Drake and stormed out. What was Drake's damn problem? I hadn't been leading him around by his balls, I just hadn't liked his crudeness.

Hellfire was the same, they spoke to their biker bunnies or skanks the same. Yeah, I didn't enjoy crudeness, but I accepted it. Accepted it from my brothers because that was who Hellfire was, and I'd have to accept it from Drake. It was part of who he was, and as long as Drake didn't speak to me the same, I could live with it. Just couldn't live with Drake picking a fight with me after what happened earlier.

I spent two hours eating and drinking and playing with the kids and avoiding Drake. It was nearly midnight when I realised I'd left my house keys at the office. With a sigh, I walked back into the clubhouse, still avoiding Drake and snagged my office keys. Darkness had well and truly fallen, and once I left the lights of the yard, the forecourt was dimly lit.

Without thinking, I walked swiftly across the forecourt, forgetting the warnings not to go anywhere on my own. Strangely, the streetlights outside Rage and HQ were out. A tingle crept down my spine, and I was going to open the door when a hand slid across my mouth.

"Hello bitch," a voice muttered. Shock hit me hard. No, it can't be, it can't be! The hand grabbed my jaw hard, and then I was spun around to face my worst nightmare. It was him! Terrified, I looked up into the eyes of my ex-husband, Martin Page. Horror hit, followed by nausea and paralysing terror.

Martin began dragging me towards a car I hadn't noticed. Parked near HQ under one of the dark lights, it had pretty well hidden. Fearful, I began to struggle, kicking with my feet, awareness dawned, if Martin got me in that car, I'd never see my kids again. This time Martin meant to finish what he started. I kicked backwards with my feet harder, and a solid punch landed on my head.

Dazed, and stopping fighting, I heard pipes and peered into bright light from a bike. In the light, a tall figure got off the bike, and the light died, Ace stood in front of us. I hadn't even noticed Ace wasn't in the clubhouse when I'd come across to HQ.

"Let Phoenix go," he growled. Ace took a step forward, and I looked in horror as Martin raised a gun and then calmly shot Ace twice.

There was no noise, Martin had used a silencer on the end of the gun. No sound, except a soft whuff when the bullet left the chamber. Ace's body jerked and then hit the floor. Crumpled on the ground, Ace didn't move. Against the hand over my mouth, I screamed Ace's name and the gun barrel slammed across my temple, and it was lights out.

Gradually, I became aware of being tied to a chair and being half-naked. Martin had removed my clothes and left me in bra and panties. Martin did that, to make me vulnerable and fear him, and it worked. I looked around, trying to see something. Was Ace alive? Had he raised the alarm? Where had Ace been shot? I'd never forgive myself if Rage's V.P had been hurt badly. Drake wouldn't forgive me after warning me not to go anywhere without guards. This was my damn fault.

At last, my eyesight adjusted, I was in a dark room with a dingy window with faint moonlight filtering through it. I couldn't figure out shapes or where the door was, everything was so dark. The room stank of damp and urine, I was gagged and tightly bound as I struggled against my bonds.

"Keep struggling bitch," Martin said from the shadows.

"Let me go," I screamed against the gag. It didn't matter Martin couldn't understand me, he knew precisely what I meant.

"Pardon?" Martin mocked and then stepped forward into the moonlight. Forced to stare up at the monster, I was terrified at being helpless again. Martin's face looked different, and I realised he'd a broken nose, and the left eye was lower than his right. There was a terrible scar on his cheek that cut across his mouth.

"Yeah bitch, look at what those cunts did. Take a good look, Marie," Martin yelled and rammed his scarred face into mine.

To piss him off, I closed my eyes and tried to block the raging maniac out. Martin shook my head, and I gasped in pain as suddenly, a knife cut into my cheek. Martin laughed as the knife sliced downwards. Fear hit another level, Martin wasn't just going to beat me this time.

"Deserved it," I mumbled. Fuck this, Martin planned to beat and humiliate me, I wasn't going to cower this time. Chance had taught me to be strong. Martin slapped my face, snapping it to one side.

"What's with your stupid new name? What idiotic name is Phoenix, what's wrong with Marie Page? My name not good enough for you?" he snarled, spittle forming at the corners of his mouth.

"We never married. I wanted nothing to do with an abusive asshole, so I changed my name."

"Bitch. Guess what? I'm divorced now." I blinked trying to work out what he meant. Martin couldn't seriously think I'd marry him. "Yeah, Marie, we're getting married. And then I'm going to kill you and take your fucking money and then fuck those kids over. Little shits." Gobsmacked, I shook my head. Martin was freaking deranged, no way was I marrying him.

"I have a will. You'll never get that money," I told him, and Martin punched me in the mouth this time. Blood dripped from my lip, another punch and he laid my cheek open, hitting the knife cut.

"Marie's going to fucking marry me," Martin screamed spit flying from his mouth and hitting me in the face.

"Fuck you!" I screamed back. "You're fucking insane. I'm never going to marry you. You'll never get my money, it goes to the kids and the Trusts."

"Marie's going to fucking marry me," Martin screamed insanity in his eyes. Who the hell was this madman talking to? "Tonight. I have a friend who's willing to marry us and do so for a nice donation. Meet Miguel Santos, he's been ordained over the internet."

Martin was warped, I'd always known he was sadistic, but now Martin was living in la-la land. A second man stepped forward. He was Mexican and around sixty and watched me with dispassionate eyes. A sudden sinking feeling hit my stomach, shit was going to hit the fan faster than I thought. I had to hang on, Chance would be looking for me.

"Screw marrying him," I snarled spitting blood. Santos laughed.

"Bitch you'll do everything Page wants. And for what Page is paying, going to be my pleasure to marry you. Twenty percent of your fortune, yeah, definitely up for that lady. I can write wills too," Santos said with a grin, and suddenly I knew this man was going to help kill me.

"I'll match whatever Martin's paying you," I

whispered. Santos threw back his head and laughed with Martin.

"Lady, I don't break my word, poor for business," Santos's hand reached down and grabbed my breast. I cringed away from him. Santos laughed again, cruelly. The knife reappeared, and Martin sliced my shoulder. I screamed in pain as Santos grabbed my breast again squeezing harder. If I survived, I'd have bruises of his fingers.

"Take your filthy hands off of me."

"I'll drop five hundred thousand off the price for a few hours with her," Santos offered with a sick grin and bile rose in my throat.

"After we're married," Martin said without interest. He was fingering the tip of the knife, and Martin looked at me and grinned. Launching forward, Martin stabbed the knife hard in my thigh, and I screamed myself hoarse. The pain was awful. Hellfire better hurry the fuck up because Martin had that look in his eye, the one I knew only too well.

"Damage the goods too much, the arrangement is cancelled," Santos said. Martin shrugged.

"Get this into your head, I'm not marrying you. You can beat me, hurt me, but I'm not marrying you." Martin glowed, because, in his eyes, I gave him permission to carry out his punishment. Martin took that permission up at once.

"Where Phoe?" Drake snarled his face in Chance's. Chance was just as pissed as Drake.

"Tell me why Phoe was avoiding you?" Chance snarled. Guilt crossed Drake's face, and then Chance slammed him against the wall. "What did you do?"

Rage moved across the forecourt and gathered close by, and Hellfire did the same taking Chance's back. Jett disappeared, but no one paid attention.

"Had a fight, Phoe was tellin' me shit about pussy I'd fucked. No pussy tells me who I fuck and when I fuck," Drake ranted, and Chance let him go stunned. He stepped back and looked at his cousin. Chance's mouth worked for a few seconds as Drake watched him, furious.

"Tellin' me, you're gonna fuck around behind Phoe's back?" Chance finally asked incredulously.

"Tellin' you, no cunt leads me by the balls."

"Phoe's a cunt? Just a cunt?" Chance asked quietly. Drake missed the warning.

"Every woman's a cunt, just different levels of them." Chance took a second step back, not in shock but in anger. His body tensed as he tried to control it.

"Treatin' Phoe as a skank, a whore. Warned ya brother, don't shit on Phoe and you just did. Clubs are done." Drake looked shocked at Chance's words and then wiped any expression from his face.

"What the fuck you on about? Clubs are done?" Drake asked anger rising in his voice.

"Warned ya not to fuck with Phoe. Treated Phoe worse than you treat the easy pussy that hangs around the club. Phoe is no fuckin' whore for you. Our clubs are done, as in done cousin." There were soft sounds of harsh breath's being sharply drawn as Chance spoke.

"We're blood," Drake snarled. Chance pointed a finger at him.

"Not anymore. Hellfire mount up, got a sister to find." Chance turned his back on Drake and began walking. Drake launched himself at Chance's back and took him to the ground. The cousins rolled around on the floor, trading punches and beating the hell out of each other.

Chance got the upper hand and sitting on top of Drake, he dragged him up by his tee and began single-handed punching Drake's face. Drake shifted his hips and jerked upwards, knocking Chance off balance and rolled on top of him and began pummeling Chance.

Apache appeared and dragged the snarling and spitting Drake off Chance. Chance scrambled to his feet and launched himself at Drake. He took both Drake and Apache down together and got his hands around his cousin's throat. Bear and Rooster dragged him off Drake, and the clubs surrounded the two men.

"What's your fuckin' problem?" Chance yelled at Drake, spitting blood.

"Fuckin' love Phoe and I couldn't save her," Drake screamed back. Silence fell.

"First fuckin' honest thing you said asshole," Chance growled. He spat blood at Drake's feet. "Hellfire mount up."

"Not without me," Drake snarled.

"Phoe's just pussy to you Drake, remember. Nothing more," Chance spat his disgust at Drake.

"I love her."

"Don't treat someone you love like that, you fuckin' prick," Chance yelled into the silence.

"Know I don't. I lost it, okay? I lost it, destroyed the woman I love, what Phoe's been through, tonight with that episode. Then finding her in the rec room taking out two skanks." Drake let the fight drain from his body. The Rage President looked defeated. "Where the fuck did my old lady learn to fight like that? Phoe shouldn't have to fight."

"We taught her," Chance replied.

"Lost Phoe, lost her tonight, I knew I was losing her, and my mouth kept engaging. Couldn't shut up. Woman's too fuckin' good for me and I won't survive it when Phoe sorts that shit out and leaves."

"Fuckin' idiot. Woman loves you, Phoe won't leave," Chance thundered struggling, to get free and get his hands back around his stupid cousin's throat. Bear and Big Rooster tightened their arms around him.

"She's too good for me," Drake whispered, and his pain hit Chance in his heart. It was what Chance feared for himself. Loving a woman way out of his league.

"Yeah, Phoe is, so what you do is value her, give her everythin'. So Phoe knows she safe and loved, don't drive Phoe away to protect your heart from her. Christ, you're as thick as fuckin' shit. Raised you better than that," Chance yelled. Drake's head shot up, and anger fired in his eyes.

"Not protectin' me, protectin' her. Makin' sure Phoe finds somethin' better."

"Woman found what she wants, and tonight you broke Phoe's heart," Chance said, taking a visible rein on his temper and calming down. "Every brother got your fear. Every single one of us, ate shit, lived shit and slept in shit for years until we could make our move. We think we ain't worth a decent woman, but we fuckin' are. Hellfire and Rage both insecure fuckers. Can't let that insecurity destroy our shots at havin' a little something worthwhile in our lives."

"She loves me?" Drake whispered.

"Yeah, you prick."

"What did I do?"

"Got a problem. Phoenix's car is still on the forecourt. Checked HQ, Phoe's keys were on the street, and there's blood on the ground. Ace is missing, his bike's not here, and brother's not answering his phone," Jett said, appearing from nowhere and holding out Phoe's keys to Drake.

"Ace? Ace hurt Phoe?" Bear asked, confused.

"No, but I think one of them is hurt," Jett said.

"Get feelers out, find them," Drake thundered. Chance looked at him.

"Head straight, or I need to pound it more?"

"Straight," Drake said and began moving.

"One more thing, my girl doesn't come back, my girl walks away from you, Hellfire walk. On my cut, I warned ya," Chance snarled, and everyone knew Chance meant it. Hellfire would go to war with Rage if their sister said so.

Regaining consciousness hurt, my entire world was awash with pain. I'd no idea how many minutes had passed. Blood dripped from open wounds on my body, and I looked at my ankle. Which had been hit with a piece of wood, I swear Martin had broken it. Pain embraced my entire body, I didn't know what hurt more, where Martin had broken bones, or where he'd used the knife.

Martin had untied my hand, and he'd broken every finger one at a time in my left hand. Damn maniac then smashed the piece of wood down shattering bones. My left hand was a ruin, and my throat ached from screaming so much. Martin had then re-tied me to the chair and carried on the beating. I thought my ribs might be broken as breathing was hard.

My face was swollen, I could feel the tightness of my skin. I lifted my right hand and touched my forehead. The skin was split open where he'd punched me wearing a ring. Martin had sliced that knife into my body again and again. My right eye refused to open, my lips were split, and my jaw was swollen.

Animalistic panting came from a dark corner, and I remained still. Unable to defend myself, I was in serious shit, Martin had been extremely thorough. Even breathing freaking hurt, Martin was still here, which meant more pain. The lunatic muttered to himself, and I did a quick recheck of my body. He'd hit and kicked me so hard, Martin had knocked the chair over and broken it. Tentatively, I wriggled my working hand and found I could get free. I froze as a door banged and realised Martin had left.

Desperately, I peered into the dim light, trying to see if Santos was there. The asshole that planned to forge my signature or something equally devious. The man who wanted to rape me. Not happening I decided there and then, I'd die before that.

Stiffly and painfully, I rubbed my wrist on my leg, trying to get sensation back. I refused to check the ruin of my left hand. Every slightest jolt of it, sent pain shooting through me. After a few minutes, I'd enough mobility to untie my legs, that was a struggle as my fingers didn't want to fully co-operate. I finally untied them and began rubbing my legs to get feeling back.

More than sure my ankle was broken, I growled inwardly, knowing it would hamper any escape. I scanned for a weapon and picked up a piece of the broken chair, one end was sharp, and it would do in a pinch. I dragged myself over to a wall and began hauling myself to my knees when low laughter echoed.

Damn, Martin hadn't left the room, the asshole had just pretended too. I heard footsteps and looked around frantically. My vision was poor and blurred, and I couldn't see him. I twisted my head, as footsteps came near to me and I lashed out with the stick, I missed, and laughter sounded. I wasn't sure if it was Martin or Santos, although it was more than likely Martin.

Martin pushed on one shoulder, and I lashed out behind me, hitting nothing again. He began humming, and terror began building. It was similar to starring in a horror film. I wanted to scream but swallowed. Aware I wouldn't be able to hear Martin approaching if I began crying. Once I started, I wouldn't stop screaming, for now, I had to be quiet.

The footsteps ran at me, and I lashed out again and yet again missed. I was knocked onto my back and kicked in the ribs, and then Martin stamped on me. I cried out in agony and shifted backwards. There was a noise at the door, and we both stopped, him hunting and me running. The door kicked open, and a tall figure filled the doorway. A torch flashed on me and then lit Martin up, and the figure lifted a gun towards him.

Martin gave an animal's scream of anger and pulled his own gun, the idiot was shooting manically before he even had the gun aimed. The figure took a step backwards and then fired his own. Martin stopped shooting and then fell towards my body. I couldn't roll out of the way, and he fell over me looking into my face.

"Stupid bitch," Martin muttered blood dripping from his mouth. Murderous, Martin began lifting the gun intent on shooting me when my arm snapped up. Hatefully, I drove the stake into his back. Martin's eyes looked at me disbelieving as the life in them faded. I began gagging to breathe, as dead weight began crushing me, and Martin was dragged away.

A man slammed next to my body. He laid down and dragged me close leaning on his left side and holding me tight. His right arm came up and over me holding the gun. He laid his wrist over my waist so he could shoot anyone coming through the door. Blood dripped onto my body, and I looked up into the stunning green eyes of Ace.

"Fancy seeing you here," I muttered, and his body shook with a laugh. Damn, we were both in a state.

"Yeah, cool place," Ace muttered back.

"How hurt are you?" I asked, scared for Ace. I'd seen him go down outside HQ, Ace was shot at least twice.

"Two in the shoulder, one in the leg, torso shot and one shot to my fuckin' phone," he growled. I got the impression Ace was more pissed about his phone than he was about his wounds.

"Need to get help." Not sure how I'd do that, I'd have to crawl.

"Help's here, Ramirez is here, gave chase to a second man. Ramirez will have heard the shots and called it in," Ace muttered again. A noise sounded, and the gun snapped upwards towards the door, I waited with bated breath, and after a minute, Ace relaxed his arm.

"Ramirez?" I asked, trying to keep Ace talking, he appeared to be slurring.

"Ramirez received info about your ex being alive and havin' escaped jail and was coming to warn us. Instead, he saw me climbing on my bike, killin' my lights and gave chase. Arrived together, a man ran into the trees, Ramirez chased him. I came here, thought your dickhead ex ran into trees. Didn't know there are two fuckers."

"Ramirez isn't here. I need to get help," I insisted as Ace closed his eyes.

"Need to fuckin' stay here where I can protect you. Brothers are on their way." Ace re-opened his eyes and looked at me. I jumped as gunshots echoed in the distance and I hoped beyond hope that Ramirez was okay. The detective appeared to be a nice guy.

"Ace we're both messed up here," I choked on blood in my mouth and twisted my head and spat it out.

"Rage will come," Ace insisted.

"How?"

"Dickhead left your phone, screen smashed, but the on light still flashed, I took it. Couldn't call for help, both phones smashed. Someone will track it. Saw asshole drive off, and chased after him, staying back and keeping lights off. Didn't get here in time to stop him beating you. Sorry," Ace mumbled not happy at having to apologise to me or so I assumed.

"You saved my life, Ace, never say sorry to me."

"Wish I'd seen you first," Ace told me, and I looked up alarmed at his pallor.

"Ace?" I asked, fearing the man was passing out. I wriggled against him, trying to turn and get his gun. But Ace stopped me and held me tight against his body. Ace's eyes opened, and Ace looked at me. Where the hell was Ramirez?

"Would've taken a risk on you Phoe. Only you had Drake hooked before my brother could do anything. Good to see my brother happy," Ace said and tightened his arm around me and then relaxed it a trace.

"Ace, I need to get help." I needed to get us both help. Neither of us was going to survive this if I didn't move. In pain, I drew in a deep, ragged breath.

"Don't leave my side. Rage will be comin', wait with you until they do," Ace whispered.

Minutes passed as Ace held me safe in his arms. Aware of Martin's dead eyes glaring at my back from somewhere in the room, I was glad Ace was there. Bike pipes roared, lots of them and then lights lit up the dark doorway and men came barrelling through. There was still no sign of Ramirez.

A light fell on us, and Ace flinched, Drake cursed, and he hit his knees beside us. Ace stared at Drake but didn't let me go. Chance landed beside Drake seconds later. Someone, sounding surprised, said there's a body in the corner. Yup, that was Martin's body, I giggled to myself. Blast, I was becoming hysterical, I took a sharp hold of my thoughts.

"Saved her brother," Ace muttered. Drake's hand hovered over both of us. Drake didn't know where to touch either one of us.

"You did brother. Let Phoe go now, we're here for both of you," Drake soothed.

"Holy shit look at that! Man's been staked, gotta be near a heart shot," Texas exclaimed.

"Yeah, that was me!" I muttered. Drake tensed and looked at me in surprise. Chance gripped my hand reassuring me.

"Proud of you, girl," Chance muttered.

Drake gently rolled me out of Ace's arms and checked my body with deft hands, and then he checked Ace. Chance hit the floor and snatched me up, a yelp of pain made Chance gentler. Apache was on the floor now beside us, his sons head in his lap, Apache stroked Ace's hair with shaking hands. Drake's face hovered in my line of sight, Axel's voice jolted me aware.

"Ambulance is on the way," Axel said quietly, his usual loudness missing. Axel should never be sad and quiet.

"We're okay, we're okay, right? Chance, tell Axel."

"Yeah, you're okay, Phoe. You're both good." But I heard the worry in Chance's voice and turned my head to see Drake holding a hand over Ace's gut wound. Ace lied, it wasn't a torso shot, it was a gutshot, and I knew they could be deadly.

"I stabbed him. Martin shot Ace, and I stabbed him in the back, not very sporting," I informed Chance as I stared into his face. Worry and anger were written all over it. Chance held me gently in his arms and looked at my wounds.

"Good, baby. You did well."

"Ace shot first, I stabbed Martin, I killed him. Martin was going to kill Ace and me. I couldn't let Martin kill us," I told Chance needing him to understand, that damn darkness was encroaching.

"Baby everything's okay, I get it, don't need absolution from me. Fuckin' proud of ya. Our girl survived, did what ya had to, to survive, that's all that matters baby," Chance muttered stroking my hair. There was blood on his hand.

"I'm proud of you too," I told him back feeling magnanimous.

"Just hang tight. Need you," Chance muttered as he bent his head and kissed me on the top of my head. I suddenly remembered something, that pesky darkness.

"Oh, Ramirez is out there. Can you find him, there were gunshots?"

Drake snapped an order at Texas and Mac, Pyro and Shee followed them. Guns in hand, they left running, to search for Ramirez. My hand groped for Ace's and finding it, I clenched it tightly. Ace weakly squeezed back and then blue, and red lights lit up the dark room. EMT's came crashing in with the police behind them. Now the darkness could take me.

Axel received my sternest look, as I struggled to move his hand, which was pushing me back into the bed. I snapped at him in a temper, the bloody man grinned, and I smacked at his huge paw.

"I want to see Ace," Axel shook his head. It was thirty-six hours after my kidnapping, and I'd been admitted to hospital and was now stuck here. Yesterday I'd been sedated for most of the day. Today I was awake and on a mission. I was black and blue with one eye swollen shut and stitches in my cheek and upper lip. And I wanted to get out this damn bed and see Ace. I had stitches everywhere but hell if that was going to stop me.

"You're not leaving this bed," Axel boomed. I narrowed my good eye at him. "That won't work either woman," I growled my displeasure as the door opened and Drake came in with a doctor.

"Get him out of here," I snarled on seeing Drake. He looked shattered, vanity kicked in, and I didn't want Drake to see me like this. I'd won, I'd beaten Martin, and at the moment I resembled a loser more than a winner. Drake had caused as much emotional hurt as Martin had physically. Panic rose in my throat, alongside my now familiar friend, bile.

"Phoe," Axel said firmly.

"Get Drake out of here. He can go fuck one of those skanks of his," I hissed at him. Drake blanched at the anger in my voice. The doctor looked over his shoulder in surprise.

"Phoenix," Drake said, and his voice was soft.

"Get Drake out of here!" I shrieked, and the doctor murmured a few words and Drake left to be replaced by Chance.

"Good, now get a wheelchair and take me to Ace," I demanded of the doctor who raised an eyebrow and then picked up my file. The doctor read through it, as I seethed in silent temper.

"I'm Doc Gibbons," the man said, and I glared. Whoopie, I didn't care who he was, I wanted to see Ace! Fully aware I resembled a spoilt brat, I pursed my lips.

"I need to see Ace," I repeated stubbornly. Axel's lips twitched, and I frowned. The massive mountain of a man broke out into a big grin. Mouth pursed, I ignored Axel and looked at Chance and the doctor, Chance looked rough. My heart squeezed in pain for him, I'd never seen Chance look so sad or pained.

"Ms Phoenix. You have a multitude of cuts and bruises, a grand total of over one hundred and fifty stitches. The surgeon reset the two bones in your ankle that was broken. Your hand is a mess, and we spent over twelve hours in surgery, putting that back together. I'd suggest you don't leave your bed for twenty-four hours at least." With a sigh, I cut into his litany of my injuries.

"I. Want. To. See. Ace," I said each word clearly and firmly.

"Take her bed to his," Chance muttered, "Phoe won't settle."

"Ms Phoenix needs rest and peace and quiet," Doc Gibbons said.

"Phoe can rest once she's in a room with Ace," Chance insisted. I lay back on the bed and grimaced, Doc Gibbons gave a sigh and then gave a nod of agreement. Twenty minutes later, I was in a private room next to Ace. After insisting that our beds be pushed together so I could hold his hand, I settled.

Once their backs were turned, I shifted over to his bed and curled at his side. I lay on my side, looking at the unconscious man and willing Ace to open his eyes. He hadn't opened them by the time I slipped into sleep. I faded away with my arm wrapped around Ace.

When I next awoke, Drake was sitting by Ace's bed, holding my good hand. My arm remained clenched around Ace's waist, Drake was asleep. I watched him for a few seconds and then pulled my hand from him.

I turned my head to face Ace. Green eyes flared briefly, and I realised I wasn't holding his waist, Ace was holding my arm there. Ace gave me a smile, the first one I had ever seen from him, and he squeezed my hand.

"Okay, Phoe?" Ace whispered.

"Yeah," I whispered back.

"Glad you made it," he said with a wink.

"Glad you did too," I told him.

"What I said…" Ace broke off. I gave his hand a squeeze and gave Ace a soft smile.

"Yeah," I drawled softly, "I'd have risked it too." His face registered shock and then Ace wiped it away.

"Make Drake happy," he told me and then closed his eyes.

"He needs to stop being an asswipe for me to do that. Drake needs to let me in and not think I'm always judging him," I told Ace.

"Prez's let you in, you got a hard job, crossing lines between two MC's, the Trusts, being a mom. If anyone can manage Drake, you can."

"I love him, I need him, but I don't think I'm what Drake needs. Too much baggage," I said tears in my throat.

"Man loves you. Strength of love Drake feels for you, had the same once. Lost it, chased it away because I didn't trust she'd understand our vision. Trust Drake, Phoe," Ace said and then turned his head away. "Enough with the girly chat shit," Ace muttered conversation over.

"I love you too," A voice rumbled, and I looked over at Drake and found his eyes studying me.

"You're an asswipe, Drake," I went on the attack.

"Yeah, got that right, I got scared."

"Bullshit," I snapped, and he looked shocked. Drake rarely heard me curse, and I decided this was a time for it.

"Woman," Drake said, narrowing his eyes.

"You were a total asshole, I didn't deserve that, I wasn't even bitching about the women you've screwed. I was complaining about the crudeness. You've never spoken that crudely." Drake was not going to wriggle out of this.

"Dunno if I can tone it down, angel."

"When did I ask you too?" Drake blinked, absorbing what I was saying.

"I was tryin' to push you away. See, my fear is that one day, you'll wake up and realise you can do better. Better than me and I'll lose you."

"Now you're just an insulting dick," I hissed and heard a muffled chuckle from Ace.

"You're still mad."

"Someone give Sherlock a medal." Yup, definitely a chuckle from Ace.

"Got fuckin' scared, jumped on that to push you away. Was tryin' to protect you from me, and then Chance made me realise that I was protectin' myself." I studied Drake and suddenly saw the bruises on his face. I thought back to Chance and remembered bruises on his too.

"You two had a fight?" Horror coloured my tone.

"Chance beat some sense into me," Drake ruefully said. I grinned at him.

"Good. Did it work?" No sympathy for Drake, tough love time.

"Yeah. I love you, woman."

"Did it hurt?" Drake's eyes narrowed at my gleeful tone.

"Yeah."

"Good," I gloated cheerfully. Drake's eyes narrowed even further at my delight in his ass-kicking. Visibly weighing up whether to continue in that vein or change the subject, Drake made his choice.

"I love you, woman, I've never said that, never wanted to. I love you, the kids, your job, Albert, the Ames. All of it Phoe, I love all of it." Drake changed the subject. Wimp!

"Drake," I whispered and began crying.

"Told ya, your mine, even when I'm an asshole," he said. I laughed through my tears, and the man next to me groaned.

"Get a fuckin' room," Ace muttered, and both Drake and I burst into laughter.

Epilogue.

Detective Ramirez came to see me in the hospital. Ramirez had taken a bullet to the leg and then got disorientated in the trees. He'd got two shots off at Santos, but Santos vanished into thin air. Mac and Texas found Ramirez stumbling back, alongside a Hawthorne detective called Max.

The detective took my statement and then Ace's and told us, it was a clear case of self-defence. Ramirez appeared rather impressed with my 'Stake the Vampire' impression. When he asked who he'd been chasing, I gave him Miguel Santos's name, the air turned electric.

Shocked, Ramirez asked me again to confirm the identity. When I did, he asked Ace if he could confirm and Ace reminded him that he'd only seen the back of the man. I'd been Ace's priority. It was obvious I was missing something judging by the looks Ace, Drake, Chance, Ramirez and Dylan Hawthorne were exchanging. The detective put a warrant out on Santos, but he'd gone to ground. A mystery for another day.

Chance returned the day after beyond furious. Roadkill just dumped Martin in the woods and thinking him dead left him there. Martin had been rescued by hikers and survived. From Chance's expression, Roadkill faced serious penance.

The kids were fine. Micah insisted on seeing Martin's corpse this time to ensure he was dead. Drake took Micah, so he got peace, I'd been ready to refuse, but Drake explained my boy needed this. I trusted Drake. Carmine and Micah made the decision alongside the Ames, and Albert to tell the younger kids from Harley down that I'd gone on a trip for the Trusts.

Ace was healing, but I left the hospital before he did. Drake took me to the clubhouse for a few days, and then I went home. The bruises and cuts faded enough that heavily applied makeup hid most, Drake and I explained the more visible ones as a car accident. The children didn't need nightmares at knowing how close they'd come to being orphans.

The younger ones bought it, but Harley, Christian, Jared and Aaron looked suspicious, but they didn't challenge it. The Ames made a fuss of me, and Drake put in a call to Hawthorne thanking him for his help. Dylan Hawthorne had kept eyes on me, that's why the police arrived so quickly after Hellfire and Rage.

Davies gave directions to Drake on the phone, as Drake chased after Ace and Ramirez. At the same time, Davies contacted Hawthorne's cousin who worked alongside Ramirez. Davies tracked my phone while Max, followed Ramirez and Ace. Max covered Ramirez assuming the same as Ace, the runner had been Martin.

All in all, I'd been covered, I just hadn't been aware of it. It had taken Martin and Santos twenty minutes to beat me. Ace and Ramirez had parked back from the hut I'd been taken to, so they didn't warn Martin and Santos they were there. Time had been lost when Ace had to explain to Ramirez why he was riding in the dark and that I'd been taken.

Drake was obviously wallowing in some of his own guilt, he felt that if we hadn't had our argument, I wouldn't have gone to HQ alone. Maybe, maybe not, who knew. The fact remained I was stupid enough to have done it.

Drake's guilt was heightened by the fact I refused to get my scars removed. I'd survived this, these were my reminders, I'd won. In the end, I couldn't watch Drake's guilt consume him, and I'd had the facial ones removed. Drake stopped wincing every time he looked at me after they'd been removed. I kept the body scars though, proof of survival.

Everyone kept a close eye on me. Drake and Chance kept waiting for my breakdown, my collapse. They didn't realise, bless them, that it wasn't going to happen. I'd won, beaten Martin Page and I stood tall, he was in a pauper's grave. In defeating him and surviving, I'd laid my nightmare to bed.

Yes, I agreed to therapy, that never hurt but I didn't think I'd collapse again. Therapy kept both clubs happy, and if they were happy, I was too. The inner strength that helped me adopt my kids, create the Trusts and trust in two MC's was dominant now. Drake had his hands full of a determined woman. I'd say Drake enjoyed it!

The case, therefore, was open and shut, and my story hit the papers. For a few days, the clubhouse was under siege, covered in reporters. Hawthorne sent more men and between them, Hellfire and Rage, not a single reporter got close.

Rage was being hailed as heroes in foiling my kidnapping, and I was lucky that the kids didn't watch the news. Mrs Ames was the first one awake in the Hall every day, she managed to retrieve the newspapers first. Hawthorne had put a security blockade up at the house so the press couldn't intrude on our privacy.

Things went back to normal. Drake and I were solid, we loved each other, he tried laying down the law, and I went and did what I needed to do. We'd a lot to learn about each other. Two days after I got discharged, Drake slipped a stunning antique diamond engagement ring on my finger. Inscribed inside was one word.

Mine.

I loved it.

Four weeks after my discharge, I stormed into the clubhouse and sought out my future husband. Drake was standing at the bar with Ace, and I barely noticed all the brothers were present. Drake had kept the kids with him today, so they were scattered around. I was shaking in shock and narrowed my eyes at him.

"Phoe?" Drake asked puzzled as he got off his stool. I held up a hand, shaking my head at him. "Christ babe what's happened now?"

"You! You! I spluttered. Drake took another step towards me. I glared at him, and he froze.

"Babe, what's wrong?" Worry coloured his voice.

"You!" I shrieked throwing a drama. Everyone began looking at everyone else.

"I what?" Drake snarled exasperated.

"You knocked me up!" I shrieked. Drake froze, and his hands fell to his side. The room went silent as everyone looked to Drake and then me.

"I what?" Drake whispered. Hope, surprise and disbelief crossed his face.

"You knocked me up! I'm pregnant. Seventeen kids!" I shrieked again. Love and pure male satisfaction spread across his face as he strode towards me and swept me up in his arms. Drake kissed me with a shit load of passion and then lifted his head, and pure happiness blazed from his face.

"I'm fuckin' pregnant! I'm having a baby!" Drake hollered, and the room broke into laughter, and we were lovingly surrounded by family.

Character Index.

There are a lot of characters in the Rage book's so I thought I'd give everyone a helping hand with who is who. As more of the Rage brothers find their girl's, we'll add them to this page!

Rage MC
Rage Patch. The patch is a barbed wire circular design, with flames interwoven. A Harley Davidson with Charon sat on the bike. Charon holds flaming scythe in one hand that curves around the back of him. On the front of the bike in place of a light, is a blue and purple flaming skull. On the back of the bike is a blue flaming eagle. At the top, it said, 'Rage MC'. At the bottom of the patch were words, 'Live to Ride.' Under them, it says Rapid City.

Drake Michaelson. DOB. 1975. His father started Rage Mc and died before Drake was old enough to become President. He became V.P and then in a hostile takeover became President. Phoenix thinks he looks like Tim McGraw with longer hair. Drake has a lean build to him but has well-defined muscles and broad shoulders. Drake sports dark brown eyes with laughter lines. He's six foot four.

Phoenix. DOB 1979. Drake's old lady. She is English and left England to escape an abusive relationship. She has five children she gave birth to and adopted eleven. She is exceedingly well off and runs three National Charities. The Phoenix Trust, the Rebirth Trust and the Eternal Trust. She has been married twice, the first husband died and her second was a bigamist. She is blond and green-eyed and is five foot tall. She met Hellfire MC first and is a sister in Hellfire.

Apache. DOB 1969. He is one of Drakes enforcers, Ace is his only son. Apache was widowed when Ace was young. He has bright green eyes and is six foot two. He is a Native American. He's described as absolutely stunning with gorgeous, high cheekbones, raven black hair that hangs past his shoulders.

Ace. DOB 1983. Ace is Drake's V.P. He looks a lot like a young Lou Diamond Philips. Like his father, he is Native American. He has bright green eyes, six foot two. He is described much the same as his father, absolutely stunning with gorgeous, high cheekbones and raven black hair that hangs past his shoulders. Ace had a girl. She left him when they were trying to get their club clean. He's been bitter and surly ever since.

Fish. DOB 1978. Fish is Drake's sergeant at arms. He's been married to Marsha for many years, they can't have children.

Marsha. DOB 1978. Fish's old lady and the one old lady the club has until Phoenix meets Drake. She's known to be kind and caring.

Texas. DOB 1965. Texas is an older man, he is the MC's secretary.

Axel. DOB 1951. Axel was one of the founders of the club. He is the Chaplin of the MC. He has blue eyes, and he is heavily bearded and very loud. He's built like a mountain. Axel has wild hair which hangs to his shoulders.

Gunner. Gunner is one of Drakes Enforcers at the MC.

Slick. Slick loves books and is happy reading quietly. He has soft brown eyes and is heavily muscled.

Manny
Lowrider
Ezra
Mac
Rock
Lex
Blaze prospect.
Slate prospect
Jett prospect
Hunter prospect

Silvie Stanton. She's looked at as an old lady even though she doesn't have an old man. She's kind and generous, the MC has a lot of respect for her. She has blond, curly hair.

Hellfire MC.

The Hellfire patch. Circular with the flames starting at the bottom and going halfway up the circle. In the middle of them is a skeleton with a devil's horns on its head and holding a pitchfork. In the other hand, the skeleton holds a motorbike and above the skeletons head was a crown of flames, Hellfire MC is written underneath in a bold freestyle script in white script.

Chance Michaelson. DOB 1973. Chance is the Hellfire President. His father started Hellfire. Chance looks like Tim McGraw with long hair. He is Drakes older cousin. They were brought up together and are as close as brothers and both fought to get their clubs clean from the filth that infected them.

There are a lot of comments that Chance and Drake could be twins. Chance is very protective of Phoenix and loves her without barriers. He has the same build as his cousin. Drake has brown eyes, and Chance has bright green eyes with laughter lines. He is six foot four with his hair hanging past his collar

Bear. Bear is the Hellfire V.P. Chance lets it slip to Drake that Bear has a dead sister.
Phoenix calls him Bearbear.

Diesel. Diesel is Hellfire's Sergeant at arms

Big Al. Al is Hellfire's Chaplin. He has an old lady called Tatianna.

Rooster. Rooster is Hellfire's Secretary

Tiny
Chatter
Pyro
Levi
Shotgun
Banshee
Celt

Roadkill. Roadkill was meant to dispose of Phoenix's ex-husband's body, his failure to make sure he was dead led to Phoenix being kidnapped. Last we knew Chance was dealing harshly with him.

HQ Staff.

Sally. Sally joined Phoe the minute they met when she came to help Phoe escape her ex-husband. She initially worked for the National Lottery in England and left to work for Phoenix. She is known as the public face of the Trusts and does a lot of the interviews allowing Phoe to hide behind the scenes.
Emily. Emily is Phoe's personal assistant. She is young and wild and likes colour.
Stefan. Stefan is incredibly loyal to Phoe. He is the Director of Fundraising. He has a crazy genius aspect and writes on walls. He is rabidly friendly and is gay. He gets kicks out of winding up Stuart. Stefan is described as wiry and slender but lightly muscled with sun-bleached almost white hair. His husband is called Bernard, who is a chef.
Diana. Diana is the Director of Human Resources
Stuart. Stuart is the Director of Legal, he is a little uptight and Stefan takes great delight in teasing him.
Abigail. Abigail is the Director of Security.
Kyle. Kyle is the Director of Finance. He is also slightly uptight like Stuart, and he thinks he works in a zoo.
North. North is the Director of public relations.
Rayna. Director of Events.
Other Directors, un-named for now. Property, Accounting, Investigations, Events, Public Relations, Advertising, Operations, Wages.
Jon. Jon is an investigator for malpractice.
Charlie SM for California.
Anna. Anna is known to be Sally's secretary.

Non-HQ People.

Liz. Liz is head of the home security team. She doesn't do security for the Trust but for the family. She came from England on a job offer from Phoenix. She is dedicated and hard-working.
Matthias. Matthias is Liz's second in command.
Albert Wilkes. Albert offered Micah a job when he knew things were bad at home for them. He also protected them when they won the lottery.
He came to the States to be part of their family, and the children think of him as a grandfather. He profoundly loves Phoenix and the children.
Mr and Mrs Ames. They have been with Phoenix just five weeks after she moved to the states. Phoenix treats them like members of the family. They work as housekeeper and groundsman.

Phoenix's kids

Micah. DOB 1995, he wants to be a mechanic and design street racing cars. He is English.
Carmine. DOB 1996, half African American half Caucasian, plays for cubs. He is from Maine. Adopted 2010
Tyelar. DOB 1996, wants to play for the Blackhawks, Tye is half Mexican and half Caucasian, Tye is from Maine. Adopted 2010
Jodie. DOB 1997. She likes tennis and is close to Serenity.
Serenity. DOB 1998, She is from Maine, she plays tennis well but also likes ice hockey. She was adopted in 2010

Harley. DOB 1999, Harley's from Maine and was adopted 2010
Cody. DOB 2000. Carmine found Cody living on the streets in Colorado, he was adopted in 2011
Christian. DOB 2002
Jared. DOB 2004
Aaron. DOB 2005. Aaron was born after his father died. He never met him.
Eddie and Tony DOB 2010. African American, adopted 2012
Timmy and Scout DOB 2014. Adopted 2014 Their mother was a drug addict. They have severe illnesses which Phoe hopes medical care will cure.
Garrett and Jake DOB 2014. Adopted 2014 Their mother was a drug addict. They have severe illnesses which Phoe hopes medical care will cure.
Baby Michaelson ?????

RCPD.

Antonio Ramirez. He is over six-foot-tall and has black wavy hair, olive tanned skin and Mexican heritage and has brown soft, gentle eyes. Tonio is lean hipped and long-legged and broad-shouldered. He is a good cop, and Drake thinks a lot of him.

Other Characters.

Andrew Wainwright. He is the congressman for South Dakota. He is loyal to his friends and thinks a lot of Phoenix. He supports the Trusts one hundred percent. He's known to have a temper.

Antony Parker-Jones. He is the senator for South Dakota. He does a lot for the Trusts, hosting fundraiser's and so on. He is known to have a hot temper.

Authors Byword.

Well now, I hope you enjoyed Rage of the Phoenix. Domestic violence is a subject I think everyone should be aware of. While some of Phoenix's injuries may seem farfetched, one only has to listen to the news to see they are not.

Phoenix's situation is one familiar to many men, women and children. It is a tragic circumstance more and more common in today's way of life. Police take domestic violence very seriously, and harsh penalties are handed down to perpetrators.

While nothing like the Trusts exist in the way, the Trusts have been described, isn't it a nice feeling to think that one day our heroes will be as valued as they should? Or victims looked after? Perhaps, one day.

The next book is the Hunters Rage. What will Ace and Artemis get up to? Please check my website for the release date!

If you enjoyed this book, please leave a review on either Goodreads.com under Elizabeth N. Harris, or Amazon! Your reviews are so important to me!

Thanks

Elizabeth.

Printed in Poland
by Amazon Fulfillment
Poland Sp. z o.o., Wrocław